PRAISE FOR *STILL MINE*

An International Bestseller

"Stuart is a sensitive writer who has given Clare a painful past and just enough backbone to bear it."

—*New York Times*

"[A] dark and deliciously disturbing debut . . . Stuart's perceptive look at addiction, abuse, and obsession will resonate with fans of psychological thrillers."

—*Publishers Weekly*

"A haunting psychological thriller that builds to a tumultuous climax. It is impossible to put down, or to look away."

—Robert Dugoni, *New York Times* bestselling author of *My Sister's Grave*

"Amy Stuart sends one missing woman out to look for another one, and the result is chilling. You'll find yourself turning the pages faster and faster."

—Elisabeth de Mariaffi, author of *The Devil You Know*

"A haunting treasure of a book that burrowed its way into my psyche as I read it . . . Not since *The Silent Wife* have I been rendered so powerlessly riveted by a psychological thriller."

—Marissa Stapley, author of *Mating for Life*

"The cliffhanger will have you continuing to bite your nails until there's a sequel."

—*RT Book Reviews*

"Twisty and swift, Amy Stuart's *Still Mine* is a darkly entertaining mystery machine. But what will really surprise you is the emotional foundation on which it has been built."

—Andrew Pyper, bestselling author of *The Demonologist* and *The Damned*

"An intricately woven thriller . . . A vivid and haunting debut."

—Holly LeCraw, author of
The Swimming Pool

"A gripping page-turner, with a plot that takes hold of you and drags you through the story at breakneck speed. The characters are compelling, the setting chilling and the suspense ever-present. Add to that, Stuart has an ability to tap into the dark psychology behind addiction and abuse, and to bring these complex struggles to life in a way that stays with you for days."

—*Toronto Star*

"A gripping mystery that I felt desperate to solve. Amy Stuart paints a vivid picture of the stark mountain town, Blackmore, and the cast of shadowy characters who inhabit it. A tense and absorbing read."

—Lucy Clarke, author of *The Blue*

"An impressive debut, rooted in character rather than trope, in fundamental understanding rather than rote puzzle-solving."

—*The Globe and Mail*

"As well as an impressive debut, this promises to be the start of an interesting series."

—PCA Mystery & Detective Fiction Caucus

"Stuart has created a likeable heroine, complete with some pretty serious flaws. Between Clare and the other characters of Blackmore, the story is both haunting and compelling."

—*Vancouver Sun*

ALSO BY AMY STUART

Still Water

STILL MINE

MINE

A NOVEL

AMY STUART

POCKET BOOKS

New York London Toronto Sydney New Delhi

Pocket Books
An Imprint of Simon & Schuster, Inc.
1230 Avenue of the Americas
New York, NY 10020

This book is a work of fiction. Any references to historical events, real people, or real places are used fictitiously. Other names, characters, places, and events are products of the author's imagination, and any resemblance to actual events or places or persons, living or dead, is entirely coincidental.

Originally published in Canada in 2016 by Simon & Schuster Canada

First Pocket Books paperback edition November 2019

POCKET and colophon are registered trademarks of Simon & Schuster, Inc.

For information about special discounts for bulk purchases, please contact Simon & Schuster Special Sales at 1-866-506-1949 or business@simonandschuster.com.

The Simon & Schuster Speakers Bureau can bring authors to your live event. For more information or to book an event contact the Simon & Schuster Speakers Bureau at 1-866-248-3049 or visit our website at www.simonspeakers.com.

Manufactured in the United States of America

10 9 8 7 6 5 4 3 2 1

ISBN 978-1-9821-2234-8
ISBN 978-1-5011-5124-8 (ebook)

For
(I could never have done this without)
Ian

STILL MINE

Sometimes I dream of my escape. In my sleep I conjure a way out, another life waiting for me beyond this one. Sometimes I am climbing, or driving, or falling through a void with no clear place to land. But most often I am running, sprinting through the field and into the trees, my clip too fast for you to catch me.

Even in the version where I'm falling there's this relief at having finally shed it all, these people, this place, you. The shame is gone, just like that. Replaced by a perfect calm. And do you know the strangest part? It feels good. I am free of your anger, and I don't care how long it will take for you to notice I've disappeared. The dream doesn't halt at the door to consider these things, because by the time it begins I am already gone.

WEDNESDAY

With the moonless sky, Clare doesn't see the mountains closing in. But then the road begins to rise and she knows she's driving through the foothills, then come the switchbacks and the hum and pop in her ears, and finally the peaks and shadows, blank spots in the ceiling of stars. By dawn the mountains crowd the long vista of her rearview mirror, she is deep among them, and Clare guesses she's covered nearly six hundred miles since sunset.

Drive west into the mountains, Malcolm said. Then cut north to Blackmore.

Clare climbs one last hairpin turn before signs of life pepper the roadside, peeling billboards first, then a scattering of ramshackle buildings. Her car lurches and revs, the ascent of this narrow road too much for its old engine. She passes a sign hammered right into rock: WELCOME TO BLACKMORE: POPULATION 2500, the word *zero* spray-painted across it in black. The road flattens out and Clare reaches the row of storefronts that marks the town proper. Most of them are shuttered with plywood, the main strip devoid of cars and people.

Beyond the lone stoplight Clare finds the motel. She turns in and parks. Weeds grow through cracks in the asphalt, the motel L-shaped and bent around an empty swimming pool, its neon sign unlit. The

barrenness washes over Clare, eerie and surreal, like
a movie set built and then abandoned. Panic cuts
through her, a grip tight around her chest, the coffee she'd picked up at a gas station hours ago still
whirring through her veins.

The folder Malcolm gave Clare sits on the passenger seat. She flips it open. On top is a news article
dated ten days ago: "Blackmore Woman Missing
Since Tuesday." Next to the text is a grainy photograph of a gaunt and unsmiling woman named
Shayna Fowles. Clare examines the photo. They
are roughly the same age, their hair the same deep
brown, their skin fair, alike in certain features only.
Is she imagining the resemblance, imposing herself
on this woman?

This is your job, Malcolm said. You will go to
Blackmore. See what you can find.

The car fills with the dampness of the outside air.
Clare leans back against the headrest and closes her
eyes. She thinks of Malcolm across from her in that
diner booth, sliding the folder over to her, his own
meal untouched. She had wanted only to get away
from him, and Blackmore was the option on offer.
Now she must gather herself up, muster the nerve
to introduce herself to strangers, tell them her name,
or at least the name Malcolm chose for her. Clare
grips the dewy handle of the car door and lifts her
backpack. Though she hasn't worn her wedding ring
in months, her finger still bears its dent.

Time to go.

At the motel reception Clare rings the bell once,
then again when no one comes. She can hear the

muffled din of a TV. Behind the desk the room keys hang in a neat row. Black mold snakes around the windows and patches the carpet in the corners.

"Hello?" Clare's voice barely rises above a whisper.

Nothing. In her exhaustion, Clare cannot decide what to do next. At dawn, she'd pulled in to a lakeside rest area, walking straight past the picnic tables and the outhouse, wading thigh deep into the lake, catatonic, transfixed by the vast, jagged landscape of snow-peaked mountains. A foreign land. She'd hoped to take a warm shower. Malcolm told her about this motel. Clare slams her hand down hard on the bell.

The door at the far end of the office opens. A man in his sixties peers through, wiping his mouth with a napkin.

"We look open to you?" He tosses the napkin over his shoulder.

"The door was unlocked."

"We're closed."

The man is gray haired and rosy cheeked. An old family portrait hangs on the wall to his right, a younger version of him the beaming father to two red-haired boys, his hand resting proudly on his pretty wife's shoulder.

"If the rooms are still standing," Clare says, "maybe I could just—"

"I'm closed."

Clare nods.

"I've never seen you before," he says.

"I've never been here before."

"You a reporter?"

"No."

"A cop?"

"No. I'm not a cop. I'm just here to see the mountains."

"Huh. Right."

"I take pictures."

"Pictures. Of what?"

"Landscapes, mostly. Anything off the beaten track."

"No one around here likes getting their picture taken," he says, his voice flat.

"Like I said. Landscapes. Not people." Clare pauses. "Is there another place in town I could stay?"

"No."

Clare gropes through her bag for her car keys. Just arrived and already she's failed at her first task. This motel might have been busy once, when Blackmore was still a bustling mining town, when there were jobs for everyone, money to go around, people to visit. Maybe this man's sons had been miners. Maybe they were underground five years ago when the mine blew up and killed three dozen of Blackmore's men. Clare detects a slight softening in the motel owner, his shoulders relaxing. He peels himself off the wall and approaches the desk.

"We had a bad melt in the spring," he says. "All twenty rooms flooded. I've barely had a customer in months. Even if I wanted to, I couldn't help you."

"It's okay," Clare says. "I'll figure something out."

"There are plenty of mountain towns. You could pick another one."

"I could," Clare says.

Already her story feels like too much of a ruse,

arriving in Blackmore alone and unannounced. On the drive she'd anticipated the questions the attendant just asked of her. Who are you? Why are you here? She'd rehearsed her answers. She and Malcolm had been hasty in picking photography as her cover, the one skill in her thin repertoire now ringing false on delivery. The attendant walks around and props the door open to usher her out.

"Turn around," he says. "Drive back down the hill. That's my advice."

Clare retraces her steps to the car. The mountains are cloaked in low clouds, Blackmore's main road fogged from view. She hears the bolt of the office door behind her. Clare knew full well the reception here would be cold. She grew up in a small town beset by the same woes as Blackmore. She remembers the way her neighbors closed rank when strangers turned up, all prying eyes unwelcome. Who knows what the motel owner sees when he looks at Clare? Maybe he knew Shayna Fowles, maybe his sons were friends with her. Maybe it rattles him, one woman gone missing and another turning up out of nowhere, a stranger in his midst.

This is what she dreams. Clare lies on the floor among shards of broken glass, her palms cut open. She looks up at him. When she opens her mouth to speak, the beer bottle hits her square between the eyes. She falls back to the cellar floor and the bottle smashes next to her. He punches the lightbulb and Clare feels its glass rain down. Then he slams the door and locks her in. She can't hear any footsteps overhead.

If you leave, he says, his voice muffled by the closed door, *I'll find you. You know that, right? I'll find you and I'll kill you.*

Clare jerks awake. The car is dark and sticky and she cannot breathe. In the black of the rearview mirror she spots movement. She fumbles with the door and drops to the wet ground, then scrambles to her feet, spinning in a circle. No one else is here. It takes a full minute before she is able to orient herself. Blackmore. The parking lot of the old hardware store. She'd driven here from the motel and climbed into the backseat to rest. That was early afternoon, and now it's dark outside.

Clare knew the bad dreams would come back, the ache of withdrawal.

The air has thinned and cooled. Clare gets back into the car and flips down the visor mirror. Her face is flushed, her hairline rimmed with sweat, her chest tight. For months she'd been spared, but she knew. Clare knew it was a reprieve only, his shadow trailing ever behind, the willpower only carrying her so far. It took Clare six months to let down her guard. Then she met Malcolm Boon.

Wrappers and soda cans litter the floor of the car, relics from her long drive. In the glove compartment Clare finds the cell phone Malcolm gave her. The brightness of the screen blinds her. No messages.

I'll be in touch by end of day Friday, Malcolm said.

Clare digs out her wallet and camera, then stuffs all her belongings into the trunk and locks the car doors.

At the edge of the parking lot, a streetlamp casts a tidy beam to the sidewalk. The stoplight is red. To the north Clare spots a sign, blinking but lit: RAY'S BAR AND GRILL. A few teenagers smoke in a cluster by the door. They fall silent and stare unabashedly at Clare as she approaches, three boys and one girl sharing a cigarette in a closed circle. The girl wears army pants and a top cropped in a ragged line just under her breasts. One of the boys breaks from the group and holds the door open for Clare with an exaggerated bow, a mock gentleman.

The bar is empty, but music plays and Clare can see the waitress and cook shuffling around the kitchen. The stares from outside follow her until she chooses a booth and props the menu to block them out, setting her camera down on the middle of the table. When Clare looks up the waitress is hovering over her.

"Kitchen closes in five minutes."

"What's good?" Clare asks.

The waitress shifts her weight but doesn't answer.

"Burger and fries?"

"To drink?"

Behind the bar, dusty bottles are lined up row by row.

"Club soda," Clare says.

The waitress pinches the top of the menu and yanks it from Clare's grasp. Out the window the teenagers swarm to the stoplight. The double doors to the kitchen flap back and forth and Clare tries to identify the song playing, something country, sounds like Patsy Cline but the voice is too young and too polished, not husky enough. Clare's soda can is delivered without a glass. It runs cool down her throat as she gulps it. Only when she's half-finished it does Clare spot the notice board on the far wall of the restaurant. She slides out of her booth and walks over.

MISSING: SHAYNA CUNNINGHAM FOWLES.

Below, the date she disappeared, two weeks ago. TIPS? TALK TO DONNA.

In the kitchen the waitress is in animated conversation with the cook. The grill hisses and flares. Clare pulls down the poster and stuffs it in her back pocket. Stapled to the lower corner of the board is another notice, this one yellowed with age. TRAILER FOR RENT. FURNISHED. CONTACT CHARLIE MERRITT. Clare plucks the staples from the corners and folds this paper away too. By the time the waitress emerges with her meal Clare is back in her booth, napkin spread across her lap. The plate is dropped in front of her with a clunk.

"You that photographer?" The waitress nods to the camera.

"I am."

"We heard about you showing up."

Clare imagines the motel attendant bolting the door, then diving for his phone. One call to his wife or his girlfriend or his sister, the highest female in his particular pecking order, and word of Clare's arrival would spread fast from there.

"What's your name?"

"Clare O'Dey."

This is the first time Clare has uttered this name aloud.

"Yours?" Clare says.

"Donna."

Donna looks to be fifty, her hair bleached yellow and tied back. The burger on Clare's plate sags out of its bun.

"I saw you making off with my poster."

Clare shrugs. Not quite as stealthy as she thought.

"You got a reason to want it?" Donna asks.

"I wondered if I might know her."

"You're not from around here."

"No."

"Then how would you know her?"

"She looks familiar," Clare says.

Donna slides into the booth across from Clare.

"You're undercover."

"I'm not."

"Some kind of private detective, then. Or a reporter? Snooping around and stealing posters."

Clare doesn't break eye contact. Whatever part she is to play in Blackmore, she must hold to it.

"I'm honestly just curious." Clare rests her hand on the camera. "It's a hazard of the trade."

"Well, there's no big story here. She wasn't eaten by a yeti. And she wasn't murdered."

"How do you know?"

"Shayna Cunningham was nothing but trouble. Popped some pills and wandered off a cliff. Down at the gorge. That's where they go to party."

One article in the file Malcolm gave her mentioned Shayna's penchant for drugs and the town's slide into addiction that followed the shuttering of the mine. Those interviewed claimed that Shayna was high the night she went missing, the consensus around here being, Clare can tell by the waitress's tone, that her status as a junkie somehow mitigates the horror of her disappearance.

"Why make a poster if you know what happened?" Clare asks.

"No one knows for sure what happened," Donna says. "I just figured. Had them printed on a trip to town. So I could feel like I was doing something."

Donna leans in and lowers her voice, her mistrust quickly eclipsed by the prospect of a fresh audience. Clare was never one for gossip, could never understand the willingness to divulge secrets that didn't belong to you. She sees she'll have no choice but to engage in it here.

"I don't mean to sound weird," Donna says, "but sometimes I picture her down there. Her body. Maybe she survived the fall but couldn't climb out or call for help. You can't be sure what happened."

"Until they find a body."

"And they might not. Too much rain. We had flash floods deep in the gorge. She could be halfway to the sea by now."

"Who's looking for her?"

"You tell me."

"The police?"

"Detachment closed last year," Donna says. "There was a search party that climbed down the gorge as best they could. I'd guess her father's looking for her. Her husband sure isn't. He's prancing around town like nothing's happened."

Clare offers the waitress some of her fries. Donna takes one and folds it into her mouth.

"So you know her family?" Clare asks.

"Sure. Grew up with her mom. We both still live in the houses we were born in. I guess that's why I bothered with the poster. Her mom couldn't."

"Why not?"

"She's gone batty. Dementia hit her early." Donna frowns. "Her husband Wilfred's out of his mind too. Too much, I guess."

"Too much what?"

"Sometimes everything falls apart at once. You know?"

"I know," Clare says.

"My husband mined with Wilfred for thirty years. They showed up in Blackmore looking for work right around the same time. Right out of high school. My husband hasn't seen him in a year. Now I heard he's building some kind of bunker up at their house. Dug a hole." Donna leans in again. "My sister says it had to be the husband. Says maybe Shayna went off the cliff, but maybe her husband nudged her. Maybe."

Stuffed in the file Malcolm gave her were a few photographs of Shayna and her husband culled online. In her wedding photograph a younger and healthier Shayna lay draped against her new husband, Jared Fowles, his arm wrapped right around her waist, his palm resting on her belly. The news article about her disappearance described the couple as estranged.

Of course he would be the point of gossip. A missing woman means a guilty husband, as Clare's own mother used to say. Clare sat glued to the TV the summer her mother fell ill, her mother next to her, frail and wispy bald from the chemotherapy. A woman from two towns over had gone missing on her way to work, and Clare and her mother watched as the woman's husband sobbed into a scrum of microphones and begged for his wife's safe return.

Guilty, Clare's mother said. You wait.

Days later, the news showed the flat hay field where the body was found and the police leading the handcuffed husband across his front lawn. Clare's mother mustered the energy to stand and jab her finger at the TV.

It's always the husband, she said. Always.

The french fries on Clare's plate are soaked brown with oil. Donna picks another one up and eats it.

"So, photographer," Donna says. "Where'd you come from?"

"A long way east of here. A small town."

"Which small town?"

"I'm sure you've never heard of it."

"Try me," Donna says.

"Long Lake?"

An answer that told the asker nothing. In six months of driving Clare had passed through four towns with this same name, registering each of them and their features. But she'd always banked on one-off interactions, moving on before the questions got too probing. She will have to find another way to stem the inquiries.

"I didn't like it there," Clare says. "I don't plan to go back."

"Where's your family?" Donna asks.

"I don't really have any family."

"So you just drive around taking pictures for a living?"

"It's not much of a living. But it keeps me moving. I like to be moving."

Clare takes hold of the soda can and squeezes it until it buckles. The give-and-take of conversation, the effort in calculating her responses, have given her a headache. All she wants is to finish her meal. Donna points a thumb over her shoulder.

"You took the ad for the Merritt trailer too."

"I need a place to stay. The motel's closed."

"Well, you can't stay in that trailer."

"Why not? This Merritt guy isn't around any-more?"

"Oh, he's around."

"So what's the problem?"

"*He's* the problem. Lost his family in the mine. Father and two brothers. His mother swallowed a loaded rifle a week later. He's been on a rampage ever since."

"Jesus," Clare says.

"He's taking the whole town down with him."

"I don't understand."

"He's supplying the junkies. That's what I've heard. I know he's selling his crap to kids a lot younger than you. Might as well be poisoning the town water. And that trailer's in the middle of the woods. Right next door to the Cunninghams."

Clare taps the poster again. "The Cunninghams? As in Shayna's family?"

"Yep. All the town's craziness is up on that ridge."

It takes Clare a minute to absorb the implications, the stroke of luck. This trailer of Charlie Merritt's sits right next door to Shayna's family. Under the bun the meat of the burger looks gristly and gray. Donna heaves herself to standing.

"You like this kind of thing? Other people's misery?"

"No," Clare says. "I was making conversation."

"If you leave now you can be in the next town before midnight."

Clare keeps her head down to ward off Donna's cautionary glare. Finally Donna retreats to the kitchen. What would Malcolm Boon do if he were here? He might tell her to be cautious, to sleep in the car instead. For six months it has been easy enough to deflect the attention of chatty strangers, gas station clerks or motel attendants or servers at diners like this one. Clare knew how to keep all conversation short. All along she's pictured a terminus, a place that might swallow her whole, a place with enough scope to let an invented past go unchallenged.

Now she's in a small town not so different from the one she left, and Clare can feel her past bubbling up again. The dread, the sense of abandon, of nothing to lose. Why not go knock on Charlie Merritt's door? Out the window the street is deserted, the stoplight switching from green to yellow to red in deference to no one. Clare will eat the rest of her burger as slowly as she can. She will stay until the waitress kicks her out. The walk back to the car is only two blocks, but she is too awake after a day's sleep. Who knows what sorts of people live here? The kind devoid of hope. The kind who refuse to leave a dying town. The kind who disappear.

It wasn't swift. It took some time. I try to chart when my woes began. That's what my mother calls them: woes. A quiet word, easy to bear. This is a cusp, I remember thinking as I swallowed what I'd been given. My fate was predetermined and I needed only to see how it would play out.

You told me. You warned me. You said we would all suffer, that people would start dying, that you wouldn't tolerate it. But still, here you are.

My mother once said that there's no rhyme or reason to who stays when things fall apart. It won't be the people you expect. But I knew you would hang on. You can't let go. You say it's love, but I think it's about control.

If I end up dead, then everyone will look at you and wonder. You'll be the one to blame, and I'm not sure you'll stand for that.

THURSDAY

A gleaming black pickup truck is parked in the driveway. Clare stops her car at a distance. The Merritt property is large and untended and dotted with old outbuildings, everything on an incline, up or down, the land climbing toward a ridge that gives way to the mountains. Even the house appears to be leaning.

At the slam of her car door, a rottweiler rounds the side of the house in a barking sprint, its teeth bared, eyes two angry slits. Clare cannot fumble fast enough for her car keys. Just as the dog lunges, its leash snaps taut and it flails backwards with a yelp.

"Timber!"

A man leaps off the porch and yanks on the leash to draw the dog back. The hair. A mop of blond gold. He is tall and strong with bulky muscle. His beard is thick, and Clare's husband was clean shaven; not an exact match, but close. The hair, that same blond hair, the hue golden like a young boy's, rare among grown men. A knot ties itself in Clare's stomach.

The man secures the dog to the porch and approaches.

"That's quite the guard dog," Clare says.

"He's trained to scare strangers."

Clare takes the trailer ad out of her pocket and hands it to him.

"The number was out of service," she says. "I looked up your address and figured I'd try you."

"Where'd you get this?"

"At Ray's. On the notice board. Are you Charlie Merritt?"

"This is five years old."

"Thought I'd take a chance."

"On what?"

"That the trailer is still standing. I'm short on options."

"You moving here?"

"No. Just staying for a bit."

"You're the one who showed up at the motel. The so-called photographer."

"Right. And the motel's closed. So here I am."

This morning Clare had washed her face with the last of her bottled water and thrown a cardigan over a clean shirt, strapping her camera over her shoulder. Now the lunging dog has made her edgy, made her tongue dry. In the breeze she can smell gasoline and smoke, the remains of a doused fire.

"Well, thank you anyway," Clare says.

"Wait a minute. What's your name?"

"Clare."

"Clare the photographer. Who sent you here?"

Clare adjusts the strap so her camera rests above her hip. "No one."

"You're not on the job?" Charlie asks.

"Do *you* have a job?"

"No one shows up here for no reason," Charlie says.

"I have my reasons."

It is written plainly on Charlie's face as he sizes her up, the sense of intrigue, curiosity. He reaches for her camera, his hand brushing against her sweater as he lifts it and turns it over, gauging its authenticity. Charlie looks to the woods.

"The trailer is still standing. You'd have to rough it."

"I slept in my car last night. Can't be rougher than that."

"I could show it to you."

"Sure," Clare says.

The dog lies next to the house and gnaws on something clutched between its paws. Charlie is disheveled, his shirt is dirty, his hair hanging over his eyes. When he starts toward the woods, she follows. From behind, the resemblance to her husband is even stronger, his shoulders the same width and rounded forward. He even walks with the same lumbering gait.

"My father dragged this trailer up the hill twenty years ago," Charlie says. "Planted a bunch of trees to box it in. Made good rent when the mine was open."

"Have you always lived here?" Clare asks to Charlie's back.

"Forever."

Charlie stands aside so that Clare might walk up the hill in front of him.

"I ran hydro up here last year. For something to do."

The trailer is an old silver Airstream, thirty feet long and resting on cinder blocks. A fire pit has been dug in front, three lopsided lawn chairs clus-

tered around it. Clare can see a makeshift shower, a
steel vat held on a platform between two tall pines,
the showerhead directly below it, nature's water
pressure.

"Water's clean enough to drink. No hot, though.
Unless you boil it."

Charlie yanks the trailer's rounded door open and
ushers Clare in.

"I could change the propane tank for you, I guess.
I've got a spare somewhere."

The trailer feels surprisingly roomy on the inside,
a kitchenette and a little seating area, the bedroom to
one end and the toilet to the other. The stench brings
tears to Clare's eyes. She pries open the curtains,
releasing a poof of dust that prompts a coughing fit.

"Pretty grim," Charlie says. "It's been empty a
while."

"It'll need a once-over."

"I can get you some cleaning supplies. Bedsheets
and whatever."

Of course, Clare thinks, it would never occur to
Charlie to clean it himself.

"I'll give you fifty bucks for a week," Clare says.

"I'd say a hundred is fair."

"I'd say fifty is better than nothing."

"Fine," Charlie says. "Fifty. Fine."

Clare fishes the money from her backpack and
hands it to him, a share of the kitty Malcolm gave
her at the diner.

"And I park my car down by you?"

"As far up to the woods as you can pull it." Charlie
rubs his beard. "What else? Keep the windows open

if you turn on the burners. The stove's old. You don't want to get gassed."

"You have neighbors up here?" Clare risks asking.

"Only to the north. Through the line of birch trees. We're not very neighborly."

"Bad blood?"

"You could say that."

Clare thinks of the waitress, the way she leaned forward in the booth, stirring the pot with her tidbits. Bad blood. Clare's husband would fit in well here.

"Be wary of the old man. He's been known to point a gun at me if my dog so much as takes a piss in his general vicinity," Charlie says. "It's just your typical small-town crap."

"I get it."

Clare would like to press him, but she must pace herself. Charlie shifts and scratches at his mess of hair.

"You look like someone I know," he says.

"So do you."

Charlie laughs. "I don't hear that too often."

Tension passes between them, two strangers alone in close proximity. Charlie doesn't seem menacing, but Clare can't trust her instincts with men, won't let herself be fooled by friendly banter. Neither Charlie nor his dog would be so easily defanged.

"I'll get you a key," he says. "And a couple of flashlights."

"I thought you said there was hydro."

"For outside. These woods get pretty dark. You got a cell phone?"

"Yes."

"Reception's spotty. Walk up the hill. You might get lucky."

"What about your dog? Is he going to attack me?"

"I'll introduce you. Let him pick up your scent. He doesn't bite friends."

It is unexpected, the warmth that comes to Clare, the familiarity of his smile. Charlie starts back down the hill. Clare lifts the camera and clicks at his back, then angles her gaze upward, absorbing the landscape that surrounds her. She digs for her phone, its signal bars flat. It is still morning. Malcolm said he would send word within two days. Clare could always make contact first, walk these hills in search of a signal, punch in an account of events so far that might suit him. *I'm settling in.* Any words she could muster to avoid sounding distressed.

Back at her car, Clare finds a bucket filled with cleaning supplies and a garbage bag of clean sheets he left for her on the hood. Charlie emerges from the house and introduces Clare to Timber, allowing the dog to sniff around her legs. Then he hands her a flimsy-looking key and heads back to his porch, settling in with a beer. Clare collects her bag and whatever else lay strewn in the car, possessions few enough that she can drag them up the hill in two trips. She fishes her camera case from the trunk, the few rolls of film she'd been able to find along the way jammed into it. Her camera belonged to her brother, a gadgety old film contraption, small and portable enough, the only thing she'd taken from home.

Her brother. Christopher.

It was Christopher who taught her how to develop a roll of film in his makeshift cellar darkroom, who taught her how to frame shots, to focus on the unexpected subject, to forgo the immediacy of digital. Christopher lives in the family home now, Clare's father transplanted to a cabin at the property's rear corner after Clare's nephew was born. The last time Clare saw her brother he'd clicked his front door closed, her money handed over. He was tired of it, of forgiving Clare over and over for the same lapses, of keeping his family shielded from the worst of it. He was scared of what she might do. You can't change what you did, Christopher said. Clare imagines her brother now thinks her dead. She hopes her nephew doesn't remember much of her, that Christopher changed the story in her absence, rendering her a better person, allowing the truth to dissolve into her nephew's young memory.

Only one day in Blackmore and already it feels harder to stave it off, these memories that blindside her. Though it forces her to stay composed, Clare has to admire the unabashed way Charlie surveys her from his perch. She makes a show of hauling the darkroom starter kit from her trunk, a yard-sale find at some town in between, and heaving it in a circle so that Charlie might read the box. After slamming the trunk closed she carries the box to the trailer, swerving against its weight, surprised at herself for hoping Charlie will follow.

By the time she reaches the trailer again, her legs burn and her back is sticky with sweat. She drops the darkroom kit next to the fire pit. These woods are replete with color, greens and yellows and browns. Without Charlie standing in front of her, without that blond hair as a trigger, Clare's physical memory of her husband evaporates. How has her mind so quickly rubbed out such a familiar face? What does Jason picture when he thinks of her? Clare doubts he could conceive of mountains as vast as these. He'd never give her credit for getting this far. He might only think her dead or lost rather than running.

Clare digs the folded poster from her pocket. Odds are that a woman missing for weeks is dead, but Clare stands in these ghostly woods as proof that this isn't always the case. Sometimes people vanish for good reason, leaving an entire life behind to escape just one part of it. Clare can feel Shayna's story weaving into her thoughts, however it varies from hers. She can picture Shayna in the gorge, alive, others with her. Clare sees that part clearly. But she cannot see what happened next; Shayna dead, or lost, or running.

The trailer is hot. It takes all of Clare's might to pry the windows open. When she succeeds, the effect is a decent cross breeze. Outside the trailer Clare strings a length of rope between two trees and hangs the blankets she'd found on the bed. Though they're moth-eaten and ragged, Clare can tell by the stitching that these quilts are handmade, probably by a mother for her young sons, both blue, one themed with trains and the other with trucks. Clare finds a long stick in the woods and beats the dust from them until their patterns brighten.

At the back of the sink cabinet Clare finds a sticky trap coated with the mangy corpses of two dead mice. The stench makes her gag. She flings the trap out the door, and the rotten smell that's hung in the trailer since she arrived is instantly gone. When the kettle whistles she goes back inside and fills the bucket with boiling water. Starting at one end and working her way on hands and knees to the other, Clare scrubs ceiling to floor, windows and countertops, cupboards and drawers, every nook and corner in this small space. When is the last time anyone cleaned here? Men don't like mess, Clare's mother would say, but they sure can tolerate filth.

When she's finished Clare carries the bucket and cleaning supplies down the hill and sets them on the front steps of the house. Charlie's perch is empty, the truck gone, the dog too. Charlie appears to live alone, and Clare knows that a man alone in his family home speaks to some kind of mitigating event, a tragedy or a death or an exodus, in this case an exploded mine with Charlie's family inside it. When Clare met her husband, he'd been living alone on his parents' farm for years, acting the part of the orphan, unable to cope with the basic logistics of a household, an only child whose father got drunk and veered his car into the path of an oncoming truck—swerving, purposefully or not, so that the truck would hit his wife's side first.

When the insurance settlement came through, Jason bought himself a pickup truck, no hired help or vacations, though he was flush with money. He rented his fields to a farmer up the road and took a job in a factory. A lot of money and only a truck to show for it. She'd admired that in him, taken it as a sign of humility. After they were married, Clare moved in and took the reins on the house and its care. She found her mother's cleaning habits had sunk in, that she too carried the need to scrub.

In the trailer bedroom Clare stuffs her things under the bed and drops Malcolm's folder on the counter. Clipped together under the photographs of Shayna are the news articles about the mine accident. A blast at the Blackmore Coal Mine five years ago killed thirty-two men and trapped eighteen others underground for three weeks. Clare flips through the clippings. The photographs of the mine site show cranes and bulldozers, the rescue crew in hard hats, huddled together, faces strained by the uncertainty of what lay beneath them, how many dead or alive. Until they could make contact below, there was no body count. The story still cried out for a happy ending.

Though it must have been international news, Clare has only vague memories of this story. Five years ago was the summer she was married, leaving her no time to take in the miseries of the outside world. No one she knew back home read the newspaper—nighttime television was reserved for game shows and sports—all of them well versed in ignoring anyone's misfortunes but their own.

In a later article, photos of the thirty-two dead line up alphabetically down the page. Midway Clare finds the three photographs with the Merritt name, each one with that same golden hair as Charlie. Clare scans the text. "Russell Merritt and his two sons found dead. A third son, also a miner, was off shift at the time of the accident." Charlie.

Out the trailer window, Clare hears the crack of a branch, the crunch of pine needles. She opens the door.

"Charlie?"

The crunching stops. It's probably an animal, Clare knows, but as she circles to the back of the trailer, her heart beats hard in her chest.

"Charlie?"

Clare spots movement in the distance. Not an animal. An upright figure.

"Who's there?"

Clare picks up a stick and holds it in front of her with a two-handed grip.

"I can see you."

A quick flash of white, a ghost. A human shape.

"Please come out," Clare says. "You're scaring me."

"*You're* scaring *me*!" A woman's voice. The figure steps out from behind the tree. She is older, her hair pulled into a silvery ponytail, the skin on her face smooth and peach in her cheeks. She wears a loose linen shirt tucked into shorts. Not dressed for the damp weather. Not a ghost. Clare drops the stick.

"This is private property," Clare says. "You're on the Merritt property."

"I must be lost," the woman says.

"What's your name?" Clare says.

"Louise."

"Louise Cunningham?"

"Yes." Louise looks up to the sky, as if considering. "Yes."

"You live next door," Clare says.

Gone batty, the waitress said. Shayna's mother.

"You've taken a wrong turn," Clare says.

"I meant to go to the creek."

"You're headed uphill. It's not usually uphill to a creek."

"I suppose not." Louise studies Clare. "Do we know each other?"

"No. I'm Clare O'Dey. A new neighbor."

"O'Dey. Is your father a miner?"

"No. A farmer."

Louise walks past Clare to the fire pit, then over to the blankets and back around to the shower, reaching out to touch everything she passes.

"I know where I am," Louise says. "This is Russell's place."

"That's right," Clare says. "I've rented the trailer from Charlie."

"Is Russell here?"

"No. Russell Merritt? Isn't he . . ."

But Louise isn't listening. She plops herself into one of the lawn chairs and uses the rocks of the fire pit to pry off her sandals.

"Shayna and I used to come here," Louise says. "We'd camp out when the trailer wasn't rented. Sometimes we'd stay for days." She laughs. "Those boys. Three of them like little animals. Always running wild."

A wave of exhaustion rolls over Clare, knowing what she must do next.

"Would you like me to walk you home?"

"That would be nice," Louise says. "You know, I saw a cougar here once."

"You did?"

"With Shayna. She was maybe nine." Louise nods as if the story is revealing itself only as she tells it. "It stood there, over there, staring at us, maybe fifteen feet away. Shayna had her back to it. She was tossing pebbles at trees. I never imagined a cougar would be that big."

"What did you do?"

"I stepped between them. I remember thinking, if I'm fierce, if I'm fiercer than this animal, it will leave us alone. So I stretched out my arms, like this, and I showed it my teeth. I bared my fangs! Can you believe that? It cocked its head, then bounded away."

Louise pivots, eyes upward.

"Clare. That's your name. Clare."

"Yes."

"You know the way back?"

"I can find it," Clare says. "I don't think it's far."

From behind Louise's gait is strong, stoic. Clare yanks the trailer door closed and jogs to catch up. She will walk Shayna's mother home, take her chances on the reception she'll receive should Shayna's father be there. There is no time for caution. Fierce, Louise said. If I'm fierce. Clare likes to think of herself as such, but she doubts she could compare to Louise Cunningham, even in the early throes of dementia. She imagines Louise as a young mother, a coal miner's wife, afraid of nothing, the sort of woman who commands even these woods, who stands up to all threats. While Clare, if her life so far is any indication, is the sort who runs.

The Cunningham driveway is enclosed by bended treetops. Clare walks five paces behind Louise until the driveway opens into a meadow, the largest patch of flat land she's laid eyes on since crossing into the mountains. Beyond it sits a white farmhouse, the paint of its red shutters much faded, its clapboard rotted and peeling. Though the house itself is run-down, the surrounding garden is bright with dogwoods, whatever plants can endure the lack of sun.

"Stop," Louise says, pointing to the field. "Shush."

In the garden, a snowshoe rabbit plucks at a head of iceberg lettuce, its nose atwitter. A man emerges from the barn with a shotgun in hand. Louise draws Clare back among the trees. By the time he is within range, the rabbit is off into the nearby woods. The man pumps the shotgun and fires a shot into the low clouds anyway. Then he stands still. Both Clare and Louise hold their breath, waiting too, until he gives up and retreats back through the wide doors of his dilapidated barn.

"Wilfred," Louise says. "He hates rabbits. He'll never leave it alone."

"They're eating his vegetables."

"Those are my vegetables. And I'm happy to share them with the odd rabbit."

"I'll wait here until you reach the door," Clare says.

"Don't be silly. Come in."

"I wouldn't want to take your husband by surprise."

"You don't know him?"

"No," Clare says.

"Then I'll introduce you."

"But you don't know me either."

"Don't I?" Louise laughs, then nudges Clare onward and up the porch steps.

The storm door is loose on its hinges. Louise takes off her shoes and wanders straight into the kitchen. Clare stands in the hall and looks around. Towers of cardboard boxes lean into each other on the living room wall. Even the couch is overtaken with blankets, a box of books, and an old rotary phone off its hook. A small space has been cleared on one cushion, the only spot in the room a person might take a seat.

Clare moves through to the equally cluttered kitchen. She lifts a box of dusty glasses off one of the chairs and sets it on the floor. Country kitchens are always the same, a square room with cupboards on every wall, stairs to the cellar, the sink under the window, and a harvest table in the middle. A kettle boils soundlessly on the stove, its whistle flipped up. Despite the clutter the kitchen bears no evidence of family, no photographs or keepsakes, only bald spots on the wallpaper where frames clearly used to hang. Louise sets about making tea.

"Why don't we sit in the living room?" Louise says, handing Clare a mug. "We could have a chat."

This time they pass through the dining room. High

stacks of boxes line the wall and folded clothes and dinnerware are piled on the table. Louise behaves as if she's noticed the mess for the first time, flustered by where to leave the tray.

"Wilfred doesn't throw anything out."

"My father is like that too." Clare takes the tray from Louise and goes to place it on a pile of newspapers on the coffee table. The headline of the top paper reads "Jury Deliberates for Fifth Day in Civil Mine Trial." Clare sets down her mug and cleans off the smaller of the two wingback chairs.

"Have you met her?"

Louise finds the bare spot on the couch and sits.

"Who?" Clare asks.

"Shayna."

Clare must fix her expression to hide her surprise.

"No," she says.

"She's married. Settled down."

"That's nice."

"She looks after kids to make money, but she'd like to be a writer. Are you a writer?"

"No," Clare says. "I take pictures."

"She writes poetry, mostly. She has piles of it."

"I'd like to read some of her work."

"You should ask her to read it," Louise says.

It will take some concentration to keep up with the way Louise passes from one era to the next, her notion of time fluid and, Clare sees, not limited to facts. Louise rises and navigates her way to the mantel to look for something. As quietly as she can Clare lifts the tray and pulls out the top newspaper. The photograph is a cloister of reporters, the man at the microphone Charlie Merritt. Clare folds the paper and tucks it into the back of her jeans. Louise returns and hands two framed photographs to Clare. The first is black and white and cracked with age, a man and woman standing in front of this very house, the woman holding a swaddled baby, the house surrounded by pine and cedar saplings barely as tall as the couple. On the papered backing of the frame it reads: *Louise Elsa, summer 1951*.

"That's Wilfred and me with Shayna."

"I don't think so," Clare says. "It says here it was taken in 1951."

"Does it?"

"Could this be you as a baby? With your parents?"

Louise frowns.

The second photograph is Louise and Wilfred's wedding portrait, they too standing in front of the house, the passage of time charted by the saplings tripled in size. Out the window those same trees now stand two stories high, cradling the house in their drooping branches. In the photo Wilfred smiles and hugs his bride, Louise raven haired and happy. Clare thinks of Shayna's wedding photograph from Malcolm's folder, Shayna the spitting image of the young Louise in this picture.

"Wilfred is foreman at the mine," Louise says, pride in her voice.

Present tense, Clare thinks, though the mine closed five years ago.

"He doesn't like it when I leave the house."

"He's probably just worried about you getting lost," Clare says.

"He's always at war with someone. He treats the whole town like a war zone."

"Maybe he's got a lot on his mind."

"Does he?" Louise says. "I can't imagine what. He goes to work. I do everything else. He's never made a meal in his life."

Clare smiles. "That sounds familiar."

"He worries about Shayna," Louise says. "Ever since she married that boy."

"Jared."

"Wilfred doesn't approve of anything she does. They used to be really close."

"They're not now?"

"Everything she does disappoints him."

"I know that feeling," Clare says.

"He's too hard on her. I tell him, our job is to love her and protect her. That's our only job. Isn't it?"

"It's not always that simple," Clare says.

Louise opens her mouth to say something but sips her tea instead. There is no sign of Wilfred Cunningham out the window, no rabbits in the garden, no sound of his fired shotgun.

Rabbits. As a girl, Clare shot rabbits and whatever else nibbled on their vegetables, stalking the perimeter of her parents' garden and piling the corpses neatly in the shed, their eyes flapped open and their coats dribbled with blood. The shooting never bothered Clare. As soon as she could hold her brother's BB gun steady the lessons started, her father standing behind her, nudging her elbow up and back, covering her outside eye with his callused hand. You see nothing but the target, he'd say. Nothing else is there. He would line up a row of tin cans for her, twenty, then thirty, then forty feet away. Then came the moving targets, skeets and crows through the bare winter branches. And the better Clare got, the more her father expected from her. The more you miss, he would say, the more they eat up our garden. Soon Clare was rarely missing, even the quickest animals no match for her dead aim.

A newer-model SUV pulls up the Cunningham drive. The man who emerges looks nothing like those Clare has seen in Blackmore so far. He is clean-cut and youthful, khaki pants and a crisp dress shirt tucked in. He opens the trunk and pulls out a black bag, a medical kit, then straightens up and waves at someone. Wilfred. From the kitchen comes the bang of a door. Louise and Clare both stand. When Clare peeks down the hall, she can see Wilfred shuffling in and out of view, his face and neck flushed.

"Mr. Cunningham?"

He cranes to follow her voice. When he tramps down the hallway, Clare aligns herself with Louise near the couch.

"Dammit!" Wilfred says to Louise. "I was looking for you."

"I went for a walk to the creek. This nice young lady escorted me home."

Both Wilfred and Louise look to Clare.

"Sorry. I'm Clare O'Dey. I'm renting the trailer from Charlie Merritt. Louise here, your wife, she came over—"

Wilfred ignores her outstretched hand. "You need

to leave. Get off my property. The Merritts aren't welcome here."

"I'm not a Merritt."

Wilfred grits his teeth. "I'm asking you to get out of my house."

"Wilfred!" Louise says.

"Sit down. You hear me, Louise? Sit down."

"I bet you'd shoot me too if I dared to pick a cucumber. Wouldn't you?"

Wilfred points to the sofa. "Sit down."

To Clare's amazement Louise obeys. Once seated she appears deflated, eyes vacant, hands upturned and limp on her lap.

"Hello?" A voice comes through the screen door. "Mind if I come in?"

The doctor strides inside, stopping at the sight of Clare.

"I'm sorry to interrupt," he says. "We had an appointment, did we not, Mrs. Cunningham?"

"You're never interrupting," Louise says, brightening. "Come right in. I just made tea."

Clare can sense Wilfred's seething, his inability to manage the sudden crowd in his front hall. And though he makes an obvious effort not to stare, the doctor clearly can't make sense of Clare's presence.

"Hi." Clare stretches her hand out again. "I'm Clare O'Dey."

"Derek Meyer. I'm Louise's doctor. Are you family? I didn't know—"

"She's not family," Wilfred says. "She's leaving."

"I am," Clare says. "Leaving, I mean."

"Tell the doc how you've been taking off, Lou,"

Wilfred says. "Disappearing. Wandering up the hill and down to the gorge in an effort to meet your death."

"Is that so?" Dr. Meyer asks. "We'll have to talk about that."

"He treats me like a child," Louise says to Clare.

The doctor kneels down next to Louise and opens his kit. Wilfred motions for Clare to follow him into the kitchen.

"You can leave through the back door," he says.

"My shoes are at the front."

With a snarl Wilfred pushes aside a chair and approaches Clare. His skin is creviced, his graying hair buzzed short. Wilfred Cunningham, a coal mine foreman, the beds of his fingernails still stained black after five years. In the small space between them Clare can smell the staleness, that of a man used to a woman's care and lately left to fend for himself.

"You tell him if I see him over here, I'll shoot him."

"Who?" Clare asks. "If you mean Charlie Merritt, I only met him this morning."

"You aren't welcome here."

"Your wife was lost. It was clear she was . . . disoriented. I was only trying to help."

Wilfred jolts to attention, his sights turned on something out the kitchen window. With a start he's out the back door, snatching up his shotgun as he passes through the cold room, the door swinging behind him. Chasing a rabbit. Clare goes to get her shoes. In the living room, Dr. Meyer presses his stethoscope to Louise's chest. Clare watches the doctor frown in concentration, his eyes fixed on nothing as he listens to Louise's breathing. Derek Meyer wears glasses but no wedding ring. Clare knows well enough that this says nothing of whether he's married. Done with his examination, the doctor writes some notes in a small leather-bound book.

"It was nice to meet you, Mrs. Cunningham," Clare says. "You too, Dr. Meyer. I should be going."

For the first time the doctor makes direct eye contact with Clare. "Can I have a quick word?" he says.

"I really should go. Mr. Cunningham will be back in soon."

"Won't even take a minute," the doctor says.

Clare is self-conscious of her clothes, her jeans and T-shirt grubby from her efforts to clean the trailer. They leave Louise in the living room and move to the kitchen.

"You're staying in Charlie's trailer?" the doctor asks.

"Yes."

He waits for her to continue.

"Louise wandered up there. She seemed disoriented."

"So you don't know the Cunninghams."

"No. I was just walking her home. She invited me in for tea."

"I see," he says.

"Can I ask you something?" Clare says. "Does Louise know her daughter is missing?"

Clare detects only a twitch in the doctor.

"Do you know Shayna?" he asks.

"No. I saw the Missing Woman poster at Ray's. The waitress there filled me in."

"There's no reason for Louise to register her daughter's absence," Dr. Meyer says. "As you've probably figured out, her grasp on reality comes and goes."

"And I guess no good comes from reminding her?"

"Reminding me of what?" Louise enters from the dining room and hands another frame to Clare. "Look! I found this one of you in the pile on the mantel. Remember this?"

The photograph shows five friends clustered in a group hug, a pristine mountain backdrop behind them. At its center Derek Meyer stands with his chest puffed, his face younger and tanned, sunglasses on. The girl next to him is Shayna. He holds her by the arm, tugging her toward him, her head tossed back in laughter. Beside them, a beardless Charlie Merritt sticks out his tongue, and next to him are his brothers, the gold hair and bulky build, standing side by side, serious.

"How old are you there?" Louise says.

"We were nineteen," says the doctor.

"Such good friends you were."

"Not really. You don't always get to choose your friends."

"Don't say that." Louise elbows him. "You love Shayna." She turns to Clare. "Don't let him tell you otherwise."

The doctor shakes his head, flustered. He leads Louise back to the living room, leaving Clare holding the photograph. In it Shayna's laughter is so carefree, all the bad things yet to come. How kindred we are, Clare thinks as she dissects this photograph, Shayna and me, two lives veering so far off the course we expected they'd follow. On the sill of her kitchen window at home Clare kept two photographs, one of her mother before she got sick, and another from the summer Clare turned seventeen, taken on a camping trip with her best friend, Grace Fawcett. Like her brother, Grace remains perfectly intact to Clare, not just the adult but also the Grace from that trip, her bouncing hair and wild smile, the Grace who inhabited the short era in Clare's life that felt both hopeful and grown-up.

Clare sets the frame down on the kitchen table and walks back to the living room.

"I really should get going."

"We haven't finished our tea," Louise says.

"I don't want to be in Dr. Meyer's way."

"Call me Derek, please."

"He's out there with his gun," Louise says. "If you leave now he might shoot you."

"Louise," Derek says. "Let's not overstate."

"You know he's done it before!"

"You're the one who's in danger, Louise," Derek says. "You need to stay close to home. No more walks on your own."

"Or what? You'll commit me?"

"It's not safe, Mrs. Cunningham. You could slip. Break a hip."

"Or I could get shot."

"That's not funny," Derek says. "You could get lost. Really lost. Who would find you?"

"You would, Doctor. That's your job."

The three of them stand shoulder to shoulder at the front window, Clare in the middle. Out in the garden another rabbit is at work on the lettuce, or perhaps the same one from earlier. Small breaks have formed in the clouds, patching the mountains with sunlight. At the far side of the garden Wilfred skulks and grips his gun.

"Run." Louise's voice is a hoarse whisper.

The rabbit stands on its hind legs, its paws holding a leaf to its face. Louise goes to bang on the window, but Clare catches her arm.

"Leave it."

"But he'll shoot."

"Then let him," Clare says.

Wilfred darts along the rows of vegetables, taking aim. When he fires, the rabbit bounds away in frantic escape, gaining ground, the shotgun blast loud and echoed. The rabbit pops in and out of the grass. If the gun were in her hands, Clare would rely on physics, aiming ahead of the animal, accounting for its speed.

"Your father's crazy," Louise says.

"Wilfred's not my father, Louise."

"He thinks I don't know," Louise says.

"He thinks you don't know what?" Clare asks.

Derek looks to Clare, widening his eyes as if to shush her.

"About what he did. About Russell. He thinks I'm stupid!"

With a strangled wail Louise lifts her mug and hurls it at the window, spraying Clare and Derek with the lukewarm tea. The mug shatters but the window doesn't, and then the doctor has Louise in a hug, restraining her as she writhes against him. He calls to Clare to grab his kit. Clare finds it and takes hold of Louise in his place, squeezing her from behind.

"It's okay," Clare says. "No one will hurt you."

"It wasn't his fault!" Louise says.

Derek plunges a syringe into a bare patch of skin. Louise jolts.

"Ketamine," he says. "Should work right away."

They scramble to hold Louise until her eyes flutter and she slackens against them, then they set her down on the couch. Out the window Wilfred shoots again, oblivious to his wife's outburst. He'll never leave it alone, Louise said. Clare watches Wilfred as he stops to reload. You can never be too vigilant, Clare's father used to say, whether he spoke of neighbors, enemies, or pests in his garden. If you leave it, her father would say, that rabbit will come back with his friends and your whole garden will be gone. And you'll think back to this moment, the first sign of trouble, and wish you'd killed it when you had the chance.

In her dream, it is dusk. The window is clouded by dust. Clare blasts through the cellar door, dashing through the kitchen until she is outside, racing across the yard, barefoot. Though she will not turn around, though his words are muddled, his voice high and pleading, she knows he is on the back porch. She must make it only to the grove behind the barn so that the trees swallow her up before he can fumble the bullets into the chamber and raise the gun to her back.

Clare is running.

Out the door and down the hill from the trailer and past her own car, past the Merritt house, Charlie's truck still gone, and into the field, sprinting. The fence that marks the back end of the Merritt field has already been pried open. From there the earth drops steeply, a makeshift path zigzagging down. Clare's momentum tumbles her forward, arms in windmills, nothing to grab. She tips over the edge of the switchback, breaking through the brush. Falling. She used to dream of falling all the time. She lands hard, flat on her back, gasping for breath.

Clare blinks. This is not a dream. The highest branches flutter far above her, the canopy so dense that little light pokes through. She blinks again. This is not the yard behind her house. This is not the grove. Jason is not here. He is not chasing her. This is Blackmore.

The pain oozes, hot up her neck. A trail of blood curls down her arm. A gash on her left shoulder.

Did she fall asleep in the trailer after returning from the Cunningham house? For months she's slept so soundly, sinking into motel beds along the way, waking sweaty and disoriented, the sleep blank and deep. She must have bolted from the trailer in a trance, in that panic that overtakes her between dreaming and being fully awake. Clare sits up. The hill she tumbled down hovers over her like a wall of rock. She pinches the gash and balls up her sweater to press into it.

Somewhere among her things is the map of Blackmore Malcolm gave her, the gorge behind the town. This must be it. It slopes in every direction, a creek gurgling not far from where Clare sits, a rusted pipe running along its far bank. If Clare can orient herself at all, this is where she must be: this gorge behind the Cunningham and Merritt houses, upward to the mine, downward to the town. The last place anyone saw Shayna alive.

When the bleeding subsides, Clare stands and gingerly removes her sweater, the T-shirt underneath torn and soaked with blood. She ties her sweater to a tree to mark the path back to the Merritt house, then crouches at the creek and cups the icy water. It tastes clean. She sits on a rock and yanks her shirt off-shoulder, splashing the gash, the pain finally sharp, her skin fanned open in a perfect line, a three-inch cut from her bicep to her collarbone. It's been years since she felt pain this clear and piercing. The first pill Clare ever took came from her mother's cancer supply, an orange bottle behind the dandruff shampoo in the medicine cabinet. It dissolved on her tongue like a snowflake and dulled all aches, damming the constant current of thoughts that had always plagued her. Calm. Clare blows on the gash, relieved by how much it hurts.

Her cell phone is not with her. There might be an hour of daylight left. Clare stands and follows the creek down. Every few steps her heel slides in the mud and she must jut her arms out for balance. Once she is awake, Clare can never remember the specifics of the dream. It is only the sensation of running that lingers, the need to get away. The thin mountain air has Clare drawing long breaths. The forest around her creaks and sways, her pulse fast and hard.

"He's not here," Clare says aloud. "You're not here."

Up ahead is a small clearing, charred logs piled high in the fire pit at its center. A tent is pitched but buckling. Sleeping bags hang from the lowest branches. The clearing is littered end to end with beer cans, crumpled chip bags, cigarette butts. In the tent a sleeping bag is gathered into a ball as though someone might still be hunched inside, passed out after a bender. It is easy to envision this place at night, the light of the bonfire, how darkness would envelop all but those closest to the fire. Shayna. A person could walk away, be led away, be carried away without anyone taking notice.

That's where they go to party, the waitress at Ray's said.

It was at a summer party around a bonfire like this one where Clare's brother first introduced her to Jason, his coworker at the plant. After the fire was doused, Jason let Clare and her friends ride in the back of his truck, and Clare remembers how he eyed her in his rearview mirror, the way her friend Grace laughed and squeezed her hand. Clare had thought him so chivalrous and mature. She wanted him to find her worthy. And so in the back of his truck she'd raised her arms overhead and screeched with abandon, giving in, the wind whipping her hair as the farmland sped by. When they started dating, her brother turned wary.

There's a side to him you haven't seen, he told Clare.

Water has pooled on the tent's canvas. Clare presses it to release the gush. On the other side of the creek the land disappears over a ledge. Clare crosses right through the water so that it soaks her shoes. Over the edge she can see trees growing upward from the gorge wall, clinging to the rock with tentacles of exposed roots. Clare takes hold of a tree to steady herself, then picks up a rock and pitches it, her shoulder pulsing with pain. The rock arcs out, then vanishes into the depths, and she waits, one beat, then two, then three, then four before she hears the rock crack against the earth. Something in that lapse, in the counting in between, has finally set Clare to tears. She tries to muffle the cries, but they come anyway, sobs bursting forth.

Sometimes Clare pictures word of her disappearance spreading through her hometown in the days after she left, what it might have stirred in those who loved her once. Though it took willpower at first, Clare made a point of never searching for news of herself online, of leaving her e-mail untouched until it would have been shut down from disuse. The tips of her wet shoes hang over the ledge. She wiggles her toes.

Perhaps it would be just like flying.

Clare lets go of the tree and holds her arms out in front of her, superhero. She bends her knees.

Don't jump.

The gray light plays tricks on her, the tent and sleeping bag too bright beyond the creek. Clare spins around. "Hello?"

Nothing moves. There is a light rain against Clare's skin. She crosses the creek again, never certain she's alone. Shayna must have felt the same way. Watched. Clare swallows against the lump in her throat. There was a version of her worth saving once, the Clare with a brother and a best friend, a father and husband she remembers loving once, a nephew and a decent job. That woman vanished long before Clare actually left. Surely such a version of Shayna existed too, a woman loved by her people. Clare will return to the trailer before it gets too dark. If she is to solve this riddle, she will have to seek out Shayna's friends and family one by one, an outsider looking for a way in.

I live with two ghosts.

Last night we found her naked in the garden on her hands and knees, clawing at the earth like an animal. Planting seedlings, she said, even though there was snow on the ground. Her skin was blue. At the kitchen table I hugged a blanket to her while she talked about the beauty of the moon out the window.

This is your fault, Dad said to me. My fault she's losing her mind? We yelled at each other across the kitchen and she sat there shivering and smiling. She's gone and he can't bring her back. Sad things never make him sad; they make him angry. I'm the same. So are you.

Sometimes I wonder if you have it in you to hurt me. Why does it have to be hard even with you? None of this makes me cry. What should be filling me with sadness is filling me with rage instead.

FRIDAY

This street has no sidewalk, each bungalow a cookie-cutter version of the one beside it, the dead end marked by a faded yellow guardrail. A few of the homes have been boarded up, "For Sale" signs tilting in neglect on the overgrown lawns. Clare parks her car and walks up the center of the road, backpack on. A young boy rides his bicycle on his lawn. He pedals in circles, his training wheels off the grass as he leans into the turns. A woman rounds the house, carrying a garden hose in one hand and holding a cigarette in the other.

"Not on the lawn," the woman says to the boy. "Driveway only."

"There's no room in the driveway. Can I ride on the street?"

"And get killed?"

"There aren't any cars."

"What's that?"

The woman points to a truck parked in a driveway across the street, its tire wells rusted out. The decal on its side reads FOWLES LANDSCAPING AND TREE REMOVAL. The mother widens her eyes when she catches sight of Clare. She is younger than Clare, thin, her brown hair unwashed and pulled into a ponytail. She flicks her cigarette onto the road and tugs the hose down the length of her driveway.

"Can I help you?" the woman asks.

"I was looking for a grocery store. The one on the main road is closed."

The little boy dumps his bicycle and sidles up to his mother.

"The mart's closed," the woman says. "Merged with the hardware store around the corner. Go looking for a hubcap and you'll find a bag of apples for ten dollars instead."

"Wow. Okay."

"You're the one up at Charlie's."

"That's right. Clare."

"Sara Gorman." The woman lets go of the hose to extend her hand. "This is Daniel."

"Hi there," Clare says to the boy.

"A photographer. Gracing us with your presence."

Clare chooses not to respond.

"Did you know that, Danny? This lady takes pictures."

The boy peers up at Clare. "Where's your camera?" he asks.

Clare slides her bag around to her chest and zips it open.

"Do you want to see it?"

"No thanks," Sara says.

"Maybe I can show it to you another time," Clare says to the boy, zipping the bag closed.

Sara squeezes her son's shoulders, then wipes at her nose with her bare forearm. The skin around the bend in Sara's arm is dotted with punctures, bruised. Clare knows precisely how long it takes for such marks to fade. Even now, if Clare runs her palm up and down her own inner arm, she can feel them, the tiny holes closed over with pearls of scar tissue. Above these, the gash from yesterday aches, her whole body stiff from the fall in the gorge.

"My babysitter's gone," the boy says. "A police car came because of her."

"Never mind about that," Sara says.

"She disappeared," the boy says.

"Shut up!" Sara crouches and gives him a shake. Daniel's lips quiver as he absorbs his mother's wrath.

"It's okay," Clare says. "I know the story."

"No one cares what you know," Sara says.

"Okay." Clare raises her hands. "I'm sorry to bother you."

"You want to meet Jared? Is that why you're here?"

"Sorry?"

"You making casseroles?"

"I'm not catching your meaning," Clare says.

"We've had a whole lot of groupies show up here from God knows where. Bringing casseroles and knocking on Jared's door. They saw his mug in the paper and figured he was a catch. Swoop in while he's too troubled to know any better. Death bunnies, my father-in-law called them."

"That's not . . . That's unbelievable. I'm not—"

"You saw his picture in the paper?"

"No . . ." Clare trails off, unable to come up with a truthful defense. She knows these things happen. In the first months after she left, Clare would often lie in her motel rooms, imagining the women who most certainly zeroed in on her husband, the ones who for years had glared at Clare at parties. Even though stories of his drunken rages wove their way through town, there was never a shortage of women beguiled by Jason's truck or his good looks, by the way he could liven a room. And though Clare had ached for years to be free of him, in those motel rooms the prospect of a woman sitting at her kitchen table wearing her housecoat inflamed her.

The boy pries himself away from his mother and mounts his bicycle. This time Sara doesn't stop him when he swoops onto the road. He brakes at the foot of Jared's driveway and bends to pick up a stick.

"Don't you dare," Sara says.

But Daniel doesn't turn around. He tosses the stick with all his might and it hits the front door of the Fowles house.

"Jesus!" Sara yells. "Get back here!"

Sara chases him down, yanking him off his bicycle and dragging him back to the lawn. Clare rests her hand over the cell phone in the pocket of her jeans, as if cueing Malcolm. The front door of the Fowles house opens and Jared steps out. He seems much older than in the wedding photo, more filled out and better looking. He wears a baseball cap on backwards and a faded T-shirt.

"Say sorry to Jared, Daniel," Sara says, heavy with sarcasm. "Tell him you didn't mean to throw the stick."

Jared collects the stick and bends it into an arch until it cracks. Then he tosses the pieces into the sickly looking bush that makes up his front garden.

"Asshole," Sara says under her breath.

Though he stands a hundred feet away, Clare can feel Jared's eyes bore through her.

"Just ignore him," Sara says. "He'll go away."

And Jared does, stepping back through the screen door into the darkness of his house. Clare feels a stab in her gut. Always the husband, her mother said.

"He was probably hoping for a casserole," Sara says. "He's as heartless as they come."

"Did his wife still live there?" Clare asks. "Before she disappeared?"

"No. She left him around Christmas. She was living up at her folks' place."

"Strange," Clare says.

The word seems to jar Sara. "It is strange," she says. "The whole thing is strange."

By now the boy is back on his bike and over at the very end of the road. He weaves fearlessly close to the yellow guardrail, yanking his front wheel to draw tight circles. There appears to be a path marked next to the guardrail, another way down to the gorge. Clare lifts her hands and mimics the clicking of a camera. Did Jared know Shayna was leaving? Did he see it coming? It might have been Sara who piled Shayna's suitcases into her car and drove her up the mountain road to the Cunningham house, playing the helpful friend in the face of a broken marriage. Was there screaming, words exchanged in the driveway? Or was it silence between them, an icy disregard?

Every marriage suffers in its own way, Clare's mother once said after witnessing a hostile moment between Clare and Jason. Some quietly, others not. But her mother knew nothing of the truth. Clare bears few scars from Jason on the pale of her skin.

He had a way of inflicting injuries that faded before anyone could catch on, of using his charm to
override any rage that seeped out in public. Surely
Shayna had her reasons for leaving. For Clare it
was the certainty that death was circling her, that
death was the only other way out. It was a fleeing
under the cloak of a winter evening, her husband
none the wiser, a panicked flight behind the wheel
of her junker car, the snow coming down hard out
the window.

The section of the hardware store reserved for groceries takes up half an aisle. At the back Clare finds a display table scattered with fruits and vegetables, and then a refrigerator and a freezer with groaning motors. With only the cash in her pocket to pay, Clare must keep tabs on what she buys. It takes all her willpower not to tear open a box of crackers and start on them right away.

Clare wanders the aisles in search of a few other supplies, duct tape and matches, ointment for her gash, a can of lighter fluid for the fire pit. She finds a plastic poncho for a raincoat and some wool socks. Though it is July, the mountains do not seem to adhere to the seasons, moving through heat and rain and fog and sun and even a sharp snap of cold in the two days since she arrived. She lands at the cash register with a full basket.

The young cashier stares dead ahead as she pulls Clare's items along the beeping conveyor. This girl with the nose ring is the same one in the crop top from the other night at Ray's, though now she wears a uniform, her eyes smudged with coal liner and her lips a blinding red. She can't be older than eighteen, an age Clare best remembers because it was on her eighteenth birthday that her mother announced at the dinner table that a marble-sized tumor had been found on her esophagus. Announced it, with flair, a swilling glass of wine in one hand and a forkful of birthday cake in the other. Her father sat still and silent in his way, almost smiling. Clare remembers feeling injured by her mother's showmanship. She'd felt ready for the world until that moment. But there was an instant loss of hope, her birthday bested by a proclamation of terminal cancer. Perhaps Clare knew what was coming, the stash of medications introduced to the house, her parents too preoccupied with their own troubles to take note of her transgressions, the hole dug in Clare's heart by her mother's cancer the perfect opening for Jason.

The high sun nearly blinds Clare as she clears the sliding doors of the hardware store, so that the sight of Jared Fowles leaning against his truck, staring at her, stops her in her tracks. He half smiles, his elbow propped against the rearview mirror.

"Clare," he says.

"Yes?"

He takes off his baseball cap, the dark of his hair falling across his forehead.

"I thought you might want to introduce yourself."

"You seem to know who I am."

"Do you know who I am?"

The plastic bags cut into Clare's hand so the tips of her fingers feel numb, her shoulder smarting. Jared's scrutiny lays her bare. A bead of sweat rolls down the curl of her back. The articles about Shayna's disappearance describe Jared as a landscaper, a former miner, a man twice arrested for drunk driving. He was at the gorge the night Shayna disappeared, but left early. Had the police interviewed him? Was he even bothered that his wife was gone?

"I know who you are," Clare says. "Sara told me."

"We don't get a lot of visitors in Blackmore. Did she mention that?"

"That's what I've been told."

"You've come to take pictures," Jared says, his tone chiding.

"I have."

"Or maybe you're a fancy private detective. A fancy PI. Here to snoop."

"I'm not a private eye."

"A cop?"

"Is this small talk in Blackmore? That's all anyone asks me."

Jared laughs. "You a runaway, then?"

One of the bag loops slips from Clare's grip. What does Jared see when he looks at her? Clare adjusts her stance.

"I'm not sure grown-ups can be runaways."

"Sure they can," Jared says.

"Then maybe that's what I am."

The words surprise Clare as soon as she utters them, the frankness of what she's just said. There was a time, before she was married, that Clare knew how to talk to a man like Jared, how to measure just the right amount of push-back, that mix of assertion and flirtation, a show of strength.

"Hiding from someone?" Jared asks.

"Not hiding. Moving. I don't like to stay still."

Jared smiles fully now. Perhaps he sees the re-semblance to Shayna, Clare same-aged and vaguely similar to his estranged wife, this arrogance a way to mask his true response. Clare nearly jumps when she feels the vibration of her phone in her pocket. It takes a concerted effort not to drop the grocery bags.

"Did you follow me here?" Clare asks.

"I did."

"Do you mind if I leave now?"

"You're staying up at Charlie's."

"I am."

"You a fast runner?"

At home, Clare *had* been a fast runner, even in the worst of times, three miles to the lake and back every morning, her body wiry because of it. She tried to keep it up after she left, find routes in whatever towns she passed through, but she could never shake the sensation of being chased.

"Don't try to scare me," Clare says.

"I'm just playing with you. A little game."

Jared points to her shoulder.

"Looks like you're bleeding," he says.

Clare glances down. Red spots have formed like ink stains on her T-shirt.

"I took a spill yesterday," she says. "Gashed myself on a stick."

"Doesn't sound like you're too careful."

"It was dark out. I tripped."

But Jared is looking past her now, suddenly bored. He puts his baseball cap back on.

"Listen," he says. "Blackmore's a pretty small place. I'm sure I'll see you around. Clare. What's your last name?"

"O'Dey."

"O'Dey," he repeats. "You want to keep up this game, come by anytime."

The playfulness in Jared's voice irks her. Where is your wife? Clare would like to yell to him. He gets in his truck and starts the engine, rolling down the window but saying nothing. Clare steps aside as he turns onto the street. She knows Jared will look for clues, type her name into a search engine. But he would be typing "Clare O'Dey," and that is not her name. A name, according to her own digging, that means "of a servant," "of a maid." Perhaps Malcolm didn't know that when he suggested it, or perhaps it is his way of being wry.

Clare dumps her bags in the trunk, then sits in the driver's seat to check her phone. It flashes red with a waiting text message.

Moines River Picnic Area, Hwy 117 South, tomorrow Saturday 10h00. A two-hour drive from Blackmore in non-inclement weather. Be punctual.

Malcolm. Clare reads the message three times. Like a telegram, curt and prompt. No questions. She would like to punch in a note about Shayna Fowles, about the people in this town, their doubts about Clare and her story, their questions always the same. But Malcolm is a stranger too. She must be careful what she gives away. Clare texts a two-letter response: **OK.**

C lare climbs the porch of the Merritt house and cups her hands to peek through the picture window. Through the sheer curtains she can see the sparse living room, worn furniture scattered on old hardwood, the wallpaper peeling in every corner. Clare's finger traces the length of the windowsill, gathering cobwebs and dust. Charlie has probably lived alone in this house since his father and brothers died in the mine accident, since his mother swallowed a rifle a week later, the waitress at Ray's said. For years Charlie has probably subsisted on canned food and beer, never bothering to run a rag over anything. She knows she will hear Charlie's truck before she sees it, time enough to scramble away.

Clare sits on the old porch swing and peels back her shirt. The gash is bright and moist with the ointment she'd picked up earlier, the skin around it flaring red. She will have to find a way to bandage it. This time there will be a scar.

A hammering in the distance startles her. Clare scans the yard. Never alone. She stands and peers over the railing to the field behind the house, but the barn blocks her sight line. The last bits of daylight linger over the trees. Clare descends from the porch and walks around to the back of the house. Through the gaps in the barn's weathered boards she spots Wilfred

Cunningham in the field, lifting a sledgehammer high and slamming it down on a rounded post. Next to him is a wheelbarrow full of more posts, and Clare can see a trail of them spaced in the tall grass fifteen or so feet apart, the first makings of a fence.

Clare gnaws on her fingernails as she watches Wilfred. She has questions for him. About neighbors, about his daughter, about the bad blood between him and Charlie. But in half an hour it will be dark, and Wilfred's face is devoid of expression, a lack of emotion more daunting to Clare than anger. Before she can retreat he catches sight of her. With a deep breath Clare waves and walks over.

"I don't mean to bother you, Mr. Cunningham. I heard the hammering."

Wilfred ignores her, tapping the post into place.

"Building a fence? It'll be dark soon."

Nothing.

"It was nice to meet your wife yesterday."

Wilfred drops the sledgehammer. "You need to leave."

"I don't mean to bother you," Clare says again.

"You *are* bothering me," Wilfred says. "You've got a lot of nerve showing your face."

"I couldn't just leave her, Mr. Cunningham. She was clearly lost."

The fence posts line up at an angle to the birch trees, cutting a pie slice out of Charlie's back field.

"I could help you," Clare says.

Silence.

"You could use some help. Does Charlie Merritt know you're building this fence?"

"Go ahead and tell him."

When the post is in place, Wilfred takes the wheelbarrow and walks it ten paces through the grass. Clare follows. She will have to be more direct.

"I know about your daughter," she says. "Shayna. Maybe I can help."

Wilfred collects another post from the pile.

"You must be worried sick," Clare continues.

Beams of light dance along the side of Charlie's house, then through the barn. Headlights. Charlie is home.

"Mr. Cunningham—"

"I know your type," Wilfred says, hoisting the post into place. He grabs hold of the sledgehammer again and bangs with renewed purpose. Charlie will soon follow the sound of hammering, as she did. She jogs back to the barn and as she rounds its corner, they nearly collide.

"Hey!" she says.

"What's the hammering?" Charlie looks over her shoulder.

"Wilfred Cunningham is building a fence."

Charlie's face is stone, eyes fixed in the distance. "Is he?"

"It's just a fence," Clare says. "You can pull the posts out tomorrow."

"Or I can set Timber on him right now."

"You can't do that."

"Does he have a gun?"

"I don't think so," Clare says.

Charlie goes into the barn and emerges a minute later, holding a rifle.

"What the hell are you doing?" Clare asks.

"I've got a trespasser."

"Stop it." She blocks his path.

Charlie pumps the rifle and fires up at the sky. Clare crouches and crawls up against the barn. She should run, find her phone, chase a signal, call the police. What police? By the time anyone arrives the damage will already be done, Clare knows that well enough. She phoned the police three times in her marriage. Three times, cowering in her bedroom, waiting, waiting. But the local detachment was small, and the officers arrived each time with their sirens off, greeting Jason by first name, the friend of a friend. Just another stormy marital spat, they'd all agree, so that even Clare questioned her version as she gave her statement. Do you really want us to take him away? they'd asked her. No, Clare would say. I guess not.

Clare scrambles up and plants her hand flat on Charlie's chest, the warm thud of his heartbeat against her palm.

"You can't shoot him," she says.

"I should. I should shoot the old man right through the heart."

"I'm begging you," Clare says. "Please just let it go. Please—"

But the hammer pounds again and Charlie is running. Clare chases him across the field, everything in grays now, the light almost gone. If Wilfred sees them coming, he doesn't budge. He doesn't even set the hammer down to brace himself.

"Old man!" Charlie yells. "Old man, you'd better stop that hammering."

"It's my field," Wilfred says.

"Not anymore. You know that."

"You think you Merritts won?" Wilfred says. "I'll end the last of you."

"We're down to the last of you too, Cunningham. You've got no one left either."

Charlie lifts the rifle and takes aim. "One more strike and I shoot."

Wilfred lifts the sledgehammer over the post, pounding it down. Charlie curls his finger around the trigger and fires. The shot rings out and Wilfred lets go of the hammer and staggers backwards.

"Feel that?" Charlie says. "The next one rips right through you."

The post has toppled over with the force of the shot. Wilfred inspects it, pressing his finger into the splintered divot where the bullet went through. Then he finds the hammer on the ground and wiggles the post back to standing. Charlie looks at Clare, eyes burning. *No*, she mouths to him, pleading, but his face is deadpan. He fires again. This time Wilfred reels in a full circle and falls, and Clare is certain she is deaf because she hears nothing, not even her own scream, not the thump of Wilfred Cunningham as he is swallowed up by the grass. Charlie Merritt is a silhouette. Gunpowder wafts over to Clare, acrid in her nose and eyes.

The sounds return to Clare. She can hear Wilfred cursing and groaning. She finds him deep in the grass, flat on his back and clutching his right arm. Clare rolls him so his injured arm is resting on her lap. There doesn't appear to be a lot of blood. Wilfred tears away from her and spreads open the rip on his flannel shirt. His bicep is streaked red.

"It's just a graze," Clare says. "Took off a bit of flesh."

"I aimed it that way." Charlie looms over them, rifle in hand. "You wouldn't drop the damn hammer."

"You missed is what you did," Wilfred says. "Your aim is for crap. You're just like your goddamn father."

"You want me to shoot you where it hurts, old man? Let you bleed out?"

"You don't have the guts."

Charlie raises the gun again, and this time Clare can see straight down the barrel.

"Don't point that at me!" Clare says.

"Then move away from him. Now."

"You want to rot in jail over a fence?"

"He's trespassing. You tell her, Wilfred. Whose land is this?"

"If your mother could see you now," Wilfred says.

"And if your daughter could see you."

Wilfred snarls and takes a run at Charlie, catching him by the waist so that they tumble with a thud to the ground right in front of Clare, the rifle falling from Charlie's grip.

"Stop it!" Clare says, circling them.

Wilfred straddles Charlie and punches him hard with his good arm. Then Charlie is on top, the one landing the punches. Clare feels her way through the grass until her hand grips the familiar steel of the gun. From her knees she pumps the rifle and fires toward the setting moon, the blast like a camera flash lighting them up. The fumbling stops at once, both men turning wide-eyed to her. She nudges the rifle's aim back and forth between them.

"Get up," Clare says, standing herself up and stepping back. "Both of you."

Charlie is on his feet first. And then, with greater effort, Wilfred.

"You wouldn't shoot," Charlie says, his tone almost playful.

"How do you know that?" Clare says.

"You ever held a loaded rifle before?"

Clare's vision has adjusted to the low light. A colony of bats streams out the barn doors. One of them dives and climbs, its movements circular, patterned. She aims, sucking in a tiny breath, then fires. The bat jerks and then drops to the ground ten feet to the left of them.

"Cripes," Charlie says.

Clare's mouth is dry, her shoulder throbbing from where the rifle pressed into it. Wilfred edges out of Charlie's reach, hands up, eyes never leaving Clare. She breaks the rifle open and lets the remaining cartridges pour out.

"Go home," Clare tells Charlie.

"You going to give me back my gun?"

"No I'm not," Clare says. "And tie up that dog of yours. I don't want to have to shoot him."

With a swat of his hand, Charlie starts back toward the barn. "To hell with you both. You go back to wherever the hell you came from! *You* go back to your crazy wife and your dead daughter, old man. Tomorrow I make a bonfire out of your damn fence posts."

When Charlie's gone, Wilfred spits on the ground, then topples the wheelbarrow with a swift kick. Even in the dusk, Clare can see his nose running with blood, his left eye nearly puffed shut.

"You need some ice," Clare says. "I can find you some."

"To hell with you," Wilfred says.

He turns and recedes into the birch trees that mark the true property line. Clare snaps the rifle closed. The barrel is still hot. The way he walks home, a shadow with his hunched shoulders and head down, Clare wonders whether Wilfred might have wanted this scene to unfold differently, wanted her to stand by and let Charlie shoot him.

In the back corner of the barn, Clare finds the storage room with an unlocked rifle cabinet. Out of habit she takes a rag from the shelf and runs it over the barrel of the rifle before reaching up to set the gun on the top rack. A single bare bulb lights this space, the rest of the barn in such bad shape that Clare can make out the curl of the low moon through the gaps in its far wall. She pulls the cord to kill the bulb and stands for a moment in the dark, peering through the slats, steadying her breaths. Then she starts back to the trailer.

The kitchen light is on in the Merritt house but Clare can't see anyone through the window. A car is now parked in the driveway beside Charlie's truck. Around front she finds Charlie and Sara Gorman sitting on the steps, Timber curled up beside them. They both drink beer and Sara holds a bag of frozen peas to Charlie's swollen face.

"Well, look who it is," Charlie says. "Billy the Kid. Sharpest shooter in town."

"Your rifle's back in the barn," Clare says.

"How nice of you to take such good care of it."

"You could have killed him."

"Trespassing is against the law," Charlie says.

"C'mon, Charlie," Sara says, pinning the peas to his cheek. "Go easy."

"I'll never go easy."

Charlie's hand rests high along Sara's thigh. They are more than just friends.

"They've been at it for years," Sara explains. "Neighbors from hell."

"What's the deal with the land anyway?" Clare says.

"It's mine, is the deal."

"Used to be Wilfred's," Sara says to Clare. "It's a long and very boring story. Don't let him corner you with it."

"Let me tell you something about our photographer friend," Charlie says. "She shot a bat right out of a dark sky."

"No kidding," Sara says.

"Really. A bat. With my rifle. I am not kidding."

With her ears still ringing from the blasts, a pain rises in Clare's chest. She sees the image of her brother Christopher standing in her backyard, arms up, pleading against the gun pointed at him. She blinks. Charlie looks down at her from the porch, almost in awe, Sara watching him, pressing the peas harder into his swelling eye.

"I'll go pack my things," Clare says.

"Where are you going?"

"I can sleep in my car."

"You don't like my mother's quilts?"

"I figured you wanted me gone."

"What, that? C'mon. Just a little gunfight."

"You pointed a rifle at me," Clare says.

Charlie pouts, licking at the droplet of blood that forms on his split lip. "You stepped into the line of fire," he says. "It's not the same thing. And you pointed a rifle at me too. That makes us even."

"Wilfred might come looking for you," Clare says.

"He won't," Sara says. "He knows better."

"I feel sorry for him," Clare says.

Charlie snatches the peas from Sara and descends the steps toward her. Like Wilfred, one eye is puffed shut. Clare holds her ground though he comes within arm's reach.

"I think you should stay," he says, almost a whisper.

"Why?"

"So I can keep an eye on you."

"That sounds like a threat."

"A threat?" His voice booms again. "I figured you'd want some protection. I don't know what your deal is, but I'm guessing you could use a man around."

Clare feels her jaw tighten at those words. "I should be calling the police," she says.

"Be my guest," Charlie says. "Three quick hours and they'll be here."

"We're doomed," Sara says.

"You might be doomed." Charlie reclaims his seat next to Sara. "I've got everything I need right here on this ridge."

When Clare turns to walk away, Charlie calls to her back.

"Does that mean you'll stay?"

Clare doesn't answer. Her heart has still not slowed to its normal rhythm. She climbs the dark hill, Charlie's sharp laughter cutting through the woods. Back at the trailer Clare secures the door closed and cups her hand at the tap to gulp some water. Then she roots until she finds the newspaper she'd taken from the Cunningham coffee table this morning. In the central pages she finds a photograph of Charlie dressed in a suit, flanked by lawyers and reporters. Three years after the accident, Charlie launched a lawsuit against the mining company and Wilfred Cunningham, the foreman at the time of the blast. The article quotes Charlie: "Wilfred Cunningham killed my father and brothers and I need him to pay for that."

There is a knock at the trailer door. Clare freezes.

"You in there?"

Sara's voice.

"One second." Clare stuffs the paper into a cupboard, then opens the door.

"Packing up?" Sara asks.

"Thinking about it. Where's Charlie?"

"He sent me up here to make amends." Sara raises a twelve-pack of beer. "I sent him to bed."

"I should probably leave."

"Not now. Where are you going to go?" Sara motions to the fire pit. "You want to build a fire?"

The woods behind Sara are dark. Clare can't think of what to say, whether to believe she is really here to make amends.

"Or never mind," Sara says.

"No. A fire sounds good."

"Great. Can I put these in the fridge?"

Clare takes the pack from Sara and pulls two cans out before stuffing the rest in the bar fridge. Her sweater is tinged with a streak of Wilfred's blood. She pulls it off and finds the other one, her warmer one, then the matches and lighter fluid from the hardware store. Outside Sara is on her knees, snapping twigs and arranging them into a teepee in the pit. It has been six months since Clare drank anything besides soda, water, coffee, juice. Beer was never her weakness. She hands Sara a can and pries her own open.

"Where's your son?" Clare says.

"With his grandfather. He spends most weekends with him."

"Your father?"

"My father-in-law."

With a single match the fire takes, tracing the thin trail of fluid Sara poured on top. Country fire, Clare's father used to say. Wood and gas. A minute later the flames dance two feet high, the wood crackling against the heat. Clare and Sara sit in the lawn chairs and sip their beer. The instant warmth that comes with the alcohol evokes a familiar ease in Clare. She sizes Sara up with a sidelong glance. Since this morning Sara has showered and changed, her brown hair clean and loose around her face, too thin.

"Charlie says you've got good aim." Sara coughs on her beer. "I think you scared him."

"I was pretty sure they were going to kill each other."

"I don't mean to laugh. Charlie can be a real idiot. He takes that patch of land very seriously."

"I can see that."

"He got it in a settlement. It was a messy deal."

They are quiet for a moment, Sara looking to the fire, its light on her. Her foot bounces in quick rhythm. "My husband died in the mine," she says. "Michael."

"I'm sorry to hear that." Clare takes another sip and risks it. "Do you ever go up there?"

"To the mine? Sometimes."

"Must be an eerie place."

"It is."

"I'd like to see it. Might make for some decent photos."

"I can take you tomorrow if you want," Sara says.

"That'd be great."

"Charlie likes it there. No one bothers him. It's his turf."

"He seems to like you," Clare says.

"You think? Sometimes I go a week without hearing from him."

"Guys can be that way."

"So why do we bother?"

Clare laughs. "Good question."

Why bother? Clare's brother used to ask Clare this very question, early in her courtship with Jason. Why do you bother with that guy? Why do you make excuses? he would say as she sat by the window, knowing he'd be an hour late, knowing he'd arrive at the door with daisies plucked hastily along the driveway to hand her as penance. At parties Jason would abandon her as they walked in, absorbed by the crowd, by the friends and the women who fell prey to his charms as Clare did. In town he walked a few paces ahead of Clare on the sidewalk, as though she were a stranger. That isn't love, Christopher would tell Clare. Don't you see it? It's closer to hate.

Sara sets her foot into the fire and kicks at the logs until the flames dance higher.

"My father-in-law watches me like a hawk. He has no time for Charlie."

"Why?"

"He's looking out for me. For Danny. I get it. Charlie's not exactly the most virtuous guy."

"It's nice that your father-in-law's involved."

"He's got nothing better to do. For a while Danny was living with him. I got a bit caught up."

"I can relate to that," Clare says.

"Used to be the worst of my problems were the hangovers. When it was just booze."

"When there wasn't the ache," Clare says.

Sara clears her throat and looks straight at Clare. "Exactly."

"I know all about the ache. My town was bad too."

Pills, small and colorful, easy enough to come by in any small town. By the time she'd met Jason, Clare was already plucking daily from her mother's supply, even versed on how to grind it up into something more potent and shoot it straight into the vein. Jason seemed to like her more when she was in the throes of it, when it rendered her cool and uninhibited yet willing to let him command.

"Charlie gives them pet names," Sara says. "The ox, the hare, the turtle. Speed you up or slow you down."

So he is the dealer, Clare thinks.

"Was that missing neighbor taking them too?" Clare asks. "Shayna?"

"Why are you asking me that?" Sara says, straightening up.

"I met her mother yesterday when she wandered up this way. She said something about it."

"I'm surprised Louise said anything about anyone."

"She seems to go in and out of it," Clare says.

"I'm glad she doesn't get what's happened. Doesn't have to wonder like the rest of us."

"You and Shayna were friends?"

"Sure. Since we were kids. We left for college together. She came back for Jared, I came back for Mike. Both of us dropped out. Both of us dumb in exactly the same way." Sara pauses to light a cigarette. "Did you go to college?"

"For a while. I dropped out too."

"Let me guess," Sara says. "For a guy."

Something tugs at Clare. To think of leaving for college. When she was twenty-two, a month after meeting Jason, Clare too left her small town to join Grace in the city, her mother's cancer in delicate remission, an acceptance to art school a chance to clean herself up. But she was ill-equipped for the city, and Grace was already well established there, already a medical student, leaving Clare adrift. After only a few weeks Jason showed up at her dorm with a dozen roses. Please come home, he said. The way he kissed her made her burn. By dinnertime she'd packed her things and left with him. Clare remembers the harvest moon out the window as they drove north, the city flickering behind them, how she hoped Grace would be hurt, jealous that no man had swooped in for her.

The fire has warmed the beer in Clare's hand. Sara is enthralled by the flames.

"What do you think happened to Shayna?" Clare asks.

"I wish I knew. She just vanished. Poof. Like that."

"You were there?"

"A dozen of us were there. At least. Jared was with some girl. Basically a teenager. Shayna was pissed about that. When Charlie and I left, Shayna was passed out on a log. I don't remember much."

"You left her there alone?"

"I just said there were dozens of us. You sound like my father-in-law. Lots of questions."

"She's your friend. She might be dead."

"She might be. What can I do about it now?"

"What if this starts happening? What if she's just the first?"

"She's the first of nothing. It's horrible, but it's no shock. You could see it coming."

"People could say the same thing about you," Clare says.

Sara lifts her beer can in mock cheers. "That's a nice thing to say."

"I'm not trying to upset you."

"No. I get it. You think I don't give a shit. You think no one gives a shit. But you're wrong."

"What about Charlie? They were neighbors."

"They were friends," Sara says. "Who knows? Maybe more than friends. They've had this thing since we were kids. This closed little circle that let no one else in."

"That must have bugged you."

Sara shrugs.

"Does Charlie talk about it? He must be worried."

"Hasn't said anything to me. Maybe he's glad. Anything to punish Wilfred."

A second wind has hit Clare full force. She sets her empty beer down and goes to the trailer. Inside she flips her cell phone open. This phone's a relic, no modern features, just a screen with the glow of Malcolm's message. She will have to be up early to make the drive to meet him. Still, she pulls two more beers from the fridge and hands one to Sara outside. Sara eases back into the chair and takes a long drink.

"There's a party tomorrow night," Sara says. "A dance. At Ray's. Town's homecoming. We'll be going if you want to come."

"I could."

"Whole town goes, pretty much. Used to be a big event. Not so much these days."

"Sounds okay."

The embers in the fire burn orange. Clare bends and collects a cluster of sticks to throw on them.

"Charlie doesn't know what to make of you," Sara says.

In her mannerisms, all hard angles and sharp edges, Sara Gorman might be the clear opposite of Grace Fawcett. Still, Clare feels a comfort with her, a willingness to share secrets that she can't fully abide.

"I'm not here to bother anyone," Clare says.

"So what's your story? Because this photographer stuff . . . sort of seems like bullshit."

"I had a hard time once. Same as you. I was married."

"Okay. And?"

"I'm not anymore."

"Why not?"

"Because he was bad."

"Bad how?"

"Just bad."

In the months since leaving it has become more difficult to itemize it, old scenes playing out differently depending on what prompts the memory, whether Clare is angry or lonely when it comes to her, whether she is dreaming or reliving it wide awake.

"What's his name?" Sara says.

"Jason," Clare says. Instantly she regrets it, whatever small power this tidbit gives Sara over her, a clue to place in her back pocket.

"And this Jason, you're done with him?"

"I hope so," Clare says.

"I'm not sure we're ever done with them. You know what I mean?"

"I do."

"Maybe you'll get lucky."

"I'm not sure it's about luck." Clare edges her chair closer to Sara's. "Will you do me a favor?"

"Sure."

"Don't tell Charlie that. What I just told you."

Sara nods without looking at Clare, an incomplete promise.

"You certainly ask a lot of questions," Sara says. "Maybe you'll wring it out of us while you're here."

"Wring *what* out of you?"

"I don't even know." Sara turns back to the fire. "The truth?"

Clare puts her second empty beer can down beside her lawn chair. She opens her mouth to speak, then closes it. She understands that Sara is not to be pushed, that this conversation is over. Still, they will stay here for a while yet, finish the beers cooling in the fridge. The fire is nearly three feet high now, its warmth licking at Clare's cheeks.

There is this photograph taken the day before the mine exploded. It was my birthday and we were all at Ray's. Nothing was ever good enough. I'm not smiling and neither are you. I blew out the candles and we lined up on the dance floor to pose. Sara and I stood at the bar and she took a shot with me even though she was out-to-here pregnant. I bought her the shot, then judged her for drinking it. Charlie was there with his brothers, and they got drunk and Charlie snatched the paring knife from behind the bar and waved it until one of his brothers landed a punch square between his eyes. You held him and stifled the bleeding with your shirt.

Remember the quiet? It went so quiet. We stood in a circle looking at each other, looking down at Charlie as he bled and barked at us. Like we knew what was coming. The ground was already collapsing beneath us, all of us trapped, even then.

My mother once said that tragedy alters a

person's constitution. She meant it in defense of my father and how he's changed. But I look at that photograph and I see that the spite was always there. The mine changed the town, it changed our circumstances, but it didn't change any of us. The good people left. We were never the good. This was in us all along.

SATURDAY

Clare drives with every window open, wind whipping through the car so that her hair dances. Blackmore is behind her and she is heading south, following the directions she traced with pencil onto her road map, her GPS long ago broken. Moines River Picnic Area, Hwy 117 south. After three days alone grabbing blindly at clues, searching for this stranger, Clare's brain swirls with angry questions for Malcolm.

Malcolm will be there before her, Clare knows. Even if she's early, he'll be earlier. At the sign for the picnic area she slows and follows the gravel turnoff along its steep descent. There is one car in the lot, a blue sedan she can't be certain belongs to Malcolm. She might have remembered Malcolm's car to be silver, but then she recognizes the dream catcher dangling from the rearview mirror, the one detail she took in before she left him in the motel parking lot days ago. Clare cuts the engine and smooths the creases in her jeans with her hands. Her head aches, her stomach rolling with the queasiness of a hangover. Last night she and Sara drank the twelve beers between them and talked well past midnight.

This picnic area is shaded with a gurgling stream at one end. Moss grows in clusters on the outhouse and the tables, the sun an infrequent visitor down here, trees as thick as houses and stretching high in search of light. Clare sees Malcolm standing at a distance. He wears a gray golf shirt tucked into dark pants, a leather case in his right hand and his jacket in his left. In the days since she last saw him, Clare has already forgotten the specifics of his features, the tall and slim of him, his brown hair clipped clean and short, blue eyes, a deep scar running the length of his right forearm. A politician's look, crisp and reserved, entirely unlike any man in Clare's life so far. Under the canopy of trees the coolness of the shade strikes her skin.

"You found me," Malcolm says.

"It took two hours. Like you said it would."

"Are you okay?"

"Depends on what you consider okay."

They choose the least mossy picnic table and sit across from each other. Malcolm sets down his jacket and opens his case, pulling out a folder to match the one he gave Clare days ago. There will be no small talk.

"You're tense."

"I'm not tense. I'm confused."

Malcolm flips the folder open. "What's confusing?"

"I don't know what you want me to do."

"I want you to look for Shayna Fowles. That was clear, wasn't it?"

"I need to know *why*. Someone goes missing somewhere and you show up unannounced and look for them? Or contract a stranger to do it for you? That's actually your job?"

"This is what I do, yes."

"Who hired you?"

"You don't need to know that."

"You mean you won't tell me."

"It's not helpful information. You need an objective outlook."

"Okay," Clare says. "My objective outlook is that Shayna's dead."

"Why do you say that?"

"Because she was a junkie who liked to party next to a cliff."

"If she'd fallen, they would have found her body."

"I went down there. That gorge is a black hole. The drop is a thousand feet. She could be anywhere along that ledge. And besides, who's looking for her?"

Another breeze passes through. Clare digs a sweater from her bag and turns away from Malcolm to wrestle it on.

"You look tired," Malcolm says.

"There's no motel in Blackmore. You said there would be."

"It still has a website."

"Right. Well, it's shuttered. The place is a ghost town. Half the houses are boarded up. The groceries are next to the mufflers in the hardware store."

"The mine was the only industry," Malcolm says. "That's what happens. A town loses its—"

"Don't lecture me on small towns, okay?" Clare extracts herself from the picnic table and paces back and forth. "The camera is so obviously a ruse. You think these people are dumb? They're circling me like hawks. Fresh meat."

Despite the shrillness of her voice, Malcolm remains dead calm, running a finger along the jagged path of his scar.

"Where did you sleep?"

"In a trailer in the middle of the woods. Right next door to the Cunninghams."

"Whose trailer?"

"A guy named Charlie Merritt. The local villain."

"You can sleep in your car. It's better to keep some distance."

"It's hard to keep distance in a town with fifteen people."

"The current population is four hundred."

Clare approaches the table and sits again.

"Is Malcolm Boon your real name?"

"It's a family name."

"Is it the name your mother gave you when you were born?"

"Clare. Please. You accepted this job. It was your choice to go to Blackmore."

"You said it was a job. It's not a job. You're feeding me to these people. I don't understand why."

"It *is* a job," Malcolm says. "You need to be methodical. Eliminate the obvious possibilities first."

"By finding a body at the bottom of the gorge?"

"You're not looking for a body. Maybe she's alive. We don't know."

"I need to know why! Why did you send me there?"

Malcolm sighs.

"It doesn't help to keep asking me the same question."

"I keep asking because you're not answering me. You sent me there based on nothing."

"I don't know much about Shayna," Malcolm says. "I know more about you than you might think."

Clare feels chilled, unable to conjure what sort of details Malcolm might have about her, a version of her story that does not match her own. From a distance comes the groan of a truck shifting gears, picking up steam in the face of a steep climb. Malcolm presses a finger into each of his temples without closing his eyes, holding them there in silence. His inscrutability bothers her, his hollowness. What life of his came before this one?

The first time Clare saw Malcolm Boon, he was sipping coffee, his fingers to his forehead just as they are now. It was one of Clare's first shifts at a café in a lakeside logging town two thousand miles from home, a job she'd taken to test her mettle, to try staying still for a bit. She noticed him as soon as he walked in, the stiff way he slid into a booth with a newspaper tucked under his arm.

Who is this man? she thought.

He came in the next day too, choosing the same booth. Beyond the newspaper, Clare took note of the way he touched his fingers to his mouth as he read, the way he frowned without a hint of sadness. The scar on his arm. That his hair was light brown but tinged with red when it caught the light. And then there was the way he seemed to be watching her. Something about him nudged her.

After her shift she went back to the housekeeping

cottage she'd rented and lay on her bed thinking of him, this man with whom she exchanged only brief formalities about eggs and toast. Here was this man so entirely unlike the rest of the café's clientele, the truckers and the locals, carrying the same leather briefcase he now lifts onto the picnic table.

"Are you hungry?" Malcolm produces two sandwiches and two apples. "I brought some food."

The sandwich sags in Clare's hand but she is rabid with hunger. She must stop herself from tearing away the wrapping and inhaling it. As she eats Clare can feel the sugar seep into her bloodstream, her anger waning. She rifles through her bag for her folder and hands it to him.

"I've listed people in some semblance of order."

Malcolm reads over her notes. He must be a decade older than her, forty or so, and up close he is not as clean shaven as he appeared on first approach.

"Can you talk me through these names?" Malcolm asks.

Her fingers pick away at the damp wood of the picnic table as she recounts the cast of Blackmore characters so far. Charlie, who hates Wilfred; Wilfred, who hates him back; Louise, suffering from dementia or out of her mind with grief or something else. Then Derek, the doctor, too clean-cut and proper; Jared, the ex-husband; and Sara, a new friend who might be of use. Clare tells him about the drugs and the squabbles over land, about her visit to the Cunningham house, every single person or crisis connecting back one way or another to Shayna. She chooses her details carefully, glossing over the particulars of last night's gunfight, about her shoulder that still aches, that doesn't seem to be healing, about the unwanted stabs of warmth that both Jared and Charlie seem to stir in her. Malcolm listens and nods. When she stops speaking, he takes out his notebook and begins writing, transcribing everything she's told him onto his page.

"Have you been taking pictures?"

"Some. Not that it's convincing anyone."

"Have your camera with you all the time. Try to authenticate your cover."

"That's hard to do. They're not stupid."

"If you tell the same story over and over, they'll buy it eventually."

"She looks like me," Clare says. "Shayna."

"I noticed that."

"Does that mean something to you?"

"No," Malcolm says. "Every case is different."

"She wanted to be a writer."

"A lot of people want to be writers."

"Her mother says she wrote poetry. I don't know if details like that are relevant."

"All details are relevant."

From the back of Clare's folder Malcolm pulls the newspaper she swiped from Wilfred and Louise's house yesterday, the article about the lawsuit between neighbors.

"Where'd you get this?"

"I stole it from the Cunninghams' coffee table."

"Was that a good idea?"

"It wasn't a bad idea," Clare says. "That house is

stuffed to the gills. I could have stolen the coffee table and no one would have noticed."

"Avoid taking risks like that."

"Risks? That's funny. Why did I risk leaving to drive all the way here to meet you?"

"I can't exactly show up in Blackmore and meet you for lunch."

"That's why e-mail was invented."

"No electronic trail. We discussed that."

"Except for the antique phone you gave me."

"The cell phone I gave you is encrypted. You can't trust other means. I like to meet in person so I know where you are."

"Where else would I be?"

"I can't anticipate what you'll do," Malcolm says.

"But you feel you know me well enough to send me in the first place."

Malcolm says nothing.

"Well, I'm there," Clare says. "And I can't be there doing this so-called job if I'm here with you."

"No," Malcolm says. "You can't."

"I'm going to a party in town tonight with Sara and Charlie Merritt."

Malcolm clears his throat, focusing again on the folder. Most of her life Clare has felt swept along by a current, someone else steering her fate, be it her father, her brother, her husband. Always a man. Now, here at this damp picnic table with Malcolm, she feels that way again, Malcolm, the architect of all this, the unlikeliest of employers directing her from the sidelines. In that lumpy trailer bed Clare has lain awake for two nights, the obvious question haunting her. Why did she agree to this job? It might have been the money, the compensation Malcolm offered more than she could make in three months at the café. It might have been her mother's voice in her head, reciting the old adage about taking the out you're given, about trusting someone who appears willing to give you a chance. It might have been that she had no other option.

Clare takes Malcolm's apple core and tosses it toward the creek. She removes her shoes, then walks across the springy earth to the stream, finding her footing on the wet rocks.

"That water will be cold," Malcolm says.

"When I was a kid," Clare says, "a boy from my town disappeared during a picnic at a conservation area. There was some kind of scene with the other kids, and this scrawny little outcast boy blew up in front of everyone. His parents took him away and locked him in the car. When they came back for him later, the car was empty. He was gone."

"Every kid runs away once or twice," Malcolm says.

"This kid was only ten, and the picnic was in the middle of nowhere. By a lake surrounded by thousands of acres of dense bush. My mom would take me and my brother up to join the search lines. Could've been one of you, she said to us. I remember staring so hard at the ground, looking for some color, a shoelace or whatever, wanting so badly to be the one to find something. After a week some hikers claimed to have spotted the boy from a distance, but he ran away from them. Sooner or later the search-and-rescue team gave up, and after two weeks everyone but his family stopped looking."

Clare pauses.

"And?" Malcolm says.

"I begged my mom to take me back but she said it was over, the story was over, the boy was dead. No one could survive that long in those woods. Then September came and one morning the kid's baby sister woke up and said she knew where he was. The parents drove her into the woods and she walked right to him. He was right there, right under her feet. The poor kid was naked and curled up barely two hundred feet from the picnic area."

"Dead?" Malcolm asks.

"Alive. Emaciated, but alive."

"Sometimes you're certain they'll turn up dead," Malcolm says. "And then they don't."

Malcolm's shoulders are bent forward, his arms folded. What an unfamiliar dynamic this is, Clare and Malcolm. She is at once electrified and troubled by it, angered even, wavering between purpose and dread, a pawn in a game she doesn't yet know how to play. Clare fumbles back into her shoes and moves to swipe her folder off the table.

"I'd like you to give me back my gun," she says.

"Why?"

"The trailer's in the middle of the woods. The cell reception isn't reliable. I have to walk around waving my phone to get your messages."

"You feel unsafe?"

"Everyone in Blackmore owns a gun. It's that kind of town."

"Do you think it makes you safer?"

"Do you know anything about guns? Because I do. And it makes me feel safer."

"I'd rather hang on to it for now," Malcolm says. "As we agreed."

"We didn't agree, actually."

Clare jams the folder under her arm.

"If you don't hear from me, assume I'm curled up in the woods. Assume I'm dead."

"Clare." Malcolm watches as she searches through her bag for her car keys.

"I don't have to go back there, you know."

"I'm not forcing you. It's your choice."

Clare's jaw clenches. He is not physically forcing her, but Clare can't be certain what he would do, whom he would call, if she backed out now. The illusion of choice, lest she forget she is under Malcolm Boon's thumb.

"Shayna's story," Clare says. "It's not the same as mine."

"You don't know her story yet."

A crow descends from the trees and plucks at one of the apple cores. Clare feels antsy, wired up. Malcolm meets her gaze with a steadiness that rankles her. What choice does she have but to trust him?

"Where will *you* be?"

"Not far," Malcolm says.

"What will you be doing?"

"Whatever I can. Whatever might be useful."

"Here's something," Clare says. "Charlie Merritt is the town drug dealer. He must have outside channels. Dig on that."

Malcolm jots something down, then stands, putting his folder back in his briefcase, the brown leather of it gouged and scratched. Until six months ago, Clare had never ventured more than a few hours beyond her hometown. Until this week, she'd never seen a mountain, and now she's cloistered among them, at work for Malcolm Boon. Clare closes her eyes to steady herself. The image of Shayna's body strikes her, dead and coiled over a rock, or facedown on the ground, unmoving. Even when she opens her eyes she cannot shake it. Clare expects Malcolm to budge, to walk her to her car, but he doesn't. He simply stands there, hands in his pockets. Without another word, Clare turns to leave.

By the time the dash lights flicker out Clare is almost on the far side of Blackmore, almost at the foot of Charlie's driveway. The clock fades in and out. It must be the alternator. The car dies just as she rolls past the house. When she cranks the keys, the engine will not turn over. Clare sets the gear to neutral and gets out to push it in a crooked line toward her parking spot. The effort renders her breathless and sweaty. Once she reaches the trees she gathers her bag and locks the doors. She cannot be angry at this car for finally dying, this car that has carried her so far without complaint.

No one else is here. When she left this morning both Sara's and Charlie's cars were still parked side by side, but now they are gone. The dog is gone too, its leash limp across the dirt of the driveway. Sara will be here in an hour to pick her up, their plan to visit the mine solidified as they said their late goodbyes last night.

Toward the Cunningham house some movement catches Clare's eye. Only a few hundred feet and a thin and trembling line of birch trees buffers the lots between these warring neighbors. Through them Clare can see Louise with her hands on her hips. The jeans she wears are smudged with mud at the knees, gray hair loose around her face. Clare approaches and fishes her camera from her bag. Before Louise sees her Clare clicks the shutter, a picture of Louise, then another of the Cunningham house. This time, she will ask her about Shayna.

"Mrs. Cunningham?"

Louise looks up and squints in an obvious effort to process who Clare might be.

"Clare O'Dey. I walked you home yesterday from the Merritt trailer. Remember?"

"Yes. Of course." Louise holds her hand out in front of her, then retracts it before Clare reaches her. "There's no one here."

"That's fine," Clare says. "I'm here to see you."

When Louise crouches to pick up her trowel, Clare spots it, the cuff around her ankle. A length of rope coils to the house. A leash. Wilfred has tied her up.

"Is everything okay?" Clare asks.

"I'm weeding. Lots of rain means lots of weeds."

"Can I help?"

Louise looks around at the gardening tools scattered at her feet. If she notices the tether, it doesn't seem to bother her.

"Is Wilfred home?"

"No. He's at work. Did I not say that already?"

"How long have you been out here in the garden?"

"Let's see." Louise looks up to the sky. "The sun was behind the mountain when I came out. And now it's not. An hour?"

"I can't see the sun," Clare says.

"Over there, behind the clouds. Just a blot."

Clare motions to the garden. "You've got enough here to feed an army."

"Tomatoes are impossible. They like sun. We don't get much sun. Peppers too. Lettuce we end up with too much. I give it away. The trick is to space your seeding so the harvest is spaced too."

"I remember that," Clare says. "My parents had a big garden."

"Your parents? Where are they now? In town?"

"My mother's dead. Cancer."

"Oh dear. And your father?"

"We aren't very close."

"Well," Louise says, crouching to pick up another trowel. "I could use some help over by the romaine." The rope slithers behind her, pulling taut as she walks. Wilfred must have measured it to extend to the far end of the garden and not beyond. She hands Clare the tool, then wanders back to her own perch and drops to her knees to dig at the soil. Clare stands there dumbly. It is impossible to imagine Malcolm here in her place. How might he proceed in the face of Shayna's mother? *Eliminate the obvious possibilities first.* On the drive back to Blackmore Clare waded through their conversation and felt a growing compulsion to defy Malcolm's warning. How can she keep her distance? Avoid immersing herself? She navigates the rows until she's among the budding heads of lettuce, then she too drops to her knees.

They work in silence, Clare bending back the heads of lettuce and yanking out the weeds underneath, a rote task she easily remembers. She never bothered planting her own garden after she moved in with Jason. Instead she spent long spring and summer Sundays helping Grace tend to hers. They were twenty-six when Grace came home to set up her medical practice at the hospital where Clare worked as a cleaner, Grace settling down with her fiancé in a rambling farmhouse just down the road from Clare and Jason. Despite the great disparity in their ranks at the hospital, it was Grace who sought out Clare's company in the cafeteria, and Clare counted on Grace to keep an eye on her, to keep her from the cups of pills that lay next to the patients as they slept. Most of Clare's friendships fell away after high school, but for some reason Grace persisted, and Clare loved her for it, but hated her too, punished her even, the straight and happy path of Grace's life a constant reminder to Clare of her own failings.

Louise's face is set in a frown as she works. Clare must take her chance while she has it.

"Does Shayna live here with you?"

"No. She lives in town."

"When's the last time you saw her?"

Louise plops back so she is seated in the dirt. She wipes her brow with her forearm, thinking.

"Yesterday. We had tea."

That was me, Clare thinks.

"Do you see her much?"

"Their house is a terrible mess," Louise says. "Wilfred can't take it. He won't even darken their door."

"You mean Shayna and Jared?"

"You can't bring a baby into that kind of place."

"Were— Are they expecting a baby?" Clare asks.

Louise shakes her head.

"No," she says. "No baby. She promised. And it can't happen now."

"Why not?"

"Because Shayna's alone. She won't see him."

There's a rumble up the drive. Clare stands and brushes the clumps of mud from her knees. Only when the truck reaches the house and the brakes squeal does Louise lift her head. Wilfred's window is rolled down. He's spotted them. Even from this distance the damage to his face from last night's fight is plain. He drives until he is nearly upon them, then jams the truck into park and jumps from the cab, covering the final distance in a limping half jog.

"You," he says, his finger at Clare. He stops short and bends down to remove the tether.

"In the house," he says to Louise.

"I'm not done out here," Louise says. "Didn't you have lunch down at the mine?"

Wilfred gives his wife a withering look.

"No. I didn't."

"You must be starved."

"I am. Can you fix me something?"

If his tone is derisive, Louise doesn't pick up on it. She pulls off her gardening gloves and sets them in the dirt next to the tools, then heads for the house, leaving Clare and Wilfred alone in the garden.

"You can't go tying her up," Clare says.

"Who sent you here?" Froth has built up at the corners of Wilfred's mouth.

"No one," Clare says.

"I'll go get my gun. Jesus."

"I'm not a Merritt, Mr. Cunningham. Get that through your head."

Wilfred appears stunned at the force of Clare's words.

"She could get tangled up. Disoriented," Clare continues. "Hurt herself."

"You know nothing about it. I'm keeping her safe."

The gash over Wilfred's lip has split open, the blood mixing with the spit that flies as he speaks. He wipes it with the cuff of his shirt.

"I could help you," Clare says. "I could take care of her for an hour or two a day. Give you a break so you can get a few things done. I used to work at a hospital."

"A hospital."

"I was a cleaner, but . . ."

"A cleaner." Wilfred scoffs. "You're kidding me."

"You've got too much on your plate. You must be looking for Shayna."

Wilfred's face goes scarlet. "You don't talk about her. Ever. To me. To Louise. Understand?"

"I get it. I'm just saying, I'm sorry. I'd like to help you. I took care of my own mother for a lot of years when she was sick. I needed help and no one offered. I'm offering. I can help you."

The clothes Wilfred wears are streaked with dirt, as though he'd been gardening along with them. Clare has known many men of the same ilk, and so she responds as she knows best. With composure, deference. Like a tree, her mother would say. Bend in their wind. Clare knows that Louise is her only way back into the Cunningham home, into their family life and its secrets.

"Who the hell do you think you are?" Wilfred says, deflated.

"Your wife has been kind to me. You've gone through a lot. I'd like to help."

Wilfred presses his thumb and forefinger into his eyes. Clare can see the cuts on his hands.

"Why don't I come back in the morning?" Clare asks. "You can decide then."

Wilfred grumbles something, then spins and strides to the house. He did not say yes to her offer, but he did not say no either. He left her here on his land, a sign the door might be nudged open. It is difficult to summon what sort of relationship this man would have had with his addicted daughter, the wars surely waged between them, an obstinacy that likely runs in the family. Clare pulls her camera from her pocket and, without lifting it to her face, aims it in his general direction and clicks.

The woods around Clare are not soundless. She tries to inure herself to the noises by identifying them. The wind. A dead branch set loose from the tree. What sort of wildlife lives around here? Squirrels, bears, rabbits. Cougars. Clare should know better than to be afraid of animals in the woods. Outside the trailer she makes a basket out of the bottom of her shirt and fills it with the empty beer cans from last night. If she had her gun, she might find a log to line them up, ping them off one by one. Instead she carries them down the hill. She will leave them for Charlie. Halfway down, she stops. Two new sounds come at her. Banging. Barking. Once in the clearing, she sees Sara on Charlie's porch, Timber in round sprints on the lawn.

"Sara. Hi." Clare sets the beer cans down next to her own car. "You're early."

"I came to let Timber out. You ready to go?"

"Sure," Clare says. "Why don't we take the dog with us? Go on foot."

"It's over two miles," Sara says.

"I could use the walk. You up for it?"

"Why not?" Sara says.

Somewhere in the folder Malcolm gave Clare are pictures of the Blackmore Coal Mine, a large bowl gouged out of the mountain, cement buildings and chain-link fences crisscrossing it, an industry built up over fifty years and then closed in a single day. Clare runs back up to the trailer to fetch her camera. At first Sara's clip is quick, but they only make it to the road before she is out of breath, wheezing.

"Are you okay?" Clare asks.

"Fine," Sara says, leaning, hands on her thighs. "It's been a bit of a rough week."

"I've had a few of those."

"This morning my father-in-law told me I look like I have liver disease," Sara says. "He'd know. That's what killed his wife. Three years ago I weighed fifty pounds more than I do now. And it wasn't like I was fat."

"We can go back and get the car if you want," Clare says.

"I'm fine." Sara's tone is sharper.

Beyond the Cunningham driveway the road to the mine climbs and winds in a pattern that disorients Clare. Sara appears to have settled into a rhythm, walking with her arms crossed a few paces ahead, bent forward with the effort of the ascent. Last night there had been an openness between them that Clare can't detect today. She will have to pry.

"Have you thought about rehab?" Clare asks.

"Did *you* ever try it?"

"No."

"Why not?"

"I never felt totally out of control," Clare says, a half-truth. "I felt like I could stop if I really needed to. Eventually I did."

"Lucky you," Sara says, sarcastic.

"I'm just saying. I get it. I know the feeling. It

took me years to quit. I was a kid when I started. Too dumb to know any better."

Sara plucks a wildflower from the side of the road, pulling off its petals one by one, eyes down. Clare can almost hear it, Sara's inner voice debating what trust might be had between them. Clare plucks a flower of her own and pulls off its petals too.

"Michael was clean as a whistle," Sara says finally. "He used to stop me after two glasses of wine. We'd never have stuck around here if he'd made it out. We'd have found someplace better. He'd have made sure of it."

Clare searches for the sun behind the clouds. The blot, Louise called it. Jason was never one to stop Clare, happy as he was to have her debilitated, beholden to him to bring her more.

"Derek would love for me to go to rehab," Sara says.

"The doctor?"

"He sent Shayna to rehab over and over again. He's trying to get me to go now too. To give me strategies, he says."

"You never know. He could be right."

"Shayna went six times. Six bloody times. Always came back worse off. She told me they have dealers who'll meet you behind a tree in the Serenity Garden and sell you a fix at a premium. Got a problem with ox? Try heroin instead. If the rehab worked at all, she'd come home and stay sober for a week, then relapse in a huge way. Worse than before. Derek's like a dog biting down on a dead rat. He insisted she'd get better if she just kept going. He's a one-trick rehab pony."

"It can take years for some. To get clean."

"I'd rather kick it on my own. I'm not leaving Danny and leveraging my house to go spend a month at some junkie spa where pushers jump out of the bushes."

Sara and Clare both laugh, a pressure valve released between them that allows for the right kind of silence. It takes thirty minutes of steady climbing to reach the gate marking the entrance to the mine. A heavy chain is woven through the links of the fence, and a sign dangles: ABANDONED MINE: DO NOT ENTER.

"It's locked," Clare says.

"There's a key in a can somewhere. Charlie pried a hole too. We could squeeze through. Timber?"

The dog sniffs out the opening where the fence meets the trees, the links cut and pried apart. Clare secures her camera against her when she crouches to wedge herself through. Sara does the same, then continues down the hill at a march, ten paces ahead. Clare is slowed by her sense of disquiet, the death this place holds. All those men, ghosts under her feet.

The first structure they come upon is the parking lot, two stories of cement jutting out of the mountainside. The entrance is sealed with another chain-link fence. A sea of empty spaces, yellow lines still visible but much faded. Before the mine closed, hundreds must have worked a single shift, a logjam of pickup trucks at this very entrance, miners with their Thermoses and packed lunches on the passenger seats, hard hats and headlamps too.

"I used to meet Mikey here," Sara says. "He'd skip out on lunch down at the mess hall and eat up here with me." She laughs. "We'd make out in the cab of his truck like a couple of teenagers. I guess we were basically teenagers."

"How old were you when he died?"

"Twenty-three. Eight months pregnant."

"Jesus. I can't imagine."

"Neither can I. Nothing. The funeral, the birth, nothing. I have a picture of Danny and me in the hospital. I swear it's my only proof that I'm the one who gave birth to him, because I have no memory of any of it. Blanked it all out."

"Of course you did. How would you cope otherwise?"

"I didn't cope. Mike's dad coped for me. I'm still not coping." Sara crouches to pet the dog. He licks her face.

From the parking lot the road curls around a sheer rock wall, then comes to a bowl and zigzags down from there. Below is a larger building and scattering of smaller structures, a long conveyor belt that would have carried the coal from the shaft to the trucks. The mine has an air of flash abandonment, as if the workers dropped everything and ran, leaving it to rot and crumble back into the ground. The clouds overhead churn and descend the mountainside like spilled milk. Clare pulls her camera out and snaps a picture.

"That camera's older than you are," Sara says.

"It's professional grade but still pretty small. I like that I can jam it into my pocket."

"Doesn't exactly look pro."

"It's vintage pro," Clare says. "And I prefer real film."

"You'd have to drive for a week to find a place to develop it."

"I develop it on my own. I have a portable kit."

"No you don't."

"It's easier than you'd think," Clare says. "My brother taught me."

Sara nods as if humoring Clare. The road overlooking the bowl makes for a good perch. They sit, feet at the edge. Sara points down into the bowl where the remains of the mine structures sit tilted and rotting.

"You see that tower? That used to be made of timber."

At the sound of his name, the dog barks.

"The year I was born they built the steel one," Sara says. "My dad used to say it'd take fifty lifetimes to get all the coal out of this mountain. I suppose they were figuring on that. Just keep digging. No one figured the whole thing would blow up."

Clare takes a long breath and decides to risk it. "Can I ask what happened between Charlie and Wilfred?"

Sara hugs her knees to her chest.

"It goes way back. Charlie's dad, Russell, he hated Wilfred. They were third cousins. Came to Blackmore around the same time. Russell bought the land right next door to Wilf. They were warring neighbors for a generation. They both worked at the mine and jockeyed for position all the way up. Wilfred got the foreman job and Russell didn't. A few months later the mine blew up on Wilfred's watch. Charlie's dad and his younger brothers all died. A week later his mom walked out to the field and put a rifle in her mouth."

"That's horrible."

"She was a shrew. Mean-looking woman if there ever was one. Louise Cunningham heard the shot. She found the body. Charlie shows up at the hospital and there's Wilfred with his hat in his hand. I heard Charlie slapped him right across the face. We all got settlements from the company after the accident, but Charlie burned right through his. Bought that dumb truck and spent weeks at a time in the city on crazy binges. Got it in his head to sue Wilfred in civil court. And he won. Some jury from three towns over found Wilfred guilty. Culpable, they said. For the Merritts' deaths. They ordered him to pay Charlie two million dollars."

"Jeez. But insurance must have covered it?"

"It was personal culpability, something like that. The mining company declared bankruptcy years ago, after the initial settlements. So Charlie gets a lien on everything Wilfred owns. Including his land."

"So how come the Cunninghams still live there?"

"Because the judge took pity on them. Because of Louise. It's her house too, she's on the title. He put a stay on the proceedings to buy Wilfred some time. But if Shayna's dead and Louise goes into a nursing home or dies, then Wilfred's the sole owner and the property transfers to Charlie."

"So it suits Charlie that Shayna might be dead."

Sara cocks her eyebrow. "You're a real cynic, you know. Do you think I'm stupid?"

"No," Clare says. "I'm not saying he killed her. But all men are angry about something."

"His issue is with her father. I know Charlie. He's not a savage."

Just wait, Clare thinks. The savagery might come later.

"I'm just saying," Clare says. "He's probably not heartbroken that she's gone."

"Nobody's heartbroken." Sara stretches out her legs. "I was with him that night anyway. If he was going to strangle anyone, it would have been me."

Timber barks. Below them a black truck pops out from behind one of the buildings, its windshield reflecting the stirring clouds. When Charlie emerges from the truck, Timber's bark guides his gaze up to them. Charlie cups his hands around his mouth and hollers up.

"You two lost?"

"Looking for you," Sara calls back.

The wall of rock behind them bounces their words in such a perfect echo that Clare actually looks over her shoulder. When Charlie sticks his fingers in his mouth and whistles, Timber takes off, back and forth in a sprint down the jags of the mine road. Sara and Clare follow him.

"Did you tell him we were coming?" Clare asks.

"He wants to talk to you."

"Here?"

"Here."

"You could have told me that," Clare says.

"Then you wouldn't have come."

Up close Charlie's face looks better than Wilfred's, the swelling around his eyes all but gone. He opens his arms and welcomes Sara into a hug.

"You two friends now?" Charlie asks.

"She asks a lot of questions," Sara says. "She likes to know other people's business."

This is why Clare was never one for girlfriends, aside from Grace, unable as she always was to grasp the intricacies of female friendship, its unruliness, how someone like Sara can act the confidante one minute, then throw Clare to the wolves the next.

The building beyond them is boxy and built from cinder blocks, its windows smashed. Behind it is another smaller building, fenced in. MINE SHAFT. Clare feels her whole body stiffen, the adrenaline coursing. Sara pouts and wraps her arms around Charlie's waist.

"This place could still be put to some use," Clare says, straightening up. "To someone with vision."

Charlie smiles. "I had a dream about you. Pointing your gun at me."

"I could say I had the same dream about you."

"There's just something in the timing," Charlie says. "Has me thinking."

"What timing?"

"You show up here right out of the blue."

Clare opens her mouth to speak, but no words come.

"She says she's on the run," Sara says. "From a husband."

"Is she?" Charlie says. He unhooks himself from Sara. "Should I be worried about you?"

"No," Clare says.

"It occurred to me last night, with that shot of yours. Maybe you're more than just a plain old cop or PI. Maybe you're some kind of special ops."

"Special ops!" Clare forces a quick laugh. "In Blackmore? I don't think so."

Charlie's face darkens.

"We've had cops up here before," Sara says. "You wouldn't be the first."

"Well, I assure you, I'm not a cop of any kind. My father taught me how to shoot. I grew up on a farm."

"Right," Charlie says. "Sniper farm girl. On the run. That's some story."

For a moment they stand in a stalemate. In the silence, Timber lets out a low growl.

"Two things," Charlie says finally.

"Okay," Clare says.

"Don't come around here on your own. *Ever.* People have fallen down the shaft before. It happens."

Clare feels the air catch in her lungs, her hands tighten into fists, the same sensation that came over her when Jason's voice began to rise in their kitchen. Anticipation. She nods at Charlie.

"And don't ever tell me you feel sorry for Wilfred Cunningham."

"I didn't."

"Yes you did. Yesterday. You don't feel sorry for him. That man killed my family. Got it?"

Clare nods again, unwilling to break eye contact first.

Charlie looks up to the sky. "Rain."

On cue, Clare feels a drop on her cheek, and then another. In an instant a torrent unleashes on them, straight and hard. Charlie tugs Clare and Sara by the arms over to his truck, opening the door to let the dog jump in first. In the cab Clare sits wedged between him and Sara, the dog panting at Sara's feet. Clare tucks her camera under her arm to rub it dry. The windshield is opaque with water.

"Open it," Charlie says, pointing.

Sara yanks open the glove compartment and extracts a small baggie of pills. Clare recognizes them at once, the round blue of them matching those taken so often from her mother's stash. Sara pinches the bag open and lifts two pills out, swallowing one and handing the other to Clare.

"No," Clare says, a deep pull within her countering her refusal.

"Think of it as a hazing ritual," Charlie says. "Welcome to Blackmore."

The drone of rain fills the truck. Clare knows what will come, that gentle euphoria, where everything feels light, easy, beautiful. Months of restraint undone in a single swallow. She can't read the expression on Sara's face, whether it is worry or anger, jealousy. Do you want to see me undone? she would like to say to Sara, the pill rolling between her forefinger and thumb. Clare tilts her head back and drops the pill in. It tastes bitter on her tongue.

"See now? That wasn't so hard." Charlie jabs Clare lightly with his elbow. "Now you're one of us."

"Aren't you going to take one?"

Charlie just laughs. "You coming to Ray's tonight?"

"Of course she is," Sara says, eyes closed.

"Good," Charlie says. "Come to the house at seven. I'll drive you down. Keep you in my sights."

Charlie eases the truck over to the switchbacks and begins the climb. Clare watches him through the windshield as he uncoils the chain and pries the gate open with a key he takes from his pocket, the way the gate gouges the wet gravel as it drags. Already the light seems different. Brighter. If she squints until he is fuzzy, she can see Jason in Charlie's place, the young Jason from their courtship, the man who incited nothing but desire in Clare. Sara's breathing has calmed from the earlier staccato, some color returned to her complexion. Charlie drives the truck through the gate, then gets out to repeat the task in reverse. Clare tilts the rearview mirror so she can see him drawing the gate closed, mesmerized by the scowl that sets on his face when he thinks no one is watching.

The warmth. It comes first to the fingers and toes, then up the arms and legs, into the core. Clare can feel the flush in her cheeks. She lies starfish on the bed and lets it wash over her, her fingers uncurling, her jaw released from tension she hadn't even known was there. The kicking in. There is a patter of rain on the roof of the trailer, the black of the tall pines out the rounded window. Clare reaches for the photograph atop the folder, Shayna's eyes two dots in the poor pixilation.

You left a hole in Blackmore, Clare thinks, her finger tracing Shayna's outline. A vacancy.

It is almost seven. Clare strips out of her clothes and wets a towel in the kitchen to run over her body. She scrubs at her skin until it is red and goose-bumped, then stands naked in front of the mirror. The sight of her own body still surprises her, the curves that have come since she left, since she stopped running. The gash on her shoulder looks inflamed. Underneath her belly button snakes a light scar. Clare rests her palm on it, this small dent of stretched skin all that remains of her pregnancy.

Clare rummages through her duffel bag for something decent, a black top and jean skirt. She walks downhill to the Merritt house. Every light is on. Through the screen door she can see Charlie seated at the kitchen table, eyes forward to an empty kitchen. She watches him for a minute from the shadows, his slow mannerisms, the way he rubs his brow, then strokes his beard in silence. Some distant part of her understands that she should be fearful of him; that part washes away for now, replaced by a strange sense of solidarity, two people having faced the loss of so much. Before she can knock on the door, Charlie swivels on his chair and spots her.

"You coming or going?" he asks.

"Coming," Clare says. "I mean, going. With you."

He motions to her skirt. "You'll be cold."

"I feel warm right now."

Charlie smiles, studying her. "You look different with your hair down."

In the trailer Clare had combed out her hair, the dark curls halfway down her back, holding up the photograph of Shayna to test the resemblance. Now she squirms under his long gaze, unsure whether it holds sadness or lust or anger. She follows Charlie to the truck, waiting at the passenger door as he returns to the house to let Timber out and tie him to the porch.

They drive to town in silence. At Sara's house Charlie stays in the car while Clare fetches her, the door opening before Clare can knock. Sara stands at the hall mirror, applying the last of her makeup. Her outfit takes Clare aback, a tight red tank top and miniskirt, towering heels, her legs thin as sticks. Next to her Clare feels like a schoolmarm, plain and prim. Across the street the lights are on through the drawn curtains of Jared's house. Clare feels an urge to go over and knock, her inhibitions muted by that pill, but follows Sara instead, the two of them sliding into the cab next to Charlie.

"Gorman," Charlie says. "That's some outfit."

"Thank you," Sara says. "I picked it just for you."

The drive takes two minutes, the parking lot across from Ray's lined with cars.

"Whole town's here," Charlie says.

Sara rolls her eyes. "All fifty of us."

As they cross the street, Sara links arms with Clare and walks in a near strut, laughing at nothing, so that Clare can't be certain who between them is commanding the sidewalk stares. Ray's is busy, a scattering of people on the makeshift dance floor. From her vantage at the door Clare can see everyone in the place. Donna the waitress mans some kind of coin-toss game. A band plays on a plywood riser in the corner, the lead singer a fiftysomething man who looks dressed for a family dinner, and though they look sort of ridiculous in their belted jeans and flannel shirts, three grandfatherly types who bob their heads to their own music, Clare thinks the band isn't half bad.

Sara drags her to a table, then leaves as soon as Clare sits, crossing the dance floor to hug someone on its far side, abuzz and happy. Charlie dips into the chair across from Clare.

"I'm buying the drinks," he says.

"Aren't you driving?"

Charlie sets his car keys on the table and pulls a quarter from his pocket.

"Winner drinks, loser drives. Call it."

"Heads," Clare says.

With a flourish Charlie launches the coin high upward and snatches it midair. Heads.

"What'd you call again?" Charlie asks.

"Heads. You know I did."

"Bah. Screw you," Charlie says, retreating to the bar.

It has been years since Clare was at a party like this, clusters of bodies on the dance floor, the lights dimmed just so, the floor sticky with spilled drinks. Perhaps even since her own wedding five years ago. Clare wore her mother's dress taken in at the bust and hips. After the meal and the slapdash speeches, when the bar was nearly dry, her brand-new husband ripped off his tie and hurled it across the room, messy drunk and wild with dance-floor abandon. From her perch at the head table, Clare watched Jason, red-faced and ignoring her, and she was filled with an aching sense of wonderment at how she ended up at her own wedding.

The music stops. Down the bar, looking right at Clare, is Jared Fowles. His collar is undone, and though he wears a smile, he still manages to look bored, disinterested, the same air about him that riled Clare so easily yesterday. The doctor Derek Meyer is at the bar too, his face in a frown. Charlie returns and sets an open beer in front of her.

"You go ahead and get hammered."

The beer is so cold it stings Clare's throat. Charlie tilts his own bottle and takes a long drink.

"Good party," Clare says.

"This?" Charlie says. "This is nothing. Thousands used to be at homecoming. Everyone came back. Kids, cousins, whatever. They'd hold the dance up at the old arena and there'd still be a line at the door. You'd have to show up at six to make sure you got in."

"It's not a bad crowd tonight."

"The room's barely full."

"The music's good."

Charlie shrugs. "You like that treat I gave you earlier?"

Clare can still feel the fuzz of it around her, the haze.

"Doesn't hurt to dabble," Charlie says.

"Some people are incapable of dabbling," Clare says. "Like Sara, I'm guessing. Or Shayna Fowles."

"See?" Charlie says. "That kind of talk makes you sound like a cop."

"And you sound like someone with something to hide."

Behind them the lead singer banters into the microphone as he tunes his guitar.

"Speaking of something to hide," Charlie says. "Tell me about this husband of yours."

"I'm not married."

"It's not hard to dig things up," Charlie says, "should I become more curious."

"I could say the same thing to you."

With a one-two-three-four from the singer and a straight pounding of the drums, the band starts up again. When Clare goes to speak, she can barely hear her own voice. Charlie appears only bemused, as though the tension between them is more playful than hostile. He leans back with his arms crossed, staring her down, the legs of his chair tilted so that

Clare is certain he will tip over. Finally he breaks his gaze and leaves for the bar to summon another drink, their coin toss nullified.

The dance floor is populated mostly with older couples like Donna and a man who must be her husband, and next to them a handful of teenagers dancing in an awkward pack. Across the room, Sara swills a glass of white wine and lines up to spin the large prize wheel. She makes such a fuss of it, reaching up on the tips of her toes for the top spoke and then yanking down, nearly pulling the wheel off the axle. As it spins Sara jumps up and down and pumps her skinny arms, and a few people gather gamely around to watch. When the wheels stops on THREE FREE DRINKS!!! Sara's yelp pierces the room despite the loud music, and then she hugs everyone within reach.

Her beer empty, Clare tucks her bag under the table and walks along the edge of the dance floor to the bar. Derek Meyer wedges over to make room for her. Even in a T-shirt and jeans and with a drink in hand, he looks stiff, the only man in Blackmore who might resemble Malcolm Boon.

"You fit in well here," Derek says.

"I'm not so sure."

"Taking lots of pictures?" he says, his tone not quite sarcastic.

"A few." Clare pulls back the collar of her shirt. "I fell down the other day. Gashed myself."

Derek leans in. "It looks infected."

"It doesn't even hurt."

"It probably should have been stitched. You might need antibiotics."

"I have ointment."

"That won't help," Derek says. "The cut's too deep. Are you taking something for the pain? Your eyes seem a little . . . unfixed."

Clare looks down. She knows this feeling well, her brother or Grace so often scrutinizing her as Derek does now. The questions, the steady doubt.

"I'm fine," she says.

"Do you know how things work around here?"

"It's a dance," Clare says. "Aren't we here to have fun?"

"I don't find this fun."

"So why do you come?"

No answer.

"The doctor!" Clare says playfully, swirling her finger through a spill on the bar. "Out to save everyone. Or so I hear."

Derek angles away from her, repulsed or angry, and signals to the bartender.

"I'd be careful," he says. "The infection could spread. Enter your bloodstream."

The bartender has come over. Derek orders a soda. Charlie stands at the far end of the bar, his finger jabbed in another man's face. Clare knows Jared Fowles is watching her from the corner. Why does she save her venom for this doctor, the one man who might actually be trying to help people in this town? Clare thinks of Christopher shuffling his terrified son to her front door as she screamed at him from the kitchen, enraged that he'd taken control of their mother's prescriptions, cutting off her easy supply. Her fury at his good intentions.

Clare takes a deep breath in an effort to compose herself. What would Malcolm do if he were here in her place? Surely he would order a soda too, say something about faculties, about keeping your wits. But the circle is closing around Clare at the bar, all of Shayna's people absorbing her into this fold. Clare orders a beer. Before she can dig a folded bill from her pocket, Derek offers the bartender a twenty.

"Thank you," Clare says.

"Let me know if that gets any worse," he says, touching her shoulder above the gash. "If you get desperate."

Soon Derek has moved away and Charlie and Sara are there, then Jared too, others she doesn't recognize. All these bodies pressed together bring a heat to the room. Someone orders shots. One after the next Clare touches the little glass to her lips and jerks her head back, the booze burning down her throat. She slams each shot glass down a split second before anyone else, again the winner. How long has it been?

The band is back and they play hard rock, no more smiles on their faces, their shirts untucked. Sara takes Clare by both hands and drags her to the center of the dance floor. Together they throw their arms overhead and spin.

Clare closes her eyes, the bass in her ears. She knows every word to this song. It even might have played at her wedding. Someone reaches for Clare's hand and pulls her into a twirl, then passes her to Jared, then to a stranger, a blur of faces. She and Sara fly around the circle, and Clare is giggling, dizzy, drunk. It was Jared who started with the shots. Each one sweeter than the last, down the hatch. The row of glasses was a foot deep along the bar, all of them partaking, even Charlie.

In the bathroom stall Clare wrestles with the buttons on her skirt. She emerges to find Donna at the sink.

"You need a ride?" Donna says.

"I'm good."

"You don't look so good."

Clare leans into the sink and splashes cold water on her cheeks.

"I heard you took the trailer," Donna says, watching Clare through the mirror.

"There was nowhere else to go."

"You're asking for it, you know."

"No I'm not. Really."

But it takes effort to enunciate, and as Donna shakes her head, Clare can only look sheepishly away. In the bathroom mirror her reflection seems the spitting image of her own mother, the circles under her eyes just dark enough, eyes not green but hazel. How old was her mother when she died? Clare clamps her eyes closed and opens them again. This time the reflection is hazy, a film over her eyes that she cannot blink away. She is struck by her sharp likeness to Shayna, the same pale skin and big eyes cradled by a mess of dark hair. She recoils backwards into Donna, who must then intervene when she can't get the paper towel dispenser to work.

"You might want to put a cork in it." Donna holds the bathroom door open for her. "Sleep it off."

At the bar Clare orders a glass of water. Jared is swiftly beside her.

"If it isn't Clare O'Dey."

"If it isn't Jared Fowles."

"We never shook hands yesterday," he says. "Yours were full."

He takes Clare's outstretched hand and holds it in place.

"It's still pretty crowded," Clare says, withdrawing from his grip.

"People like to party. It's the common denominator around here."

"I guess no one has to work tomorrow."

Immediately Clare regrets the words, but Jared laughs.

"I did some recon on you."

"What did you find?" Clare must plant her hand on the bar to steady the incoming spins.

"Nothing. The only Clare O'Dey I found is a wedding planner in California. Not you, I'm guessing."

"Not me. I hate weddings."

"I heard you shot a bat out of the night sky."

"Charlie seems to like that story."

Jared presses his hand into the small of Clare's back. She arches against his touch.

"Aren't you the one with the missing wife?"

"Missing *ex*-wife," Jared says without a beat.

"I saw the poster and I wondered. Because of the name."

"She dropped my name when we split, actually. Went back to Cunningham."

"I'm sorry about that," Clare says.

"About what?"

"Must be hard. Missing wife and all."

"Ex-wife. Like I said."

"Missing ex-wife might be even worse. The optics aren't great."

"Right. So you're afraid of me?"

"No." Clare must articulate the word. She is surprised by her own audacity, how emboldened she still gets by a few drinks.

"If you want to talk to someone about it, talk to him." He points to Derek Meyer. "He's got his nose in everyone's business. Loves to keep his nose in ours."

"Isn't that his job? He's a doctor."

"Yes. He's also a prick."

"Sara said he's trying to send her to rehab."

"That's his thing. If he really wanted her to stop with the pills, he'd take away her kid."

"Can he do that?"

"Of course he can."

The dance floor drains when a slow song comes on.

"As much as I love uplifting conversations, maybe we could dance instead? Do you dance?"

Clare lifts her elbow in an attempt to decline, but Jared takes hold of it and guides her to the center of the dance floor. Then they are pinned close, the width of a fist between them, so that Clare's chin touches his shoulder and she cannot see his face. She inhales the scent of his shirt, a mild aftershave detected only at close range. He is broad, lean, tall. Clare is too muddled to speak. Next to them, Sara's face is planted in Charlie's chest. Surely Clare has been bantering with Jared all night, sharing drinks, jokes, glances. Surely she did not just end up in his arms on the dance floor out of nowhere. She is not losing herself in this place or these people.

Jared's heartbeat is slow, calm. The scratch of his stubble is in Clare's hair. He seems to be bearing most of her weight, and Clare feels that she could fall asleep like this, her body limp against his. The rest of the night will have to unfold in a daze, because nothing is sticking anymore. Clare lifts her head to look around. Sara looks glassy eyed too, under Charlie's spell.

Sometimes, in a crowd, Clare is certain she sees her father. Sometimes, she sees her husband. Or Christopher. Or Grace. It is never actually them, of course. But that initial trick of the light always brings a patter to her chest. This time, she blinks and blinks again. It could not have been Malcolm Boon she saw passing through the doors to outside. Out the window she sees only shadows, the brake lights from departing cars. She sets her cheek on Jared's shoulder. It could not have been Malcolm. Malcolm is not here.

The air is like a cool cloth against her skin. Clare is relaxed, her body sweaty under her clothes. Charlie's truck is right where he left it, the parking lot across from Ray's almost empty. She feels in her bag for his keys. The walk back to the trailer is over two miles, and her joints still feel loose. The moon must have set long ago. The road will be dark.

The gravel of the parking lot slips into Clare's shoes. She sits on the bumper of Charlie's truck to shake out the pebbles. These old leather sandals are not the best for walking. Clare lifts one of the shoes to her face to examine it, its shine scratched away, the leather of the strap curled into a ringlet. How old is this shoe? Clare has no idea where it came from, when she bought it, how long it has been with her, stuffed into her bag with her flats, her boots, her sneakers. Four pairs of footwear bought secondhand along the way. Even when she had a bedroom and a closet of her own, Clare always wore the same things over and over anyway.

"Please don't break my ankles, you stupid shoes," Clare says aloud.

What a cliché I am, she thinks, the silly drunk. Clare digs for her pad and pen and leaves a note for Charlie under his windshield wiper, unconcerned as to whether it might anger him.

I have your keys.
You are too drunk.
So much for the coin toss.
Walking back now.
You walk too.

On the last stretch of town road, Clare meets a few stragglers still clinging to half-empty bottles of beer. Past town the road is dark and devoid of cars. Clare can't be sure how far she's gone. She is thirsty, and her ears ring, but she keeps a decent pace, her eyes on the ground. One foot in front of the other.

At the sound of a car behind her, Clare steps to the shoulder. The headlights come at her. The car is moving more slowly than it should be. It passes her without stopping, but then she sees the brake lights and the car is turning around, and the headlights are on her again, she is washed in white light, and all she can think to do is clutch her bag and stand there blocking the car's path, frozen.

"Dammit. Get in."

This is Malcolm's voice. This can't be Malcolm's voice.

"It's me. Get in the bloody car!"

Me, Clare thinks. As if there is only one person who could be *me*.

Clare touches the heat of the hood and feels her way around to the passenger door. Malcolm leans over and opens it for her.

"I thought I saw you!" Clare says. "At Ray's. An apparition."

"Get in."

Only when Clare sits in the warmth does it register that her legs are sore with cold. The car is moving before she can pull her door closed.

"Other way," Clare says. "The trailer's the other way."

Malcolm yanks the car into reverse and turns around, driving in silence until the Merritt mailbox appears and Clare motions for him to pull over. The dashboard glows, and Clare can see the shadows of Malcolm's face, the angle of his jaw, the white of his hands as they grip the wheel.

The second time Malcolm walked into that café where she'd been working, a strange calm overtook Clare. He ordered the same breakfast and plucked out his cell phone, leaving it on the table next to his napkin. He was finished with his meal and Clare was standing over him, pouring coffee, when his phone rang. The name on his call display came up as two single letters: J.O., and right away Clare understood. She understood that J.O. stood for Jason O'Callaghan, that this man was here for her, chasing her, the one she knew would eventually come.

If you leave, Jason used to say, his thumb pressing into the softness of Clare's throat, I'll find a way to find you.

In the café that morning, the phone vibrated on the table, and Malcolm rested his hand against it without looking up.

Aren't you going to answer that? Clare asked.

No need, Malcolm said. In the glance exchanged, Clare wondered if he understood too.

It was sunny and warm, the morning of his second visit. The café was busy, the griddle in the kitchen crackling with bacon and pancakes. Clare walked behind the counter and set the coffeepot back on the burner. A family occupied the booth next to Malcolm's, a young girl fiddling with the salt and pepper shakers while her parents debated the menu. In the kitchen, Clare pulled off her apron and left through the back door. She drove her car to an empty parking lot tucked behind the elementary school and sat with her face in her hands, the early July heat prickling her legs through the windshield. She knew enough to have her things packed and with her at all times, just in case. A few minutes later she was on the highway headed north.

To think of that as only days ago. To think of Malcolm as that man in the café, the same man now fuming and quiet in the driver's seat.

"What are you doing here?" Clare asks.

"I came to find you."

Clare puts her hand to her mouth to stifle a hiccup. "Wow. Sorry."

"I was there long enough to witness the show you put on," Malcolm says.

"You said you weren't coming."

"I said I'd be nearby."

"You'll blow our cover."

"I'm sure everyone was too busy watching you."

"You know what? I had a few drinks. Is that a crime?" Clare feels dizzy. She drops her chin to her chest.

"What are you doing?" Malcolm asks.

"I'm resting."

"No. I mean, what are you doing *here*?"

If she tries to speak, Clare might well throw up instead. She shakes her head. Malcolm drops an envelope into her lap.

"More notes. I figured I'd get them to you directly. Since you're supposed to be working."

"It feels like you're spying on me."

"You have a job to do."

"Here's the thing. Whatever this job is, I'm doing it."

"Didn't look that way to me."

"I'm sorry, Malcolm. I thought you were staying out of sight."

"I am out of sight."

"You came to the only bar in town. That's actually the opposite of out of sight."

"I stayed in the background. You didn't even see me."

Malcolm starts the car. All Clare can do to stop herself from retching is open the window and lean out to gulp the fresh air.

"Can you give me a minute?" she says. "I don't feel very well."

"Get out."

Something in Malcolm's voice sets Clare alight, sobers her, the annunciation, the bite in his tone so much like her husband's. She edges along the seat until their faces are inches apart.

"Don't you want me to fit in?" Clare asks. "Isn't that why I'm here instead of you? I keep asking you that question and you won't answer me."

"I don't think it's working."

"Isn't this exactly what you want me to do?"

Clare's voice is measured, raspy. "Live like the locals? That's what you said. You said, 'Be methodical. Eliminate the obvious possibilities first.' You want me to get right in there. I can ask them anything I want. I can eat off their plates. I haven't been here three days and I'm *in*. I'm not an outsider anymore. They think they know me. I might as well be Shayna. How convenient is that? And I haven't told them a thing. Even Jared. He's asking me to dance. They all want to be my friend. They're that lonely."

"No one here wants to be your friend," Malcolm says. "And you're not Shayna."

"I know that," Clare says, stung. She sits up straight. "Do you have any friends? Because that's how people act with friends. They open up."

Malcolm is silent. Clare slumps back and fingers the envelope on her lap.

"What is this?"

"Articles. Some history I thought might help." Malcolm pauses. "They are not your friends, Clare. You're being reckless."

"No I'm not."

"She could still be alive, you know. You don't have any time to waste."

"I wasn't . . ."

But Clare trails off. She leans into the headrest and closes her eyes. It shouldn't matter if she's dead, this woman a stranger to Clare. Malcolm reaches over her. She can smell him, his scent alien to her. Has she ever touched Malcolm before? Clare can't be sure. He pulls a drawstring sack from the glove compartment and sets it on her lap atop the envelope.

"What's this?"

"Your gun."

"You're giving it back to me?"

He withdraws it and sighs. "Shouldn't I?"

"No. I mean yes, you should."

"Now I'm not so sure."

"Malcolm. Please. I'm not an idiot. I haven't had a drink in a long time. It hit me quick."

The familiar contours of the barrel reveal themselves to Clare as she feels the gun through the canvas of the bag. How many hours has she spent in motel rooms staring at the door, this very gun loaded on the table in front of her, a split second from her reach? Waiting. Waiting for someone to knock, for him to come looking for her. Clare takes Malcolm by the arm and squeezes until she feels his biceps contracting under her fingers.

"You scared me. Driving up on me like that."

"I was angry," Malcolm says. "Shayna's fate rests in your hands."

"This is all on you," Clare says. "Between you and me? Believe me, you're not the angry one. Don't ever sneak up on me again."

And then Clare is out of the car, standing again on the side of the road. Malcolm turns his car around and passes her without a glance. Her breaths are quick. She would like to pick up a rock and throw it at his rear windshield. But as his taillights ebb, Clare's fury soon gives way to a kind of shame, the thought of Malcolm watching her as she flitted from the bar to the dance floor and back, flirty in her denim skirt, putting on a show, filling the void. Clare sways and nearly bumps into the Merritt mailbox. She fumbles to open the drawstring sack Malcolm gave her. It is always a surprise, the surge that comes when she takes hold of this gun. The urge to fire it, to point it at someone and pull the trigger. To end it. She will have to find a hiding place back at the trailer. Tomorrow, she will start again. She will do her best to remember what she can from tonight, anything useful. But in the cold and dark she feels only anger. How did she end up here? What happened? In her mind the details are already liquid, the evening seeping its way out.

My sharpest memories are the dark ones. Driving in a heavy rain to the city with my father. Was I nine, or ten? A car bobbing downstream with its trunk in the air. My father pulled over and waded into the water ahead of the car. I rolled down my window and watched as he took hold of the fender before he dove under. Why did he drag the body back to shore by the collar? I would have let it float away.

The dead man was wearing a shirt and tie and his eyes and mouth were open. I was out of the truck by then, crouching next to them in the rain, the three of us soaked through. I'd never seen a dead body before. The man's face was distended, his skin a pale gray. He must have tried to escape, my father said, because the driver's-side window was open and his seat belt was undone. My father crossed the man's arms over his chest one by one and pressed his swollen eyes closed. Don't worry. That's all he said to me.

My mother used to complain that my father never hugged her. As a kid I'd hide in the cold room and watch him eat a bowl of cereal after a shift, his face smeared black from the coal. He almost never mustered a smile. But he never flinched either, even that day at the river, his grip on that dead man's collar. He never flinched in the face of terrible things.

SUNDAY

As she walks down the hill from the trailer Clare feels it, the flood of wanting more. The ache that always came the morning after. She pauses at her car, tracing the path of the dog's leash from the porch to track whether he is tied to it.

"Timber?" she calls. Nothing.

Clare climbs the porch to tuck Charlie's truck keys into the mail slot. She wears her camera around her neck, her flimsy decoy, the roll of film half finished. It is barely five hours since Malcolm left her on the dark road. Where would he have gone? Driven hours to find a bed or slept hidden somewhere in his car? A man of few traces. Popping through the line of birch trees, she finds Louise waiting on the porch chair, purse already in hand. The screen door is latched, but when Clare calls for Wilfred he appears right away from the living room. He's been expecting her. He does not unlatch the door.

"So you're okay if I take her for a bit?" Clare asks.

"I'm ready to go," Louise says, standing.

Wilfred shifts from foot to foot on the other side of the storm door. Clare makes a point of adjusting the camera around her neck. The photographer.

"I'll take good care of her, Mr. Cunningham."

"Have her back in two hours," Wilfred says without making eye contact.

"We'll go for a short walk. Not too far."

They will walk the length of the gorge, down to the creek where Louise was trying to go the other day, see if anything stirs, if any clue or memory bubbles to the surface. Clare guides Louise around the house and across the back field, surprised by how nimble she is, how deftly she manages the steep descent at the back of the property. Giddy at her freedom, Louise walks too far ahead of Clare to manage any conversation, her purse swinging. All Clare can do is pant with the effort to stay close. She used to be fit, used to be able to run far and fast, chased as she always felt. But all those months of driving, of motel living, have taken a toll on her body, and now her legs burn, her shoulder aches.

By the time Clare catches up, Louise stands over the waterfall, the clearing with the fire pit up ahead. If anything stirs in Louise, any sense that this was the last place her daughter was seen alive, she doesn't show it. Clare lifts her camera and snaps a photograph.

"It looks like someone lives here," Clare says.

"It's a gathering place," Louise says. "We used to come here to have campfires."

"Is this the spot you were trying to find the other morning?"

"I'm sorry?"

Clare tries again. "Who comes here now?"

"The younger folk, I guess. Shayna and her friends."

They navigate their way down to the fire pit. Clare is certain there are more discarded beer cans than there were the other day, that someone has partied here in the meantime.

"What a mess." Louise bends to collect the cans and toss them to the center of the pit.

"Tell me about your daughter," Clare says.

"She's a good girl. She'd never leave a mess like this."

"Maybe it was her friends. Does she have a lot of friends?"

Louise does not look up from her task. "I'm sure she does."

"Do you like Jared?"

Awaiting a response, Clare clicks a photograph of Louise at work. She seems not to have heard the question.

"She was always Daddy's girl," Louise says. "I gave her whatever she wanted, but he was the one for her. I couldn't compete. They're so alike. Both so serious. He used to bring her down to the mine on his days off. He was issued a citation once for letting her ride a coal car. They adored each other. Then she grew up and she just got so fiery. When she was a teenager they fought like mad. He couldn't bear to let her go."

"Do you worry about her?"

Finally out of breath, Louise sits on a log.

"Do you have children?"

"No," Clare says.

"When you do, you'll see. All you do is worry. All he does is worry."

"Do you see a lot of Shayna?"

"Every day."

Clare brushes the log next to Louise and sits. She will have to navigate this conversation carefully.

"Do you know where Shayna is now?"

"She's not here," Louise says, a shadow passing across her face. "Wilfred takes me to see her."

"Where?"

"In the garden."

Clare thinks of Sara's description of rehab, the dealers in the garden.

"He drives you to town?"

"No," Louise says. "She planted the cucumbers."

"Who, Shayna?"

"No. The other one."

It feels almost shameful, pressing this woman, muddling any lucidity still to be had, capitalizing on her frailties. They both fall silent and listen to the sounds. Honking. Music.

"What is that?" Louise says.

"It must be the parade. In town."

"Well, we *have* to go," Louise says, taking Clare's hand and squeezing it.

Clare remembers Sara saying something about it last night, Sunday's celebrations, the last remnants of homecoming. Before she can muster a next move Louise is already on foot, headed downhill into territory Clare has yet to explore. The sounds grow louder. After a few minutes they come to a path that takes them up, Clare scrambling to keep Louise in sight as they reach the dead end of a side street. Clare recognizes it, Sara's house and then Jared's across from it, both of them parked in their drives. The gorge connecting everyone. Louise is already halfway down the block. Clare hooks her camera under her arm and runs to catch up. She is parched, a headache taking strong hold, the hangover no longer at bay.

The fog retreats against the heat of the sun breaking through the clouds. The road is scattered with cars and trucks in vague formation. Louise and Clare stroll arm in arm on the sidewalk. Two young girls with batons stride alongside a fire truck, *Blackmore Volunteer Fire Brigade* scripted in gold against the dulled red of the cab. The odd person stops them and greets Louise, old friends introducing themselves again in case she happens not to remember. Clare knows enough not to let the conversations meander to hazardous territory. To Shayna.

Clare is surprised by the bustle. Still, like everything else around here, this parade must be a shell of its former self. The sidewalk is not crowded. Most of the townspeople must be in the parade, leaving few as spectators. Clare and Louise wander north and find a stretch of open sidewalk, then sit on the curb, knees tucked up. Clare looks to the sky to absorb the sun. Around them a few children sit on their parents' shoulders with balloons tied to their wrists, their faces turned south to where the parade crawls toward them. She can imagine what homecoming might have looked like when the mine was open, when Blackmore was alive and well, when those who'd left still bothered to come home for a visit. But Louise seems enthralled anyway. If the parade is a trickle, she doesn't notice or care. Clare makes a show of taking photographs, lifting her camera every time she makes eye contact with a stranger.

Every man in Blackmore looks loosely the same, descended from the brawn of their miner fathers, thick shouldered and strong. The parade is led by a convertible with a banner on the side that reads MAYOR BILL MCGRATH: SERVING BLACKMORE FOR TEN YEARS RUNNING! The man perched on the backseat is Donna's husband. Donna waves to the crowd from the front seat. Their conversation in the bathroom last night washes over Clare. You might want to put a cork in it and go home, Donna said to her. You're asking for it. Perhaps she'd been right.

"She's nuts." Louise points to Donna. "Look at her. Waving like the queen."

"That's Donna. She works at Ray's."

"I know who she is."

Next come the fire truck and the pair of out-of-sync baton twirlers. Louise clucks when they both drop their batons. A man squeezes into the space next to Clare and sits. He wears an old baseball cap that reads MINEWORKERS LOCAL 118. Alongside him is a boy Clare recognizes as Sara's son.

"Hi there, Louise. Nice to see you out." The man waits for some flicker of recognition. When none comes, he offers his hand to Clare. "Steve Gorman. You must be Clare. Blackmore's lone tourist."

"I am. Nice to meet you."

"This is my grandson, Danny."

"We've met." Clare winks at the boy. "He's quite the cyclist."

"We're headed home to see his mother. He's got a bit of a stomachache. Don't you, Dan?"

Daniel buries his head in his grandfather's lap.

"You're Sara's father-in-law," Clare says.

"I am."

"She was telling me you look after Danny on the weekends."

"I do what I can," Steve says, lowering his voice. "You looking after Louise?"

"Just helping out. I'm staying next door. I offered Mr. Cunningham some help."

"I'm surprised he took you up on it."

"So am I. You know him?"

"We worked together for thirty years." Steve Gorman leans closer to Clare. "Listen," he says. "I'm about to stick my nose in, but would you take some advice from an old man?"

"I might."

"I heard about last night. At Ray's. They're latching on to you because you're new. All of them. Be careful. They'll suck you in."

"Who will?"

"Just take it easy. That's my lowly advice."

Next to his grandfather, Danny holds his head between his legs.

"I should get this boy home," Steve says. "Just wanted to stop and say hello. Louise? It was great to see you out. Give my best to Wilfred."

"I will," Louise says, her gaze distant.

On the sidewalk Steve Gorman rolls the boy over in his arms and sets off. Clare and Louise wander up the block in search of another vantage point. The light and sounds of the parade disconcert Clare, a crushing pain forming between her ears. Before falling into bed last night she'd loaded her gun, sliding bullets one by one into the chamber, then peeling back a loose piece of wall paneling in the bedroom to hide it. She feels swarmed here, anxious, wishing she'd brought it with her. What good is a gun tucked away?

Clare guides Louise to sit on the curb in front of Ray's.

"Wilfred will be here any minute," Louise says.

"I don't think he's planning to come."

"Of course he is. They just had to pick something up after his shift. Shayna wouldn't miss this."

Next comes a group of veterans, Blackmore's War Heroes, two pushed along in wheelchairs and three others upright and spry in their faded uniforms. At a break in the parade Clare's eyes land on Jared Fowles. He stands directly across the street, tipping his ball cap in salute, a water bottle in his hand. Who knows how Louise will react to her estranged son-in-law? Clare tries to shoo him with a slow shake of her head, but Jared doesn't stand down. Please don't come over here, she wants to holler at him. But he crosses anyway, placing his hands on the last veteran's shoulders as he passes. Only when he hovers over them does Louise take notice.

"Hi," he says.

"Sit down," Clare says. "You're blocking our view."

Jared sidles up to Clare so that their arms touch.

"Hi, Louise," Jared says. "You look well."

"Thank you," Louise says without looking away from the parade.

"Not even a flicker," Jared whispers to Clare. "Should I be insulted?"

"Be quiet," Clare says.

"Is Wilfred here?"

"Do you see him?"

"Jeez," Jared says. "It's nice to see you too."

She nudges him over, out of Louise's earshot. "I'm worried you might upset her. She thinks Shayna is on her way here. Sometimes she thinks I'm Shayna."

"Wouldn't that be convenient?" Jared says. "Lets me off the hook."

"Don't you care what people think? Everybody is looking at us."

"I know what they think. It doesn't matter if I care." Jared reaches over and tugs on the strap around Clare's neck. "And they're looking at *you*. At this camera."

Clare straightens up and takes his water bottle from him, draining its contents.

"You disappeared last night," he says.

"I needed some air."

In the midday light Jared shows his age, the skin around his eyes lightly cracked. But he is handsome, still disarmingly boyish. A group of small children dressed in flags of the world walk by. Louise stands and claps for them, reaching out to touch their little hands as they pass.

"She has no idea who I am," Jared says.

"That could change any minute. You really should leave."

"You're not being very nice."

"This is making me uncomfortable. Show Louise some respect. Isn't she your family?"

At last Clare sees it, the smallest wince across his face. He tilts toward her.

"What are you up to? Pretending to be Shayna?"

"Don't say that. She might hear you."

"You can tell Louise not to worry. Her daughter's not dead. There's no tragedy here. She took off."

"Took off where?"

"Hell if I know."

"Have you heard from her?"

"No."

"So how do you know she took off?"

"Because she was threatening to do it for months. Said she hated it here. Hated everyone. Hated being dragged to rehab. Hated her father. Hated me. The world was an awful place and this town was the worst of it."

"Surely she'd know people are worried about her."

"Sure," Jared says. "Whatever drama she can muster. She loved to torment us."

There is scorn in his words, but still, Jared's look bears more sadness than anger. He may well be right, that even necessary escapes can be partly motivated by the need to punish those left behind. Seared precisely into Clare's mind is the image of her husband's shotgun perched high on the wall of their mudroom, the ammunition nearby. Sometimes, as Clare stood in the kitchen washing dishes, he would take it down and fiddle with it at the table, pointing it to her left, then to her right. You'd never leave me, right? he would say. After he'd go outside, Clare would watch him through the window as he fired at any living thing that dared traipse across his property.

I will leave you, Clare would think, studying him as he paused to reload. I will leave you with nothing.

The blast of a horn rights Clare back to the parade. The makeshift marching band has lost its configuration, the saxophonist about to knock up against the trumpeter. Clare's hand rests on the damp concrete of the sidewalk. She squeezes her eyes closed to ward off the throb in her head. Louise isn't there.

"You okay?" Jared says.

"Where'd she go?" Clare says to Jared. "Where'd Louise go?"

"I didn't see her walk away."

Clare jumps to her feet. She walks against the parade's flow, her pace quick but restrained. Behind her, Jared keeps up. It takes them less than a minute to reach the tail end of the parade.

"We're looking for Louise Cunningham," Jared announces to the group.

"Where is she?" a man asks.

"If we knew that, we wouldn't be looking for her, would we?"

At this admonishment the man grits his teeth, then turns from them to fiddle with the float. This must be the parade's main event, this large papier-mâché rendering of a mine's entrance. Four children in overalls and hard hats with headlamps sit along the edge of the flatbed truck. One boy fiddles with a costume mustache taped over his lip, his cheeks and hands smeared with black, the look of coal dust. The banner draped across the float reads Blackmore's Mining Museum: Our Men, Our

History. The pickup truck starts its engine and the float lurches forward. The parade will soon be over.

"You walk back up the other side," Jared says. "I'll head down this way. Give me your number."

"I don't have a cell phone," Clare says, though she can feel it wedged into her pocket.

"Seriously?"

"Seriously. Can we focus?"

"Jesus. Meet me at Ray's in thirty minutes whether you find her or not."

"What will you do if you find her?" Clare asks.

"What do you mean? I'll bring her back."

"She doesn't recognize you. She might refuse to come with you."

"I can convince her."

"Shouldn't we—"

But Jared is off in a jog. The miner's float is already a hundred feet ahead of her. The boy with the mustache watches Clare, his eyes bright against the dust on his face. The onlookers fold down their lawn chairs, gawking at Clare as though she were famous, a small-town novelty.

Clare retraces their earlier path up the main road, then down Sara's street, her wits dull. Louise. White sweater, white hair, blue jeans. Everyone should know her. How could she disappear so easily? Where might she go? Should she wander toward home, back to the Cunningham house, it will be Jared who finds her. Or Wilfred. The gorge. Clare slows when she spots Charlie sitting shirtless on the front stoop of Sara's house, cigarette in hand. He stands and wanders down the walkway to meet her.

"I was just about to go looking for you," he says. "And here you are."

"Louise Cunningham is lost."

"She's always lost."

"Did you see her pass by?"

"Nope. But I just got out here. Old man's home and he doesn't like me hanging out with the boy."

Charlie flicks his lit cigarette onto the lawn. Clare watches it, the curl of smoke rising from between the blades of grass.

"My truck's still at Ray's. I blame you for that."

"I put your keys inside your door."

"I'm stranded."

"You were drunk," Clare says.

"Don't you want to know why I was coming to find you?"

"I need to find Louise."

"And why is that old lady *your* problem?"

"I'm just trying to help."

When Clare makes a motion to move past him, Charlie steps out onto the road and faces her. With his shirt off he looks stronger, taller. Two hundred feet beyond him is the guardrail, Blackmore falling away, a residential street cut off by a precipitous drop.

"I want you to be my guinea pig," Charlie says.

"What? Not now. Please?"

There is a pleading to Clare's voice. She can feel the desperation setting in, Charlie tapping at that rousing part of her. He reaches into his back pocket and pulls out a folded wad of paper towel. Inside it is a ragged, pea-sized rock. The headache grips her now. She knows what this pill will do. Wash it clean.

"It's a prototype," he says. "A special blend. All the good stuff rolled into one."

"No."

"Take it for later. Just take it. Put it in your pocket."

They do a small dance, Clare trying to step around him, Charlie moving side to side to block her. He laughs as though it were a game, but Clare wants to cry, the tight swirl returned to her chest. Finally Charlie grabs hold of her wrist and pries open her hand, planting the rock in her palm. Instinctively she closes her fist around it.

"There," he says. "Was that so hard?"

"I need to go," Clare says. She stuffs the rock into the pocket of her jeans.

"No one goes to the gorge alone," Charlie says. "That's the rule."

He crosses his arms, still smiling. Something catches his eye over her shoulder. Clare spins around.

"Hey!"

Jared stands at the main road, his hands cupped over his mouth.

"Hey!" he hollers again. "They found her!"

"Is she dead?" Charlie hollers back.

"Shut up, Merritt," Jared says, jogging toward them. "They found her up the road. She ran in front of the mine float. Got knocked over."

"Is she okay?" Clare asks.

"Banged up. I'm not sure."

Clare turns back to Charlie. He makes a gun with his hand and points it at her pocket.

"I'll expect a full report," he says.

"Full report on what?" Jared asks.

"Ask her," Charlie says. "My guinea pig."

Charlie hugs himself as if suddenly beset by a chill, then wanders back to Sara's walkway, patting Clare on her sore shoulder as she passes. She flinches. How can someone as malicious as Charlie seem almost a child in his actions? Though Jared faces Clare, his gaze has turned down the road. She raises her camera and snaps his picture, the sun replaced in only minutes by swooping clouds. Louise has been found. It should be a relief, but instead Clare feels only a sense of impending doom, Louise slipped from her grasp and hurt, the rock Charlie gave her sharp in her pocket, digging into her thigh. Jared takes hold of her arm. The rain begins, setting them to a run, the torrent soaking them anyway.

At the hospital the nurse gives Clare a towel and a set of scrubs to put on. Jared sits next to her in the waiting room, soaked and shivering, the nurse offering him nothing but a sharp glare. Clare hands him her towel when she's done with it. Louise had wandered off, the nurse said, and spotted one of the missing-person posters on a boarded-up window. She tore it down and rushed out onto the road, hysterical. The truck pulling the float was able to brake just in time.

After a while Derek Meyer comes in, the nurse behind him. Jared stands but Clare stays in her seat, demure and defiant at the same time.

"She okay?" Jared asks.

"You should have left by now," Derek says.

"She's my mother-in-law."

"Not anymore."

"What's your problem?"

"Is she okay?" Clare interjects.

"You're the worst possible person to be here," Derek says, ignoring Clare. "Louise hasn't processed that Shayna is gone. Then you show up and she sees the poster."

"Right," Jared says. "Because I handed it to her."

"Of all the people who make things worse for Louise, you are number one," Derek says. "I had to sedate her. She's suffering."

"You love it when people suffer," Jared says, stepping closer. "It's the only time they need you."

"Shayna was done with you, Fowles. She hated you."

The nurse wedges herself between the two men.

"Calm down," she says. "You're embarrassing yourselves."

"You think she wanted you to save her?" Jared says. "All she wanted was her pills and her junk, and money for her pills and her junk. Whatever concoction Charlie had lying around. You're the only guy in town she wouldn't touch." Jared jabs Derek's shoulder. "Where'd you hide her?"

"Jared," Clare says, pulling him back by the shirt. He tugs free from her grasp.

"Call security," Derek says to the nurse.

"Security?" Jared laughs. "You're going to sic the last of the town geriatrics on me? You're really something, you know that?"

"You're a murderer," Derek says.

Jared spits at Derek's feet. "Wouldn't you love it if I was."

"Jared Fowles," the nurse says, a tremble in her voice. "You need to leave."

Jared snatches up his jacket and bumps Derek's shoulder on his way out. Clare wonders if he expects her to follow, but he turns the corner out the doors without a word or a glance. It takes a moment for the tension to leave the room.

"I've called Wilfred," the nurse says. "You're Clare?"

"Yes."

"Eleanor. You'll need to be here when he comes. He'll want an explanation."

"I don't work for him," Clare says.

"You were supposed to be watching her. That's what he said." She points to the scrubs on the chair. "Go change. I'll throw your clothes in the dryer. There's a locker room at the very end of the hall." She looks to Derek. "You go to your office. Calm yourself down."

"I am calm," Derek says.

"Jesus, no you are not. Your neck is covered in blotches. I'll move Louise into a proper room and come get you both when Mr. Cunningham arrives."

Eleanor may be a small woman, nearly sixty, but Clare admires her efficiency. Clare takes the scrubs and wanders down the darkened hall. She feels numb, tired. She pulls the rock Charlie gave her from her pocket and tucks it into her bra. Derek's office door is closed, but along the hall she's able to peer into the few rooms still in use. On her shifts at work Clare made a habit of looking into every room she passed, of gleaning the details, the machinery, the presence or absence of visitors, the touches of home, the cups of medication on their trays, each patient's story like a painted scene through the door to their hospital room. By the time Grace moved home Clare had been married for three years, her husband's cycle of rage and remorse constant but unpredictable. She figured it was a matter of time before she ended up in the hospital too, her best friend tending to a broken jaw or a cracked skull or too many pills swallowed. But it was her mother who ended up there first, skeletal and depleted from a survival effort that went years longer than doctors predicted it would. Her mother's impending death brought a new resolve.

I'm going to clean right up, Clare said in that hospital room, her mother unresponsive, comatose from the morphine. I'm going to leave him.

When it looked like only hours remained, the length of a day or two, Grace took a turn at the bedside so that Clare's family could go home to shower. She found Jason at the table, eating oatmeal for breakfast, hugging his bowl as a child would. Clare sat down across from him.

I don't think this is working anymore, she said.

It took a minute for his expression to change, for the life to spring to his eyes.

You leaving me? he asked.

What Clare felt in that moment was stillness. She'd witnessed the coming of death, the peace in it. This could be no worse than that.

I need help, she said. *You* need help.

The way Jason curled his fingers around the edge of the table, Clare was certain he thought to over-turn it and crush her with it. Instead, he stood and came around to her. He brushed the hair from her forehead and kissed her, a touch so light that Clare could feel the texture of his fingertips against her cheek. I'll do better, he said. And then he led her up the stairs to their bedroom, and Clare had allowed it, some body memory taking hold, the heat of his skin against hers. Why had she allowed it? When it was over he even managed to summon tears. I'll do better, he said again, propped on one elbow and facing her. We'll both get better. She fell asleep next to him, a deep slumber. Only when she woke and showered and dressed did the timing occur to her, the lack of protection. She set her hand against her belly and counted back through the days of the month.

At her mother's funeral, Jason held her hand firmly and deferred to her in conversation, standing in the background while she greeted the long line of neighbors and friends. When she alluded to the possibility of a baby, to the waves of nausea, he'd offer her the small smile of someone in on your deepest secret. He's changed, Clare said to Grace. She even showed Jason some photographs she'd taken and talked about signing up for a class or two, working part-time toward a degree, taking his silence as permission. For weeks, she stayed clean.

Then, shortly after Clare buried her mother, she came home from a trip to the city with Grace, a bag full of darkroom supplies tucked under her arm. Jason was at the table, drinking, his face already a deep red. The positive pregnancy test was in Clare's purse, and she set down the bag to dig for it, meaning to rest it on the table in front of him, a silly riddle, a moment she'd planned the entire drive home. But before she could find it Jason was already against her, her darkroom supplies crushed underfoot, pressing her into the refrigerator, his forearm into her neck, lifting her right off her feet. If you leave me, he said, I'll come for you. She'd almost forgotten the sensation. The perfect fear. Though she gagged and struggled and he only hissed, she could hear him clearly, the exact words he said, repeated under his breath after he'd released her and sat down again to finish his drink. Wherever you run, I'll be right behind you.

Wilfred is in the corner, his fists in angry balls. At the foot of Louise's bed Clare stands next to Derek, the scrubs Eleanor gave her loose on her frame. Eleanor hovers close to Wilfred, caging him in. In the bed Louise looks frail and bewildered.

"Louise?" Eleanor says. "You're in the hospital. You took a spill at the parade."

"I was looking for Shayna. She was supposed to be there. Is she here?"

Derek coughs.

"You saw a poster, Louise," Eleanor says. "It upset you. She's not here."

Louise shifts her smiling gaze to Clare. "Yes she is," she says.

"I'm not Shayna, Louise. I'm Clare. We went for a walk today. Remember?"

"Don't ask her if she remembers," Eleanor says under her breath. "It's not helpful."

"We should discuss restraints," Derek says. "Until we can calibrate her medication. See if that helps."

"So she needs a leash," Wilfred says.

"Well, no," Derek says. "She needs reliable, constant supervision. We'll make a plan. She may need to go into a home for a while. There are devices you could wear, Louise. Beepers, sort of, but with GPS."

"You mean a collar?" Wilfred says, no lilt to his voice.

"Mr. Cunningham," Eleanor says. "Please keep in mind that your wife is very much able to understand you."

"At this rate I could just stick her in the cellar and lock the door. Would damn well be cheaper."

"Watch your tongue, Wilfred," Eleanor says. "For God's sake. She hears you."

"Does she?" Wilfred waves his hand in Louise's face. "Hey, Lou! Hey! You there?"

"Stop it, Wilfred," Eleanor says.

Louise smiles at her husband, blinking as he waves, reaching to take hold of his hand.

"Hello," she says.

"See? She has no goddamn clue who I am."

"She knew who you were this morning," Clare says. "She talked about you today. You and Shayna."

"Shut your mouth," Wilfred says to Clare. "I know Charlie sent you here. He wants her dead."

"What?" Clare says. "That's not true at all."

"Mr. Cunningham," Derek says, "I know you're angry. I think you know that anyone could lose track of Louise at this point. She appears very determined to get away."

"I know who you are," Louise says to Derek. "Don't think I've forgotten. Shayna will be here any minute to get me."

Wilfred throws up his arms. Derek opens the drawer next to Louise's bed and pulls out a folded piece of paper.

"Louise was trying to show me this earlier," he says. "She kept trying to fish it out of her purse."

The paper is a poem written in the large cursive of a child's writing. Derek hands it to Louise. She stretches it taut and holds it to her face.

"She won a poetry contest at school," Louise says.

"Who did?" Eleanor says.

"Wilf and I took her out for lunch the day of the ceremony. She got a certificate and everything." Louise laughs. "They even published her poem in the newspaper. She made the front page, if you can believe it."

"When was that, Louise?" Derek says.

Louise considers the question. "I'm not sure. Last month?" She shakes her head. "You'd have to ask Wilf."

"Where is Wilf?" Eleanor says.

Louise scans the four of them standing in a semicircle at the foot of her bed.

"What day is it today?" she says.

"Sunday."

"Sunday? He'd be at the mine. He's working weekends this month."

Wilfred yanks the paper from Louise and tears it in two. Louise shrieks.

"That was twenty years ago. Twenty years ago, Lou!" Wilfred hurls the pieces to the floor.

"Stop it right now, Mr. Cunningham," Derek says, yanking at Wilfred's arm.

"Some damn poetry. You're nuts. Your daughter's no writer, Lou. She's a junkie. Remember? The booze and those pills? Those little crappy pills and that

garbage she'd snort? She even started shooting up."
Wilfred tugs himself free from Derek's grasp and
sits on the bed, leaning close to his wife, squeezing
her arm. "Remember the time we found her on the
kitchen floor? Foaming at the mouth? Remember
forking over our life savings to pay for rehab? Remember when we found her in the barn sniffing at
the gasoline can? You don't remember any of that.
You spoiled her! You always let her off the hook.
Everything's perfect and sunny in your world. Then
you come begging to me to fix it!"

"You shut your mouth right now, Wilfred Cunningham," Eleanor says.

The fight is gone from Wilfred all at once. He
stands and straightens the blankets over Louise.
From her vantage Clare can see his pained look,
the scowl of suppressed rage. He sidles to the door
and withdraws down the hall followed by Eleanor.
The room is quiet but for Louise's whimpering cry.

"He's gone," Clare says. "It's okay."

"Shayna," Louise says, her eyes wild with fear. "Is
Shayna here? Is she dead?"

"Shayna isn't dead." Derek hesitates. "She's
just . . . not here right now."

"That's right," Clare says. "We hope she'll be
back."

Derek bristles at Clare's words, frowning at her.
He opens a drawer in search of surgical gloves, a
stethoscope, the blood pressure cuff, then eases Louise over on the bed so that he can sit next to her. Louise soon cries in gulping sobs. After a minute Eleanor
returns with a syringe. Derek Meyer means business

now. Clare watches him, the way he tends to Louise, as he would his own mother, the way he'd raged at Jared in the waiting room, the way he'd chastised Wilfred. She's just not here right now, he'd said, as if there were more to that answer. Clare steps to the door so she is out of Eleanor's way.

"Horrible," Eleanor says. "Just horrible, all of it. What a thing to say to your own wife."

"He's struggling," Derek says.

"We all are," Eleanor says, flicking at the syringe to prepare it. "That's no excuse."

The needle goes in and Clare watches as Louise falls limp for the second time in only a few days. Sedated, released from her pain and her questions, Clare knows, in a way Wilfred will never be.

The chocolate bar has melted on her fingertips. Clare licks them one by one. She sits on a bench in the hospital garden, Blackmore's main street stretched out below her. Beyond the town Clare can see the road to the mine cut out of the mountainside. Somewhere along that ridge is the trailer, the Merritt and Cunningham homes. Whatever it was that Charlie gave her now presses into her bra against the flesh of her breast. She lifts her hand to it, jagged on her skin, a tiny bomb. The gash on her shoulder is redder than it was yesterday. It stretches taut with jabs of pain if she moves her arm too quickly.

The next town might be fifty miles away as the crow flies, but by road it would take three or four hours. Clare considers what she would pack to make such a journey on foot. Good shoes. A tarp of some kind. Matches. Her gun. A coat. She wouldn't weigh herself down with food or water. She could drink from the creek. Clare and her brother used to play this game as kids. Runaway. Survival. He'd show her which berries she could eat and how to huddle into a ball if hypothermia was setting in. Just try not to die, Christopher would say, as if not dying were the only goal a runaway could realistically set.

Her chocolate bar finished, Clare jams the wrapper between the slats of the bench. The rush of sugar sets in right away, dulling the ache in Clare's head. How strangely normal it feels to be here, to be absorbed into this town and its secrets. The camera sits on the bench next to her, her cell phone stuffed into the pocket of the scrubs. No message from Malcolm. No word since he left her in darkness on the road. I have things to tell you, Clare would say to Malcolm now. I have leads, I have suspects, I know their motives.

How long will he make her wait?

The scrubs are baby blue, an exact match for those Grace used to wear. In the days and weeks after Clare left, as she picked her way along the backcountry roads, driving ever west, she would narrate speeches to Grace, all the truths finally told.

I hated you, she would say aloud in the car. I hated that you had it so easy.

Of course Grace knew. She must have felt Clare's wrath. When Clare showed up at Grace's office last April, the pregnancy test in her purse, Grace had hugged her tight, then pulled her own positive test from the drawer of her desk. Talk about perfect timing, Grace said. Clare had wanted to slap her, as if their pregnancies meant the same thing, Grace married to a well-established doctor and settled in their renovated farmhouse with a nursery already in place. As she took Clare's blood pressure during her first prenatal exam, Grace braced Clare by the shoulders.

You can stay clean, she said. You can leave. I could help you.

Who says I want to leave?

On those drives, those endless hours of oncoming

headlights and maps folded every which way on her lap, Clare had confessed it all. I hated you and I loved you, Clare would say, speaking aloud to the empty passenger seat. I wanted to spare you and I wanted to hurt you, she would say. I was afraid he'd come after you too.

A familiar sedan pulls into the hospital parking lot, snapping Clare from her reverie. Sara slams the car door. She sees Clare on the bench and walks over. Up close Sara is unkempt, mascara still circling her brown eyes. Clare shimmies over on the bench but Sara doesn't sit.

"You okay?" Clare asks.

"Steve says Louise got lost. Danny said he saw her at the parade."

"They found her. She ran out in front of a float."

"Jesus. Was she hurt?"

"She's fine," Clare says. "A few bruises. Seems to have already forgotten the whole thing."

Sara points to Clare's scrubs. "You work here now?"

"My clothes got soaked in the rain. I'm waiting for them to dry. The nurse gave me these to wear in the meantime."

"You really get around, you know."

"I know I do. It's a skill."

They both laugh. Despite her gauntness, Sara's features are pretty, her skin so fair and smooth, as if never touched by the sun. She plops down on the bench.

"Is Derek here?" Sara asks.

"He's inside. Do you need him for something?"

"We had an informal appointment." Sara faces forward, avoiding eye contact. "Listen. I'm sorry about springing Charlie on you at the mine."

"It was a bit of an ambush," Clare says.

"It was his idea. I mentioned you wanted to see it. He took issue with that. Had me convinced we should be watching you."

"Charlie can be a convincing guy," Clare says.

"After last night I think he thinks he can bring you on board."

"On board with what?"

"Nothing. Never mind. All I can say is try not to piss him off."

"Or what?"

"Or . . . whatever," Sara says. "He loves drama."

"Do you love it? Must be exhausting."

"Danny and I are about to starve and Charlie comes over and leaves a wad of twenties under our last apple on the counter. Steve wants to help but he's struggling to make ends meet too. It's hard to know what to do. So I play Charlie's game."

"I get it. Believe me."

Sara arches and pulls her cell phone from her pocket, checking the time.

"You're meeting Derek?" Clare asks.

"I don't know what I'm doing," Sara says, shifting to face Clare. "Do you think you'll stay in Blackmore awhile?"

"Not forever," Clare says.

"You were dancing with Jared last night."

"Don't remind me."

Clare thinks of his hand on her back, a rush of shame running through her. Nothing is clear, the evening playing out in broken scenes, like a film she watched years ago.

"Jared and Derek Meyer nearly tore each other's throats out in the waiting room just now," Clare says.

"Of course they did," Sara says. "Jared gets him every time."

"Do you think Jared could have hurt his wife?"

Sara shrugs. "I heard he found her in the winter."

"Found her where?"

"Fully overdosed on her parents' kitchen floor. She was back living with her parents by then. Rumor has it he just stepped over her and walked out. Left her there. Her father found her a few hours later. She was in a coma for four days."

"How does anyone know he was there?"

"Charlie saw his truck pull in," Sara says. "Then pull out."

"That's not the same as murdering her."

Sara raises her eyebrows at Clare. "It isn't?"

"He wasn't the one giving her the drugs."

Lifting her sleeve, Sara scratches at the red skin on her arm. "Everyone was in love with Shayna," she says. "And now no one cares she's gone."

"Derek seems to care."

"Derek just needs to win. To beat Jared. What's Jared got? On paper, nothing. Lost his job, lost his wife, will probably lose his house. But it doesn't matter. He's just so unflappable. He oozes it, you know? He can still get Derek all twisted up in a knot. The guys below said Jared was the one who kept his cool. He came up the hero. It just added to the mystique. Derek can't stand it."

"Below? Jared was one of the trapped miners?"

"He was the good news story. Handsome guy, married to the foreman's daughter, taking charge, keeping all the guys from killing each other in the chamber. Made up for everyone who died. Once they pulled him out and he did a few interviews, all the reporters felt they could pack up and leave. He was the only worthwhile story."

"Imagine," Clare says.

"Shayna loved it. Jared lost nothing and he still got to be the hero. She didn't want the attention to die down."

Sara leans forward, her elbows propped on her knees, her face blank. Imagine. Men darting as the earth caved in around them, hedging their bets on which way to run. Jared Fowles made the right choice, and Sara's husband didn't, Sara's life forever altered by someone else's mistake. In her previous life, Clare often wondered whether widowhood might be better than her marriage, whether it could seem like freedom in comparison. She used to think of the police knocking with news of an accident at the factory, those same officers who'd arrived at her door just a little too long after she'd called them, cowering in her bedroom, begging for help. Clare wondered whether it would take effort to feign grief. But feign it she would have. She would have done a better job than Jared, or anyone else in Blackmore. Where was their grief?

"No one talks," Sara says. "No one ever talks about this stuff."

"I'm not trying to pry," Clare says, a lie.

Sara turns a wary gaze on Clare. "What do *you* have to talk about?"

"Nothing," Clare says. "For me there was nothing to salvage. The story's over. You're still here, at least. That's more than you can say about Shayna."

"You know the worst part?" Sara says. "I wished it on her many times. Danny loved her. Everyone did. I hated her for it. I wanted her gone."

"Friendship can be complicated," Clare says.

"I like to think that I'm a pretty good friend," Sara says. "I'd help her out. Hired her to look after Danny. Listened to her whine about Jared. I did a lot for her. She was incapable of gratitude."

"Maybe she resented your goodwill," Clare says, thinking of Grace.

"Maybe, but it wasn't just me. She worked her way through everyone. She'd latch on to you and give you the world, and then she'd bail. She'd flirt with Charlie right in front of me. He was in her sights. She had no shame."

"Wouldn't Wilfred kill her for dating Charlie?"

"That was the point. She made a sport out of pissing off her father. When Charlie sued Wilf, Shayna offered to testify. Tell the court that her own father hated the Merritts and bragged about killing them off. Anything to butter Charlie up. But she was such a junkie that Charlie's lawyer wouldn't even let her on the stand. They knew she'd be crucified. A junkie whoring herself out for the drugs."

"Does Wilfred know that?"

"That his daughter's a traitor? It's no big secret."

Clare will have to write everything down, keep it straight somehow, all these details, riddles. Sara could be making this all up, and Shayna is not here to defend herself. Back home, Clare thinks, people might be inventing all sorts of stories about her, about her husband, reasons why she might be gone, death or dalliances or affairs, rumors about abuse or infidelity, whatever makes for the best tale. When you don't leave a clear story behind, Clare knows, someone will make one up for you.

"Tomorrow's my birthday," Sara says, her knees bouncing.

"Do you have any plans?"

"Ray's, I guess. Pops will have the boy for the night."

"I met your father-in-law today at the parade."

"He told me."

"He seems nice."

"He tries."

"I could come over," Clare says. "Bake you a cake or something. Keep things quiet. We could hang out."

"Charlie doesn't do quiet."

"Well, I'm game for whatever you have planned."

Sara nods. Clare's clothes will be dry by now, but she stays on the bench with Sara and watches the street below, a lone pedestrian ambling empty-handed up the sidewalk. Hot and cold as she is, rough and prickly and even unfriendly, these talks between Clare and Sara, these little confessionals, might be what Sara sees as the start of a friendship,

another female finally in her midst, a more suitable
match to Clare than the faultless Grace. But Clare
was never a good friend. She never held Grace's son,
though he was born two weeks before she left. By
then there was no warmth left in her, no desire to
ask forgiveness again, no strength to cradle someone
else's baby in her arms.

Clare feels a tug of loneliness, her eyes closing
in an effort to call up Grace's features. When she
opens her eyes Sara has edged away from her on the
bench. Clare knows she can't trust her. She knows
there is more to Sara's story, some crucial detail she
isn't sharing. She also knows better than to wish the
events of her life reversed, to waste time regretting
the choices that brought her to this place. These
people in Blackmore, they are not Clare's friends,
Derek and Jared and Sara and Charlie. They are not
even one another's friends. They were not Shayna's
friends. They are only characters in Shayna's story,
and Shayna is not here.

Louise sleeps, her wrists relaxed in the restraints. The clock reads 4:50 p.m.

She asked for you, Eleanor said when Clare returned for her clothes.

Clare tries to match her breathing to Louise's, but it takes a concerted effort to slow hers down, to draw in through her nose. Louise opens her eyes and shifts to face Clare.

"Is he gone?"

"Is who gone?" Clare asks. "Wilfred?"

"That wasn't Wilfred."

"Yes it was, Louise. That was your husband."

Louise shakes her head. "Wilf's not like that. He's not a bad man."

"He's under a lot of stress," Clare says.

With some effort, Louise hoists herself to sitting. Clare finds the controls and adjusts the bed so Louise can lean back comfortably.

"Have you ever wanted to kill someone?" Louise asks.

Clare is struck by the question. "Have you?"

"I asked you first."

In his slumber Jason always looked sweet, benign. But still, Clare would lie next to him in bed and imagine it, a knife into the soft spot under his ribs, the gun to his temple, the turmoil his death would bring in exchange for the liberation.

"Sure I have," Clare says.

"Who?" Louise asks.

"Lots of people."

Louise frowns and looks out the window. They itemize for Clare, all those she's wished dead. Jason. Christopher. Grace. Her father. Even her mother by the end, in that purgatory where the cancer had ravaged her but modern medicine kept her alive.

"What about you?" Clare says.

"I always told him," Louise says. "I always said I'd kill for us."

"For who?"

"For my family. If it came down to it, I'd kill to keep my family together."

"Has it ever come down to it?" Clare asks.

"No." Louise rests against the pillow and closes her eyes. "Are you married?" she asks.

"No," Clare says.

"Have you ever been married?"

"Yes."

"Are you divorced?"

"No."

"Is your husband dead?"

Clare clears her throat. "No. At least I don't think so."

"I don't understand."

"I haven't seen him in a while," Clare says.

"But you're still married?"

"I left. But I didn't officially get a divorce."

"Do you have any children?" Louise asks.

"No."

"I was pregnant seven times." Louise places her

hand on her abdomen. "Seven babies in my belly and only one baby in my arms."

"That's terrible," Clare says.

"The doctor said it was the water. Living downstream from the mine. Sometimes it came out of the tap brown. Wilf said it was just dirt. Harmless. But I'm not so sure. A lot of women had trouble. Women who shouldn't have been having trouble. There were a lot of only children in town." Louise pauses. "Did your husband want children?"

"He did. He figured he did. I'm not sure he would have wanted one if it came."

"But none ever did?"

"I was pregnant once," Clare says.

"But you don't have a child."

"No. I lost the baby in a fall." Something breaks open in Clare, a flood of sadness, a need to tell the true story. She bites her lip, Louise watching her expectantly. "Not a fall, really," Clare continues. "My husband pushed me down the cellar stairs."

"Oh no. That's awful."

"It was just one of those things. I was fine but the baby wasn't."

"I hope your husband suffered for it."

"I'm not sure he's ever suffered. And I wasn't . . . It was my fault too."

"But you said he pushed you," Louise says.

"You know Shayna's troubles?" Clare says. "The drugs?"

Louise frowns. "Wilfred took care of that."

"Did he? How?" Clare says.

"That place," Louise says, waving a hand. Clare

waits for her to continue, but Louise's eyes are heavy again.

"I had those troubles too," Clare says, unsure of why she is still talking, of whether Louise is even listening. "I had trouble with drugs. When I got pregnant it was easy to stop. Cold turkey. But one night my husband was on a rampage and something just snapped. I wanted to punish him. I thought about taking a razor to my wrists. Instead I took pills. Five, maybe. Then I drank. I'm not even sure what I was trying to accomplish. The worst part is that he thought it was funny. He liked it when I was wasted. I needed him more. Everything's blurry from there. I know we were in the kitchen and I took a knife from the drawer."

Louise's eyes pop open, a bright blue. "You were going to kill him."

"Maybe. He snatched the knife from my hand and we were wrestling. He had me by the shoulders. It wasn't so much a push as a letting go. But my senses weren't fully there, and you're off balance when you're pregnant anyway. So I fell. There was nothing to grab hold of on the way down."

When she blinks, the tears curl down Louise's cheek.

"You poor thing. You poor darling."

"I wanted to kill him."

"He gave you no choice."

"I tried to cup my belly, which was ridiculous. I remember that. Futile, right? As soon as I landed, I knew. I lay on the cement floor and I knew. It was like I could feel it leaving me. He came down to get me. He tried to get me to go to the hospital but I couldn't do it. I couldn't go."

"Why not?"

"Because she was my friend. The doctor was my best friend. I couldn't bear it. She'd know I'd been using. She'd hate me."

"But he pushed you."

"Maybe he did. Maybe I fell."

"So you never went to the hospital?"

"When I started bleeding, he took me. On the way he asked me to recite what happened. 'You fell,' he said. 'I got home from work and found you down there.' He was coaching me. I remember sitting in the passenger seat, and there was no pain anywhere. I was completely numb. I remember wanting the truck to crash so badly. He wasn't wearing his seat belt, and I wanted to grab the wheel and steer us into the embankment."

"Did you ever tell your doctor friend what really happened?"

"No."

"And where is this man now? This husband of yours?"

"I assume he's still home."

"Where's home?"

"Way east. We had a house on two hundred acres. Five miles from where I grew up."

"And you left."

"I left. I lost the baby in September. I left in December. Here we are in July."

"It's like your father always told you," Louise

says, pointing a finger at Clare. "That man deserves to die."

Clare takes Louise's hand and squeezes it. Did she expect solace, that Louise might hear this story and absolve her of any blame? Clare can never be sure whom Louise sees when she looks at her.

"He *did* deserve to die," Clare says.

"Maybe he suffered when you left."

"I doubt it."

"Does he know where you are?" Louise asks.

"I hope not."

"He doesn't," Louise says. "We'll make sure of that."

With a start Louise sits up and tries to raise her hands. The restraints snap. She looks down at them quizzically.

"They're supposed to keep you from wandering," Clare says.

"Do I wander?"

"You seem to get lost."

"I'm not lost. I know exactly where I'm going."

"Where?"

"Can you remove them?"

"I'm not supposed to. Doctor's orders."

"Shackled," Louise says. "What have they done to me?"

"Where are you trying to go?"

Again Louise yanks her hands upward, pulling the restraints taut.

"They won't let me see her," Louise says. "I need to go! She'll be waiting for me at home."

"You mean Shayna?"

"That's what this is about. They don't want me to see her."

"Louise. Do you know where she is?"

Now Louise claws at her wrists, her face red with the effort.

"He knows!" she says, pointing to the door.

"You mean Derek?"

Louise whimpers and shakes, sitting up, her eyes unfocused. Clare presses Louise's arms to hold them to the bed. In the final weeks her mother had been restrained too, waking too often in her hospital bed and thrashing herself loose from the sheets, buckling in her efforts to stand. After a minute Louise's arms relax, too tired to fight. Her head lolls to one side, her breathing slowed by sleep. Clare's chest aches. She reaches into her bra and pulls out the home-made pill Charlie gave her, rolling it between her thumb and forefinger, the urge to swallow it making her mouth water. She tucks it back in. All this time Clare's sights have been on Jared, on Charlie, relying on the imperfections of Louise's memory to point her here and there. Derek. She needs to think clearly.

Clare flops back into the chair and blinks to stem the tears. She can still picture the gown draped over her pregnant belly as she lay in her own hospital bed, the movement she'd felt for months entirely gone. For hours Clare lay unmoving on that bed, restrained by her own grief, by a self-loathing that felt worse than death. Grace gave her something to help her sleep, waddling in and out of the room, their babies due two weeks apart.

There was a birth after all. They put tubes in Clare's arms to prompt it, and then came the cramps, and then the pushing. Grace handed him to Clare, tiny and translucent as he was, cupped by the palm of her hand. Grace had told Jason to go home before they wheeled Clare into the delivery room. He'd obeyed. Grace knew. She knew Clare would not bear to let him hold their baby. But, if she could do it over again, Clare would have wanted him to stay. She wants to own the image of him holding his dead son in his hands. She should have witnessed his despair. In time Clare's mind might skew the story to include it, revise the story so he suffers the depths of that moment too.

The next morning they discharged Clare, and in the passenger seat of Grace's car she steeled herself for the next few months.

Please leave him, Grace said, her voice cracked. Please leave him.

You don't get it, Clare said.

Her rage spared no one. Everyone was to blame. It was early September, the first shades of orange and red lacing through the branches of the maple trees. The fields out the car window were tall with corn and wheat bending in a breeze, ready for harvest. Clare would abstain. She would start running again to build up her stamina. By Christmas, these same fields would be blanketed with snow, and Clare's stomach would be flat again. By Christmas, she would be gone.

Clare allows the hot water to pour down her face and chest. When Eleanor left her in the hospital locker room Clare bolted the door and stripped down, the promise of a warm shower too good to pass up. The stall fills with steam. Clare kicks at the shower curtain to set some of it free. When the water runs cold she steps out, dripping, the gash throbbing, its red edges expanding outward on her shoulder. As she dries, the first *beep beep beep* bubbles up from the pile of clothes on the floor. Her phone. She crouches and fumbles. The *beep beep beep*. A message:

Parking lot of old hardware store.

Outside, the rain has started again. By the time Clare reaches the parking lot her hair is beaded with water, her camera tucked into her shirt, the effects of her hot shower erased. The lot is empty but for Malcolm's car. She pauses at the perimeter to ensure no one is watching. This is what an affair must feel like, she thinks, clandestine and sort of silly. The passenger door flies open and Clare climbs in. Malcolm wears a different shirt, clean but wrinkled. He's still unshaven. His duffel bag is zipped closed in the backseat.

"Where'd you sleep last night?" Clare says.

"I stayed close by. You didn't reply to my message."

"I figured you wanted me to come straight here."

Malcolm's face is unreadable.

"I was angry last night," he says. "I lost my composure."

"I had too much to drink," Clare says.

"I'll say this. You definitely get your hands dirty."

"You said to eliminate the obvious possibilities first."

"We must define the concept of *eliminate* differently."

If this is sarcasm, Clare can't quite detect it.

"I wasn't expecting to hear from you," she says. "For all I knew you were going to ditch me here."

"Do you want to be ditched?"

"What's that supposed to mean?" Clare says.

"Do you think you'll have trouble leaving when we're done with this?"

"No."

"You've made some friends."

"You said they weren't my friends," Clare says. "I'm just doing what you told me to do. I've found a way to get people to talk to me."

Clare waits for a response.

"What else can I say?" she continues, reaching to touch the dream catcher that dangles from the rearview mirror. "They're different from you, these people."

"I'm not sure you know enough about me to say that."

"I know you wouldn't fit in. Just based on your shirts. No one in Blackmore plays golf."

For the first time since she met him, Malcolm smiles. Clare turns away, this small show of warmth unwelcome. She does not want him to be congenial with her. She is unwilling to trust even a smile.

"You certainly fit in," Malcolm says.

"You must have figured I would."

The car is damp. Malcolm unzips the duffel bag and pulls out a folder.

"You asked about Charlie Merritt," he says. "I've done some research. Four arrests in the past five years. All drug related. Most recently for trafficking. He's out on bail. The trial is in a month. If he's convicted, he's looking at ten years or more."

"Who put up the bail?"

"Sara Gorman."

"Of course she did," Clare says. "Stupid girl."

"I wrangled a copy of the prosecution's list. Shayna's on it. She was with him the last time he was arrested. She's been subpoenaed to testify."

"He's not bold enough to kill off a witness," Clare says. "This isn't the mafia."

"Maybe not, but this goes deeper than him. He could choose to plead. Name everyone higher up on the chain. Without Shayna, the case against him is much thinner."

"Wouldn't the cops piece this together? Show Shayna a little more concern?"

"You never know," Malcolm says. "These towns are connected. They're small. If money lines the right pockets . . ."

Clare reaches into her shirt and retrieves the small white rock.

"What's that?" Malcolm says.

"Charlie's. He isn't just dealing drugs. He's cooking them too."

"He gave it to you?"

"He's on to me," Clare says. "He's calling my bluff. If I don't play along, I'm in trouble."

When Malcolm reaches for it, Clare closes her fist and pulls her hand away.

"I can dispose of it," Malcolm says.

"So can I."

"You won't take it," Malcolm says.

"Won't I?"

"Clare. Please."

By the look on his face, Clare can guess that Malcolm knows enough of her history to warn her from repeating it. It irks her, how little she can glean of him, how he rebuffs any talk of personal things, the imbalance this creates between them. Clare pulls the lever so that her seat angles back.

"Did you go to college?" she asks.

"Yes. Why?"

"What did you study?"

"Sciences."

Sciences. Vague and specific at the same time, an answer that tells Clare what she would have already guessed: Malcolm Boon is well versed in the objective. It might be something in the way he speaks, the thoughtfulness of his pauses. Clare spent three weeks at school before Jason arrived to whisk her away. She can still call up dreamlike images of a cloistered downtown campus, cafés and parks and younger versions of Malcolm sitting next to her in airy lecture halls. Funny, Clare thinks, how we like to fiddle with our past, to debate how a single choice made differently might have altered our entire course. If she had known what was to come, she never would have left school with Jason. She would have stayed and finished her degree. And then her trajectory would have been so unimaginably different that she would not be here in this sticky car, in the mountains with Malcolm Boon.

"I have a question for you," Malcolm says. "Let's say Shayna Fowles is dead, and not by misadventure."

"Her name is Shayna Cunningham. They're not married anymore."

"Either way. She's dead. Not by accident or overdose or anything like that. Let's say someone killed her. Let's say I had the name of the person who killed her written on a piece of paper."

"That would make things easy."

"Tell me," he says. "Whose name would you expect to see written down? From your gut. Tell me."

"My gut has a bad track record."

"Just think about it. Hazard a guess."

Clare should be better practiced at this, the art of listening to her own intuition. In hindsight she sees it was there all along, the churning dread about Jason that rose up well before they were married. But she's always questioned this inner voice, her own intuition. Jared is the obvious choice. She should suspect him. She does. Yet she has seen Charlie angry, the menace he stirs up, and he has motive, Shayna privy to his dealings. Even Sara seems to hold Shayna in dangerously low regard.

"And?" Malcolm says.

"Derek Meyer."

"The doctor?"

"There's something off about him. I think he's hiding something."

"Derek Meyer," Malcolm says, shaking his head. "I did not see that one coming."

"You think I'm way off?"

"Your gut is telling you something."

"It's a stab in the dark," Clare says. "I don't think Derek Meyer murdered her. I don't think she was murdered at all. I just think . . . he's weird. He's hiding something."

"I don't like that word," Malcolm says. "Weird. It means nothing."

The rain has stopped, the car windows fogged. Clare won't tell Malcolm that she wonders if Derek might be hiding Shayna, stashing her away for himself, shackling and drugging her mother to avoid getting caught. That of all those in Blackmore, it is the doctor who feels most off to Clare. There is a small thrill in keeping these thoughts from Malcolm, in asserting herself as the one doing the actual work.

"Shayna's mother has been wandering," Clare says. "I think she's looking for her daughter."

"She has dementia. You said so yourself."

"She does. She's confused, but then, out of nowhere, she can seem so clear. It's like she's wandering with purpose."

"That's an oxymoron."

"No it isn't."

"Listen," Malcolm says. "You've got three more days. Follow your leads. And your gut. Without getting reckless about it."

"And then what?"

"We move on."

"Just move on? Forget about Shayna? That's it?"

"Like I said at the start, Clare. You have a week. After that, the trail will dry up."

"Don't you ever feel invested?"

"It can't get personal."

"Why do you know so much about missing people?"

Malcolm ignores her question. "Our only responsibility is to the person who hired us."

"And I don't know who that is," Clare says. "Because you won't tell me."

Malcolm rolls down his window and lets a rush of cool air into the car. Clare reaches to roll down her own, flinching with the movement.

"What's wrong?" Malcolm asks.

"Nothing."

"You winced. Are you hurt?"

"No." Clare plucks at her shirt to pull it away from her shoulder. Malcolm will surely notice if dabs of blood soak through. "I'm just stiff. The trailer bed is lumpy."

Clare keeps her eyes straight ahead, Malcolm's gaze heavy upon her.

"It's about to rain again," he says finally. "You should go. Where's your car?"

"It broke down. I think the alternator's dead. I can walk from here."

"It's two miles at least. It'll be dark soon."

"I need the air," Clare says. "I need to clear my head."

Clare pries her camera out and turns it on him.

All Malcolm does is lift his hand to his face, but Clare has already clicked. He lowers his hand close to where hers rests.

"Clare," he says. "You're on the edge."

"I'm not."

"Are you sure?"

Without looking his way, Clare opens the door and jogs from his sedan. Malcolm is obscured by the fogged windshield, but Clare knows he is watching her. Back on the road she takes the rock from her pocket, holding it tight until Malcolm's car pulls out of the lot and disappears down the main road. No one else is here.

The edge. Clare can feel herself hovering over it. She flicks the rock into the trees.

The day Malcolm Boon found her, Clare bolted from the café and headed north. It was two days before she saw him again. She didn't then know his name, but she knew that he would track her, that anyone smart enough to find her, six months later, was smart enough to follow her. On the highway, she weighed her options. Drive fast, take a lot of turns, try to shake him. Kill him. She had a gun. Or turn herself over to him, wager on his humanity.

She drove overnight and into the next day, due north all the way to the oil fields. From the window of her roadside motel room she could see the wells pumping, transport trucks in convoy on the highway. She would not sleep. When the sun was gone, Clare pulled the notebook from her duffel bag and sat down to write to him. It took her eight drafts to get it right. She folded the note and stuffed it into a plastic bag. Then she sat at the window and waited, fighting sleep. It wasn't until the sky lit up with morning that she saw his blue sedan pull into the lot. She watched him from a tiny slit in the curtain. He walked to the motel office, and as soon as the door closed behind him she darted out and placed the note under his wiper, catching sight of the dream catcher through the windshield.

> Sir,
>
> I used to be Clare O'Callaghan. But you already know that. Let me tell you about my husband, Jason. In the second year of our marriage, he swung a hammer at my head and fractured my skull. Last September he pushed me down the cellar stairs and I lost our unborn baby. You don't know what he's capable of. If you tell him where I am, someone is liable to end up dead. Either me or him. Or, possibly, you. Meet me at the motel restaurant at 10 a.m.
>
> C

Back in her room Clare yanked the curtains closed until they overlapped. From the bottom of her duffel bag she dug out the towel and unwrapped the gun. She'd bought it on sale the week after Christmas, less than a month after she left. A handgun and a few boxes of bullets. When she checked a few minutes later, the note she'd left on the windshield was gone. And so, that morning in the oil fields, Clare rested her hand on the gun and waited. Three bullets in the chamber. Then came the knock, a gentle rap an hour

before the meeting time. She'd braced for it, gun in
hand, but when she unlatched the door he shoved his
way in and kicked the door shut behind him. Please,
Clare said. Please. After the struggle, after the gun was
knocked from Clare's grasp and he retrieved it, Malcolm used the ties from the curtains to bind her to the
chair. He paced her motel room, her gun in his hand.

You'd better shoot me, Clare said. Because I'm
not going back.

You were going to shoot me, Malcolm said.

He'll kill me, she said. I might as well die here
instead.

Clare did not know what this man knew, why
Jason had hired him. This man before her, the clean-
cut stranger from the café, she knew nothing of him.
He could shoot her between the eyes, let the force of
the shot tip her back in her chair, leave her to die on
the musty carpet of this motel room. Perhaps Jason
had charmed him. He could be very charismatic
when he needed to be. He might have told Malcolm
that Clare took off on him, took his money and his
heart, an addict wife who left him bereft. I only want
closure, Jason might have said. I only want to know
she's okay. Or, he might have said, I want her dead.
He might have hired this man to kill her.

An hour passed before Malcolm stopped pacing.
Then, he sat on the bed across from Clare and made
his offer.

There's a job in the mountains, he said. I might
consider hiring you.

What are you talking about?

I look for people, he said. People like you. People

who disappear. If I don't turn you in, you must agree
to help me. That's the deal.

I don't even know your name.

Malcolm Boon.

He untied her, taking her gun and leaving her
to meet him in an hour at the restaurant. Clare sat
still in the chair, rubbing at her wrists, unable to
process the choice she'd just been given. It seemed
a ridiculous proposition to trust this stranger, but
what were her options? Go forward, her mother
used to say. Take whatever option moves you forward. Never go back. Before noon Clare crossed the
parking lot to the restaurant and slid into the booth
across from him.

Tell me more, she said.

I look for people. The ones who disappear.

Why should I trust you?

Because if I was going to turn you in, I would
have done it already.

Why don't you just let me go?

You need work, don't you? This is work. It will
keep you moving.

For a long moment Clare stared at him, the echo
of her mother's words in her mind.

How do I know you won't hurt me?

You were tied up, Malcolm said. I had your gun.
If I was going to kill you, you'd already be dead.

And if I say no?

Then I'll have a choice to make, Malcolm said.

A minute might have passed, Clare searching this
stranger's face for a hint, a sign of what might come,
Malcolm breaking the impasse by turning to watch

the passing trucks out the window. He'd framed it as an offer, an out, but Clare saw little choice in it.

So what do I do? she asked. What's the actual job?

You go to this town, Malcolm said, sliding the folder across to her. And in that town, you try to find this woman.

It took half a day. An afternoon for Malcolm to brief her and use the kit he carried with him to make her fake identification. Clare O'Dey. Half a day to brief her on the story. To talk her through the clippings. All Clare could do was listen to the bass of this man's voice, baffled at why he would trust her to take this on, at how the arrangement benefited him. If she had questions to that end, he did not allow for them.

When do I start? was all she could say.

Now. Drive west into the mountains, he said. Then cut north to Blackmore.

And so Clare set out that afternoon, leaving Malcolm in the parking lot, the bald tires of her car kicking up a cloud of dust so that she could not see him in her rearview mirror. For the first hour of that drive, she fingered the cell phone he'd given her, unable to keep rein on her heartbeat, to focus on the road. At every intersection she debated veering off course, shaking him, running again, never showing up in Blackmore at all. But something compelled her. Anticipation and fear. Her mother's voice in her head. Trust it. This man, Malcolm Boon. This woman, Shayna Fowles, alike in looks and basic circumstance, vanished with the same swiftness as Clare. Finally a destination, a place to go after months of existing in the empty distance between nowhere and here.

You knew it all along. Admit it. It suited you that I was bad at being married. I have to tell the stories I know will make you mad. I think back to the first time Charlie gave me a pill. The night of his mother's funeral. What are you going to do now? I kept asking him. You've lost everyone. He pulled this pill from his pocket. Prescribed to keep his mother calm. Try it, he said to me. The next day I asked him for another one. You sure, Cunningham? he said.

I don't blame Sara for hating me. I like the way Charlie always comes to me first. That night I ended up in the hospital, I'd been to see him. We met in the barn. She wants another kid, he's telling me. Thinks it'll solve things. He told me I was the easiest on him, the only one who understood. He tucked a baggie of pills into my pocket, free of charge. Told me he'd never liked Jared. Then we were in the storeroom and I was pressed up on the worktable. It was cold enough to see my breath. I wasn't even thinking of you.

I know you don't want to hear this story, but I'm writing it down anyway. You look for color when everything is dulled. That's my only excuse. I don't know why I'm telling you this now. Maybe because these words are supposed to be the truth, because you seem to love me no matter what I do.

MONDAY

Twenty-four pictures. Even a sliver of light and it won't work. The dark of the trailer is so absolute that Clare can't see her own hand waved in front of her face. Still, it feels familiar, the steps in blindly handling the roll so as not to expose the film, motions as rote as brushing her teeth. She thinks of her brother and his do-it-yourself photography, her teacher from a young age, all the little tricks he showed her, the alchemy in conjuring an image from liquids and the absence of light.

As she works Clare traces how far back the photos on this roll will carry her. It took her the rest of September to heal from the birth, three months to save her money and plot her escape. After burying her son she'd managed to stay clean, to go back to running, her brain too rigid with grief and purpose to take note of any ache the abstinence might have brought upon her.

The trailer fills with the smell of the chemicals. Clare aligns the photo paper in the enlarger. One by one the photographs count her back through time, Malcolm's hand lifted in the car, then Jared on the road, his head craned to the side, Louise in the gorge, strangers at the parade, the bowl of the mine, Wilfred storming away, Louise in her garden, Charlie receding down the hill from the trailer, and then the blur of towns between here and home. The first picture on the roll, she knows, will be Jason.

In the last days before she left, Clare descended to the cellar to dig an unused roll of film out of the same box of Christopher's castaways where she'd found the camera. Jason dozed on the couch, his hands folded almost daintily across his chest. Peaceful. Drunk. She could tell by the pink in his cheeks. Clare loaded the film in the kitchen, then snuck up and stood over him, framing his portrait with the camera, emboldened by his long and slow breathing. Click, she said, actually said it out loud as she took the picture. He didn't flinch, and Clare stood over him, thinking of the gun secured over the doorway in the mudroom. In their entire marriage she'd never pointed a gun at Jason. She'd dreamed of it many times, but the actual logistics of his death remained unfathomable.

Now his form takes shape on the photo paper, fingers interlaced on his chest, his head dipped to one side. Clare can feel a bulb rise to her throat. Despite the hard drinking Jason always kept his good looks, his skin honey brown even in winter. His lips red and full. This black-and-white photo betrays nothing of those colors, the shades of his face, but still Clare is taken aback by the sight of him. Hatred. She is used to the hatred. But there is longing too, a stab of longing so unexpected that Clare must look away to stave it off.

All those conversations with herself in the car, Christopher's or Grace's voice in her head: Why did you stay? Why didn't you fight back more?

Because I was afraid he'd kill me.

But the other answer, the one she never actually uttered, is about love.

The first years with Jason built up so much of it in her, lust and yearning and devotion, that it lingered for too long after he proved himself unlovable. And then the dependence, Jason the only one who never questioned Clare's use, who enabled it, allowed it, enjoyed it, even celebrated it. Even now she feels it, the thrill, whatever small wave this photograph brings. She draws the picture from the solution before it is fully saturated and hangs it next to the ones of Malcolm and Jared, of Wilfred's back. These men, each angry in his own way. The stench of the chemicals burns her nose now, this space too enclosed, too claustrophobic. Clare knocks the trailer door open and stumbles out into the fresh air.

Slouched in the lawn chair, facing her, his hands gripped to the armrests, is Jared Fowles. Clare recoils back toward the trailer, swinging the door closed so that Jared can't see inside.

"Jesus!" Jared says. "Watch yourself."

"You scared me."

"You looked scared before you saw me."

Clare's eyes ache from the onslaught of light.

"What are you doing here?" she asks.

"Checking on you. I was driving past. I'd have called, but apparently you don't have a phone."

"I'm kind of in the middle of something."

"What?"

"Developing pictures."

"Come on. How?"

"I have some portable darkroom equipment."

"In there?"

"It's a tight space. The chemicals got to be a bit much."

"So you really do take pictures," Jared says.

Where is your grief? Clare would like to say to him. She thinks of her father's coldness in the aftermath of her mother's death, his wife's clothes dropped at a consignment shop the same day as her funeral, as though he'd held her in no higher regard than one of his barn hens.

Everyone has their own version of grief, Clare's brother said in their father's defense, and yours is no better than his. Carrying on, Christopher said, doesn't make him a bad man.

"Where are you headed?" Clare asks. "If you're just driving past."

"Uphill."

"To the mine?"

"To commune with the dead." Jared smiles. "The miners, I mean. You want to come?"

Whatever that photograph of Jason incited in Clare, the mix of hot and cold, Jared brings out the same. She hesitates, leaning against the trailer.

"I'm not done here," Clare says. "I should finish up."

"You *are* scared."

"I know better than to go to dark places with a stranger."

"Am I a stranger?"

"Your wife is missing."

"Ah," Jared says. "And you think you might be next."

"Why not?"

"Meyer's got you on board. I'm the murderer in plain sight."

"Are you?"

Clare cannot detect her own tone, whether she is being bold or foolish, or worse, coy. The sensation of her heart wild in her chest has the effect of warming her body.

"Come on," Jared says. "I promise you'll come out alive. Good enough?"

Reckless, Malcolm called her. Clare's mother used to call her much the same, the young Clare who jumped into the hay from the height of the barn roof or fired at targets dangerously close to her brother. You don't think of the consequences, her mother would chide her. You just dive headfirst. Reckless; Clare's entire life unfolded as it has because of it.

"Give me a minute," Clare says.

In the trailer Clare scrubs her hands and face in the sink. Last night she made a rudimentary effort to bandage the gash, slathering it in ointment, but she can feel it, the oozing, the heat of it creeping outward from the cut. She puts on a clean shirt long enough to cover the silhouette of her phone in her pocket. Then she rests her hand on the wood paneling. Her gun. Will she bring her gun? No. Clare knows too well what can happen when you bring a gun, how easily it can end up in the wrong hands.

Outside, Jared waits for her some distance away.

"Sara's expecting me at her place later on," Clare says. "It's her birthday."

"You think she'd notice if you didn't show?"

"Stop it."

"Where's your camera?"

"I'm almost out of film," she says. "There's no-where around here to buy more."

Clare follows Jared downhill to where his truck is parked next to her dead car. He unlocks the passenger door for her. A sharp bark startles her, the dog running at them from Charlie's porch until his tether yanks him back.

"Go on!" Jared says to the dog. Timber stands there, expectant, his tail wagging. A dog much like his owner, Clare thinks, friendly only until his fangs must be bared. The truck starts with a long rumble. In the driver's seat Jared's shirt shows his form, his broad shoulders, and it stuns Clare that she danced with him on Saturday, pinned herself up against him shame-lessly, and that Malcolm was watching as she did.

"Do you go to the mine a lot?" Clare asks.

"Once a year. To honor it."

"Honor what?"

"Five years ago today."

"The accident?"

"No. The accident was weeks earlier. Five years ago today I got pulled out alive."

"So you come here alone?"

"The first anniversary there was a ceremony," Jared says. "The whole town was there. The second year it was just me. It's been just me ever since."

"Sara brought me up to the mine the other day," Clare says.

"I heard about that. Charlie's keeping an eye on you."

"It's easy to guess what he's doing there."

"Reclaiming the family grave?" Jared says.

"If he's cooking drugs, shouldn't he at least try to hide it?"

"There's no one to hide from. Everyone's afraid of him."

"Are you afraid of him?" Clare asks.

Jared taps on the steering wheel, thinking. "Charlie's loyal," he says. "He's got a strange way of showing it, but he is. He's loyal to his people. I swear he thinks he's keeping the town afloat. That he's being benevolent. Giving people what they want. Whatever they need to dull the pain."

"He gave me a pill to try yesterday. Something he cooked up. A prototype, he said."

"Did you take it?"

"No."

"Good. It'd put you through the roof."

When they reach the gate, Jared jumps out to unlock it and pull it open. As they drive down the switchbacks, Clare detects a change in Jared's breathing. A slowing. A wave of nausea hits her, the quiet of this place, the ache in her shoulder. Jared parks. He climbs out of the truck and wanders alongside the larger building, waving at her to join him. There is a ringing in Clare's ears. She jogs to catch up.

"You look pale," Jared says.

"I'm not feeling great."

"Are you afraid of me?"

"You keep asking me that. Like I should be."

"I didn't kill my wife," Jared says.

"Every husband says that."

"For some stupid reason I need you to believe me."

"I'm not sure I do," Clare says. Again, coy.

Jared laughs. "You're here. That says something. You came with me."

"I did," Clare says. "Maybe that was my mistake."

They've walked beyond the large building to where a fence squares the perimeter of a smaller structure with steel doors. DANGER, the sign beyond the fence reads. MINE SHAFT. Jared points just beyond it to a manhole covered and bolted shut.

"We popped out right there," he says. "Eighteen of us. Five years ago today."

"Do you remember much of it?" Clare says.

Jared eyes her. "What do you want to know?"

"Why are you alive?"

"Because I got lucky," Jared says. "It was a toss-up. Heads or tails. I made the right call."

"And Charlie's family didn't?"

"Guys thought they could get out. Your instinct is to get out."

"So what happened?"

Jared shakes his head. "We heard the blast and everything shook," he says. "You have nightmares about it and then one day, it happens. I followed the guy in front of me out of our tunnel. All I could see was this line of headlamps. My father-in-law was the foreman. Wilfred. He was trying to radio up top, but he couldn't get through. He was doing this mad head count. By who's missing we figured the first explosion must have been in the third tunnel. Fifteen guys died right there. And then there was this standoff between Wilf and Russ Merritt, Charlie's dad. Wilfred was yelling at us to get in the chamber. Wilfred was technically in charge, but Russ had two of his boys there and his chest was puffed out. He said we should climb the shaft, get the hell out of Dodge. Or if the shaft was blocked off, then we'd make our way to the egress."

"What's the egress?"

"An escape tunnel that runs out the side of the mountain. For emergencies."

"Didn't Wilfred see the logic in trying to get out?"

"He knew the deal. The tunnels are gonna fill with methane, he said. It'll blow again. He ordered us into the chamber. It'll hold us all for thirty days, he said. Four days of reserve oxygen. I'm thinking, Thirty days of *what*?"

"But you stayed."

"Wilf and Russ were yelling at each other, and you could see the group parting like the Red Sea, forty-some men split right down the middle. I was picturing popping out and trying to explain to my new wife why her father was stuck deep in the mine."

For a long moment, Jared is silent.

"Once the door was sealed, that was it," he continues. "Wilf called it a submarine. You can't open the hatch underwater. You have to wait until someone comes to get you. The group split clear in half. Mikey was gone. Mike Gorman, Sara's guy. He went with Russ. I remember thinking, I hope he's right. I hope he gets out and meets that baby of his."

"And he never did," Clare says.

"Mike was this really good guy, you know? The rare kind, salt of the earth. I pictured him up there, leading the charge. I told myself he'd made it for sure. That he was up there trying to rescue us."

"That's what people do," Clare says. "We tell ourselves what we need to hear."

"In there, especially. Eighteen of us like sardines in that chamber. I was the youngest by ten years. Wilf found the control panel and made us sit down along a wall. He told us, 'Once that chamber hatch is closed, it cannot be reopened. Get it?' He repeated that over and over, like he had some sixth sense. He sealed us in, turned on the oxygen, the fans, these overhead lights. It was like the inside of a jet engine. Wilf kept telling us not to worry, he was up there like a teacher, describing this goddamn rescue chamber and how it all worked, how we were all gonna be just fine. But when he sat down you could see the fear in his eyes. Like he knew it was fifty-fifty if we were lucky. The guy next to me was an oldie. 'Six more shifts and I retire,' this guy kept saying to me. Wilfred sat down between us. He said nothing but he kept patting me on the back. Trying to be fatherly. Wouldn't look me in the eye. Then, boom. Everyone screams bloody murder. The lights go out and come back on."

"Another blast?"

"He knew it. Wilf knew it. Methane buildup. Trapped gas is like water. It looks for a way out. Up the shaft. Probably caught a flame. The lights were flickering and all the guys were freaking out. But Wilf was calm. You could see his look. Doing the math on the time between blasts. Maybe twenty minutes. He knew it would take thirty to climb the shaft ladder if you're fit, twenty to walk the egress if the path is clear. On a good day. He said to us, 'I'm sure they made it.' The guy next to me wanted to be assured. 'You think so?' This old man, he said that fifty times in five minutes. 'You think they made it out?' What was I supposed to say? How do I know?"

"Why is Wilfred the bad guy in this story?" Clare asks. "He did everything right, didn't he?"

"No one blamed Wilf for the split. But some people said the blast was his fault in the first place. He failed to perform the right safety checks. That's how Charlie won his case in court. The jury found Wilfred negligent."

"Even so," Clare says. "If they'd followed his orders they'd still be alive."

"Right. But it wasn't the split that caused the war." Jared fixes his eyes on the shaft door. "It was the banging."

"What banging?"

"A few minutes after the second blast, we heard this knocking. Wilf cupped his ear against the hatch. He said, 'There's methane out there. If we open it, we all die.' We couldn't hear actual voices, but the knocking got really loud. Pounding. We knew there were guys on the other side. The guys with time enough to turn back before the second blast hit. Maybe one, maybe all seventeen are behind the door. We knew they had their gas masks, but those things don't last long. Five minutes, maybe. The old-timer ordered Wilfred to open the hatch. He stood up and yelled 'Those are our men!' or some righteous crap like that. Wilfred was calm. He held his ground by the door. 'We can't open it,' he said. Over and over. 'If we open it, we all die.' People can say what they want about Wilf. But he owned it. He didn't open that chamber door. Guys in the chamber were weeping, pressing their hands to their ears, begging it to stop. You knew the guys on the other side were suffocating, choking, wondering why the hell we weren't letting them in, and you knew one of those guys was probably your friend. Maybe one of them was Mikey. Some part of me was screaming it. Why weren't we opening the goddamn door?"

"You took Wilfred's side," Clare says, edging closer to Jared along the fence.

"I guess I did," Jared says. "There was no clarity. No rhyme or reason. Wilf just seemed so sure. The whole time, he owned it. He stood at the door. I'm trying to play the deputy. 'Wilf's right,' I'm saying. 'Do we *all* die?' Then the banging was fading and the old-timer started really losing it. 'Your men! Your men!' he's yelling at Wilf. We had to hold him back. It took eight minutes for the banging to stop outright."

"That's . . . that's hell," Clare says.

Jared looks down to his feet. "No one said a thing after that. The old-timer just slumped down and buried his face in his hands. I think about him sometimes, that old-timer. He had eight grandkids. He never spoke a word of it after we got out. No interviews, nothing. He died of a heart attack a few weeks after the rescue."

"Jesus," Clare says.

"Traumatized, I guess."

"And you were down there for a month?" Clare asks.

"Twenty-four days. The first night was actually hell. Guys huddled and crying. Then on the second day the radio buzzed to life, and they started calling to us from the surface, and right as the oxygen was getting low in the chamber they broke through with an air shaft and found a way to pump out the methane and pump fresh air in. Even the old-timer sprang back to life. No one told us anything about the other guys, so we start thinking, Maybe they made it? We weren't asking. But we knew. I was picturing Mikey alive and well. I had to keep myself from falling apart, but I knew."

"How did you survive for that long?"

"That's what the chamber is for. Like a spaceship. There were water rations and dried food, and eventually they got stuff down to us, this high-protein liquid diet that tasted like shit. Every mine rescue crew east of the Pacific was up there trying to get us out. It was all over the news. They brought in equipment from around the world to drill the rescue shaft. They made a show of letting the dads in the group talk to their kids over the radio. Wilfred was on his game, keeping tabs on everyone. I'd wake up and he'd be the only one awake, keeping watch. Then the rescue shaft was a go and you knew your odds still weren't great. Still a million variables. We knew it would take each guy nearly an hour to get winched up. Wilfred would be the last to climb it."

"And you?"

"Second to last."

Clare has some memory of this scene, the news images of men being plucked from a narrow hole lit by a floodlight, a ticker across the bottom of the TV screen flashing the miners' names as they emerged one by one, bearded and dazed. It strikes her as strange, the revisionism, the way the memory cements itself more urgently now that she knows one of them was Jared Fowles.

"Everyone went crazy when Wilfred finally came up," Jared says. "Louise and Shayna were there. It was the main event. A family reunited. But Wilfred was having none of it. He refused all interviews. Batted away the cameras. Like the hero just drained out of him as soon as he hit the surface."

"He lost thirty men," Clare says.

"Thirty-two," Jared says. "Even Charlie was there. Putting a face to the dead miners. He didn't hate Wilfred yet. Didn't have the full story."

Clare and Jared both turn and lean against the fence, facing out. Clare points to the cinder-block building.

"What's that place?"

"Used to be the mess hall," Jared says.

"Were you friends with Charlie back then?"

"We've always been friends. Even after I married his girl."

"Shayna was his girl?"

"Shayna was everyone's girl."

"So Charlie loved her but hated Wilfred," Clare says.

"There's a picture of Charlie and Wilfred shaking hands right after we got out. For a while it was okay.

No bad blood. Then Charlie started hearing from the guys who'd been below. The mine company began questioning Wilfred's safety checks, looking for someone to blame. People said the captain should have gone down with the ship. You know what? That's what Wilfred tried to do. He tried to go down with the ship. That's what Charlie doesn't get. His father and his brothers are dead because they tried to abandon the ship. They jumped overboard and drowned."

"Everything gets foggy in the aftermath," Clare says. "It's hard to blame the dead for anything."

"You know what?" Jared says, his shoulder against Clare's. "That's the first time I've told the story in years. After the news cameras left, no one ever asked." He taps at his temple. "Clearly it's all still there."

"Did they ever find out who was banging?"

"Three bodies. Take a guess."

"The Merritts."

"Russ and his two boys. The retrieval crew found them piled up outside the chamber. Theirs were the only bodies they recovered. Everyone else was ash. Charlie's been on a rampage ever since."

The sun peeks out of the clouds, warming Clare's face. She closes her eyes, her stomach roiling. Has she eaten anything today? Jared faces the fence. He grips the links and scales it, landing with a thud on the other side.

"Where are you going?" Clare asks. "Come here."

Jared's back is to her, the chain-link fence between them. He approaches the steel door of the mine shaft and easily pries it open, only black beyond it.

"Charlie took an industrial saw to the door last year," he says. "Opened it back up. He traps animals and throws them down the shaft."

"You're making that up," Clare says.

"Am I?"

"Step back!" Clare says. "You're too close to the edge."

Cupping his mouth, Jared hollers into the void. The echo is muffled.

"They call it a lost mine," he says. "All the tunnels down there. Miles of them, abandoned."

"Please. You could fall in."

"People have fallen in," Jared says. He takes hold of the frame and leans into the darkness.

"Please," Clare says, a crack in her voice. She sees the top of the cellar stairs, the darkness below. That tipping sensation that comes right before you fall. Jared presses away from the door and walks over so that their faces are inches apart through the fence.

"Sorry," he says. "I'm just playing around."

"Who's fallen in?" Clare asks.

"No one, really. That's just Charlie's dumb joke. But it would be the perfect place to hide a body. Wouldn't it?"

"It doesn't sound good when you say things like that."

Jared steps back to take a quick run at the fence and climbs it again, landing on the other side right next to Clare. He takes her by the arms so she is facing him squarely.

"Let me make it clear," he says, drawing out the words for effect. "I didn't kill my wife. I didn't throw her down the mine shaft. She never came down here. Not even with Charlie. No one threw her down the mine shaft."

"You didn't kill your wife," Clare repeats, blinking, nauseated again.

"Swear to God. Last time I saw her, she was in the gorge, out cold by the fire."

"You left her down there?"

"I had my hands full with someone else."

A flash of awkwardness passes between them at this revelation, Jared going home with another woman. His thumb presses into Clare's shoulder, prompting a stab of pain. She shakes herself free from his grasp.

"She never would have come home with me anyway," Jared says. "She was looking for reasons to hate me. She didn't want me, but she didn't want me to move on either."

"So what do you think happened to her? You must have a theory."

"I think she woke up and walked upstream. She knew the route like the back of her hand. Got home and drove away."

"Drove away in what?"

"Someone's car."

The way he looks at her, Jared is willing Clare to piece it together.

"Derek? You think Derek took her?"

"Why wouldn't he? Suits him perfectly. He gets to keep her, and everyone else looks to me."

This is the version Clare presented to Malcolm last night. It strikes her now that she might be grasping at whatever theory absolves Jared.

"What about Wilfred and Louise?" Clare asks. "Derek just steals their daughter right out from under them?"

Jared shrugs. "Maybe they're in on it."

"What? No way."

"They always listen to the doctor."

"You're just pointing fingers."

"So are they."

Clare frowns, considering.

"If I ask you something," she says after a minute, "will you tell me the truth?"

"Would I admit to a lie?"

"Sara told me that you once found Shayna overdosed at her parents' place. She said you left her to die."

Jared bends to pick up a rock. He tosses it over the fence so that it lands and rolls into the open door of the shaft, clanging its way down.

"That's the kind of story people invent when they need a bad guy," he says. "You never knew Shayna."

"So you didn't find her?"

"I went to see her up at her parents' place. She'd moved out a month earlier and we had some decisions to make. I wanted to file the paperwork but she was stalling. She was jonesing, actually. Off-her-head desperate. She begged me to find her something to take the edge off and I refused. Tried to talk her down but she was having none of it. Believe me, she was alive and sober when I left. I guess Wilf found her a few hours later in a coma. She must have hit up Charlie in between. I wasn't even allowed to visit her at the hospital. I was the evil one by virtue of my wedding ring."

Clare spots four birds circling, hawks or falcons, she could never tell the difference. She squints up and watches them swoop and glide overhead. It's been months, years, since Clare has bantered like this with a man, a back-and-forth both calm and fraught. An equal footing. Jared studies her.

"You really do look pale," Jared says.

"Can you drive me to town?"

"I didn't kill my wife," Jared says again.

I believe you, Clare thinks. But she can't say it out loud. Jared is standing too close to her. Please don't, she wants to say. She'd almost forgotten the energy that signals a kiss, the ground gathering charge. Clare steps around him and walks back to the truck.

"I told Sara I'd meet her soon," Clare says. "I need to make a quick stop first."

"I told you my story," Jared says, following behind. "Now you owe me yours."

"I know I do. Just not now."

In the truck Clare rolls down the window and leans into the breeze to ward off further conversation, to settle her stomach. She thinks of Shayna and Jared's wedding picture, of the photographs of Malcolm and Jason hanging in the trailer, those framed photos left behind on her kitchen windowsill at home, she and Grace, that last healthy picture of her mother. You owe me your story, Jared said. What if Clare isn't sure of her story, whether she's remembering any of it correctly? What if she's altered it to spare herself some key truth? If all those photographs were here, Clare would pile them into the pit at the trailer and light a fire, watch all their faces swirl together. What she wouldn't give to be free of it, like Louise, to remember nothing, to have it all melt away.

The driveway is marked by a hand-painted sign nailed to a tree: *Meyer*. The walk from the hospital has disoriented Clare so that now she is almost teetering, her mouth dry with thirst. It took some convincing to get Jared to leave her at the hospital, insisting she needed only to pick up something left behind in Louise's room, that she'd soon head to Sara's.

Derek's driveway is narrow and rocky, a trailer up ahead much like the one at Charlie's, his SUV pulled up beside it. No house. Flies swarm her. Clare feels anxious, shaky. You are not yourself, Clare thinks. Settle down. This is just the infection setting in.

A light is on in the trailer. Before she nears the door, Derek opens it and steps out. He looks disheveled, his shirt untucked, a day's growth on his face.

"I'm surprised to see you," Derek says. "No one comes up here."

"The nurse told me where to find you," Clare says. "My shoulder is bad. I'm out of sorts."

"Did you walk here?"

"My car is dead," Clare says. "I thought the fresh air would help."

"So you're stranded?" Derek says, his expression blank. "That's not good."

Clare feels the familiar patter in her chest. Fear.

"Is someone here with you?" Clare asks.

"Who would be here with me?"

"Shayna?"

"Don't be ridiculous. Come in."

"Maybe you should take me back to the hospital."

"We'll go if we need to. Let me have a look first. Come in. You need something to drink."

There is nothing else to be done, nowhere to go but in. Clare hoists herself up the steps and into the trailer. It is laid out just as hers is, the small kitchen and banquette at the center and the bedroom at the far end. Except Derek's is immaculate, the counter wiped clean, the sink scrubbed and devoid of a single dish, no comforts of home. He places a glass of water on the table.

"Sit down. I'll get my kit."

After a minute, he returns from the bedroom with his medical bag.

"You're the town doctor," Clare says. "Why do you live in a trailer?"

Derek washes his hands at the sink. "I had plans to build a house on this lot. There's a great view from higher up. I was about to break ground when the mine blew."

"Why'd you stay in Blackmore? You must have had better options."

"They needed me," he says. "The other doctors left. Most of the nurses too. Everything would have fallen apart if I'd gone."

"But everything fell apart anyway."

There is a small clench in Derek's jaw at this slight. A dizzy spell comes over Clare. She sips the water, then rests her forehead in her hand to quell the surge. Derek sits beside her and removes some supplies from his kit. He pulls on a pair of surgical gloves.

"Let me have a look," he says.

Clare pushes her bra strap aside and wriggles her arm out of the neck of her shirt so that her left shoulder is bare. Derek presses gently into the skin surrounding the gash.

"It's warm to the touch," he says. "A bit swollen."

"I don't feel very well," Clare says.

Up close Derek's eyes are too deep a brown for Clare to distinguish his irises from his pupils. He squints.

"Do you see how the edges of the surrounding redness are jagged?" Derek traces the perimeter of the wound. "The infection is starting to spread. You need antibiotics."

"You like to fix people," Clare says, studying his face.

"I'm just doing my job. That's why you're here, isn't it?"

"You tried to fix them. The women. Shayna and Sara."

"Not anymore," he says, leaning back. "I know a lost cause when I see one."

Derek reaches into his kit for a gauze, then douses it in antiseptic. When he touches it to Clare's shoulder, she jolts.

"That burns," she says.

"It's not the infection that's making you sick," Derek says. "I've seen withdrawal before."

Clare shakes her head. It's always obvious, Grace

used to say. You think you can hide it but you can't. We aren't blind.

"What have you been taking?" Derek says.

"Nothing. Not recently."

"You know it'll eventually kill you, right? There's no surviving it. You either stop, or you die."

"It's not that simple," Clare says.

"My mother was a drunk," Derek says. "She could have stopped. Willed herself to stop. She just didn't. It *was* that simple."

"You don't give her much credit."

"She didn't deserve my credit," Derek says.

Clare thinks of Grace and Christopher seated together in her living room, pitted against her as she seethed at them, their intervention ill-timed, days before her planned departure, Grace's tiny baby tucked safely at home with Grace's husband. She thinks of Christopher following her into the kitchen, insisting she hear him out, Clare's rage steering her to Jason's gun in the mudroom. Clare braces herself when Derek presses the antiseptic to her skin again. It bubbles and hisses as it seeps into the cut.

"Was Shayna pregnant?" Clare asks.

"Where did that question come from?"

"Louise said something about a baby."

"She has early dementia. She says a lot of things."

"She says things about Shayna. About you."

"Are you working for someone?" Derek says.

"No."

"Are you working for someone?" Derek says again.

"No. It's hard not to be curious."

Derek presses harder. Clare flinches. "Sorry," he says. "I've got to get it clean."

"I'm trying to help Louise," Clare says. "I think she's searching for Shayna. You know a lot about that family. Maybe you know something that could help her. Or help the authorities track her down."

Derek unpacks some fresh gauze and tape and sets to fashioning a bandage over her shoulder.

"No one in Blackmore gets pregnant anymore," he says. "The whole town is poisoned. The water, the air, the soil."

"Were you her doctor?"

Derek sighs. "I'm everyone's doctor."

"Louise seems certain you know where Shayna is."

"Louise is also certain the mine is still open and that she sees Shayna every day."

"So you think there's nothing to it?"

"Why don't we cut her loose?" Derek says, losing patience. "Let a woman with dementia run the investigation? A wild-goose chase. See what she finds."

The door to the trailer flaps open in a breeze. Derek fixes the bandage to Clare's shoulder.

"Believe me," he says. "I wish I knew where Shayna was. She vanished and no one who was there remembers a thing."

Clare brushes her hair aside to keep it from tangling into the tape, Derek focused on his task. She inhales deeply in an effort to pick up his scent. When the bandage is in place, he removes the gloves and stands again to wash his hands. Clare struggles to readjust her shirt.

"I know the theory floating around," he says.

"That I've squirreled her away at rehab somewhere. Stolen her to heal her."

Clare says nothing.

"Why would I do that?" he asks. "What rehab clinic would take someone against their will? Why would I jeopardize my whole life and livelihood for that?"

"You and Jared hate each other."

"That's nothing new. I'm not about to kidnap his wife."

"Ex-wife," Clare says.

A cell phone rings. Clare rests her hand against her pocket. Derek lifts his phone from the counter and answers it. Clare watches him frown as he speaks, his words clipped, yes and no. Though he hides it well with his poise, Derek Meyer's anger is palpable, the same anger all the men she's ever known have bared in the face of things they cannot control.

"I have to go see a patient," Derek says, hanging up. He reaches into his kit again and sets a full pill bottle on the table. "Take these. Three times a day until all the pills are gone."

"You just carry a pharmacy around in your bag?"

"I make a lot of house calls," Derek says. "They're standard antibiotics. Just take them. You'll feel better quickly."

"Thank you," Clare says, rolling the bottle around in her hand. She twists off the lid and drops one of the pills into her palm. Derek nudges her water closer.

"They're bitter," Derek says.

Clare lifts her head and drops the pill to the back of her throat. It occurs to her that the bitterness might be born of something other than the antibiotics. That the pill could be laced, unable as she is to trust even this doctor.

"Can I catch a lift with you to the hospital?" Clare says. "I'd like to check in on Louise."

Before she can stand up, Derek takes her by the wrist, closing his grip when Clare tries to pull free.

"Let go," Clare says. "You're hurting me."

"I know what this is really about," he says. "This is how you control people."

"Excuse me?" Clare says.

"You play the victim. You don't let anyone turn away from it. That's how you get your way."

"I don't know what you're talking about," Clare says.

When Clare yanks her arm away, Derek sits so she is pinned in the banquette.

"You're mad." Clare's voice is quiet, shaky.

"You're just like the rest of them," Derek says.

Clare feels her fists clench. "So are you," she says.

With a cough Derek appears to snap out of it, the focus returned to his face. He offers her a contrite smile, then stands. Clare waits until he has gathered his things before she stands too. In the broad daylight Derek must know that Clare isn't Shayna, just as she knows that he isn't Jason, Christopher, or Malcolm, the scorn between them meant for people who aren't actually here. Clare lifts the glass and drains the last of the water before following Derek out the door.

It had only taken a few months for Clare to plot her exit, her lunch money dutifully stored in a mason jar on the highest pantry shelf, a trip to the city under the guise of a Christmas shopping excursion to acquire fake identification and buy an unregistered car she'd hide overnight at the far end of their fields. Clare remembers feeling astounded by the magnitude of online resources dedicated to shedding one's identity. It would be easier than she ever dreamed.

Outside, Clare watches as Derek opens the trunk of his SUV and drops his bag in, the view behind him a cluster of snowcapped mountains. There must be something that keeps Derek in Blackmore beyond his duty as a doctor. Some reason he has not plotted his own escape.

When Clare dreams, it is of the cellar door nailed shut, the darkness of that place. Sometimes she is tied. Sometimes the rope is long enough that Clare is able to run, only to be yanked back when she reaches the end of the tether. She never dreams of him tying her up, because he never actually did. He is never in the dream. Jason's face never actually appears. And then once, the night before she met Malcolm Boon, Clare dreamed instead that she was running across the field. This time, Jason was chasing her.

I'll find you, she heard him call. I'll find you.

As she turns the corner toward Louise's room, Clare nearly collides with Steve Gorman, still wearing the mine workers' cap he had on at the parade.

"Hello!" Clare says. "Are you here to see Louise?"

"I came to check on her," Steve says. "Sara told me about the fiasco with the poster."

A thin band of fluorescent light casts a gray glow down the center of the hallway.

"I figured she won't be getting many visitors," he continues. "Thought I might run into Wilf."

"Is she awake?"

"She was," Steve says.

"How is she?"

"Confused," Steve says. "Asking me about Russ. Telling me she thinks he and Wilf don't get along."

Steve shakes his head. "She doesn't know the half of it."

"She's mentioned Russ before. That's Charlie's dad, right? She seems to have a soft spot for him."

Steve lifts his eyebrows. "That's one way to put it."

"Wow," Clare says. "How long ago was—"

"Forget it," Steve says. "I'm not interested in gossip. This town has more than enough of it. I just came to make sure Louise was okay."

"Of course," Clare says. "Sorry."

Along the hallway Clare can see rows of boxes, stretchers folded up.

"What's with all this stuff?"

"Hospital's closing next month," Steve says. "They're bringing in a team to strip it down. Shutter it."

"What will happen to Louise?"

"What'll happen to any of us old-timers?" Steve sighs. "We'll end up wandering into the woods like wounded animals."

"There certainly isn't much left in this town," Clare says.

Steve ends the conversation with a bat of his hand.

"I'm heading over to Sara's place soon to celebrate her birthday," Clare says. "Will you be there?"

"She asked me to take Danny for the night. Keep him out of your hair."

"She said Charlie was coming too," Clare says.

"He's already over there." Steve removes his cap. "I hate that guy."

"I don't blame you."

"I showed up at Sara's place a few weeks ago and he was sitting at the kitchen table with Danny on his lap. Two shady types were at the table with them. Doing business."

"You should have called the police."

"He's already on charges. Her house is the collateral. If I call the cops, she pays. She and Danny are kicked to the curb." Steve rubs his forehead. "I'm not a bad man, but I could put a bullet in Charlie Merritt and not lose a minute's sleep over it."

"Don't say that. It's no good for Sara or your grandson if you end up in jail."

"He's got no respect for anyone," Steve says. "His whole family was like that. Above the law. Boys who'd push cars off cliffs just to watch them blow up."

The light above cackles and flickers. Every door down the hallways is closed. Steve puts his cap back on.

"I'll leave you," he says. "Say good night to Louise for me."

"I will."

"Do me a favor?" Steve asks. "Watch out for Sara. She could really use a friend."

Steve reaches out to shake Clare's hand, his grip callused from a lifetime of shoveling coal. Clare watches him until he is out of sight, then opens the door to Louise's room.

The smell. Sterile, sharp. Clare knows it well. She will leave the door ajar. Give Louise some air. A way out. Clare finds Louise fitful but asleep, her forehead warm. The sound of Clare pulling up a chair wakes her.

"Hi," Clare says. "It's me."

"Your cheeks are rosy," Louise says.

"So are yours."

"I'm very tired."

"It's getting late," Clare says.

"Don't be angry with your father."

It is dark in this room, easy to mistake one face for another.

"I'm not angry," Clare says.

"He doesn't handle it well. It upsets him. I don't think he's coping. That terrible place."

"It's hard for him," Clare says. "All of this."

"He can't just lock you in. But I can't reason with him. He needs help."

"Lock me in where?"

"You know he loves you."

"I know he does," Clare says.

"He's only trying to protect you. To save you."

"Louise," Clare says, the ruse too much to bear. "Where is she? Do you know where Shayna is?"

Louise blinks, trying to focus. "He's taken her. Down the hill. I saw them. I tried to follow you."

Now Louise is agitated, her breathing hard and fast. She looks to Clare, scrutinizing her, her eyes welling up.

"Who's taken her?" Clare asks.

"They were here for her. And then they were gone."

But Louise has clamped her eyes and mouth closed, whimpering. Clare presses her hand into the warmth of Louise's forearm, holding it there until Louise's breathing settles again and she is sleeping.

Clare looks around the room, pulling open the
drawers of the bedside table. She opens the cupboard and searches through the pockets of Louise's
clothes. Stuffed in the back of the cupboard is the
purse Louise had with her at the parade. Clare takes
it and sits again with the purse heavy on her lap,
unzipping it as quietly as she can. It is stuffed full as
Clare's mother's used to be, a hairbrush and tissues
carried everywhere. Clare rifles through it, reaching
to the bottom. She feels the shape of a book and
pries out a small hardcover, its brown front worn
and embossed. *The Short Stories of Ernest Hemingway*.
Clare opens it. The inscription is dated April.

S—

   *I found this First Edition at that antique store
in the city. He is a romantic in his own way, this
Hemingway fellow. He writes about survival. I
know you will soon be fine, if you trust me. We
will be fine. In time, right? What we need is time.
Time and a place.*
   D. xx

Clare snaps the book closed. D. For Derek. S. For
Shayna. The only man in Blackmore who would
enter an antique bookstore in search of something
like this, a poetic symbol, a profession of love.
Shayna Fowles and Derek Meyer. Of course. Just
as Jared suggested. The rage between them in the
waiting room.

Tucked into the middle pages of the book are
folded sheets of lined paper. Letters. Addressed to

Derek, the script shaky but legible. Clare unfolds the first one and begins to read:

Sometimes I dream of my escape.

A surge of panic cuts through Clare. Why is Louise carrying this book? She tucks it back into the purse and returns it to the cupboard. In her sleep Louise's face is twisted into a frown, her lips tight. If only she could shake Louise awake and insist on a lucid truth, answers beyond the snippets her wayward mind allows.

Derek's words at his trailer come back to Clare. *Why don't we cut her loose?*

Clare can't waste any time. She finds the keys on a hook by the door. As daintily as she can, Clare unlocks Louise's restraints, each wrist and ankle, then positions them open-side down so she still appears secured. Only when Louise wakes and yanks at them will they fall away, will she realize she's been untied. Will she be free to escape.

The night Clare left, there was no snow but the ground was hard with cold. She wore her running shoes, the camera clenched in her fist and the single key to the car tucked into her shoe. Jason would be home in an hour. It would take another hour before he began to wonder, before he sat in the old leather chair by the window and waited for her silhouette to appear up the driveway. Out for a jog. Clare did not lock the back door behind her. She sprinted the length of the hay fields, westward. The car was parked nearly a mile from the house, hidden so well under a navy bedsheet that even Clare couldn't see it at first. Then, she was driving, down to where that side road met the paved highway. West. She'd only been driving for ten minutes when the snow started, a swirling galaxy of flakes out the windshield. By the time she reached the next town, the blizzard had fully set in.

In the warmth of her car Clare imagined Jason, home for certain by then, his routine unfolding like clockwork, so that by the time he opened the front door to come after her, by the time he revved his truck and flew down the driveway, Clare would already be two hundred miles from home.

That snow, covering her tracks, a small and perfect mercy.

Louise is sound asleep now. Clare puts the restraint keys back on the hook. She leans in and pulls the hair away from Louise's ear.

"Where's Shayna?" she asks again, hoping. "Do you know where she is?"

Nothing. If Louise hears her, she doesn't stir.

The hallway is clear. Clare leaves by the same route she came. The emergency room is empty. Down the hall a nurse fiddles with one of the beds, her back turned. Clare sneaks out the doors unseen.

Outside the hospital, the light is gone. The streetlamp on the main road has burned out. As she cuts across the rise of the parking lot, Clare can see down to where Charlie's truck is parked across from Ray's. Clare thinks of Louise asleep in her room, untied. She might well wander away in search of Shayna. Or she might wander home. Something terrible may come of this. Perhaps they will blame that nurse for the breach, no working cameras in the hallway to prove otherwise.

On the sidewalk, Clare pauses. Why did you do that? she thinks, turning her gaze back to the hospital. Why? Because she can't bear to see a woman trapped, held down, tied up, no matter what her state of mind. Because she had to set her free, because she wants to know where Louise will go. Because no one in Blackmore is watching.

Warm rain pelts her cheeks. Clare widens her mouth to catch the flying drops on her tongue. Sara sits with her legs stretched the width of the truck bed, her arms draped over the side, the two of them in the back of Charlie's truck with Jared and Charlie in the cab. Cigar smoke wafts from the driver's-side window, and occasionally Jared glances over his shoulder to catch Clare's eye. Beyond him the dashboard lights are fuzzy and bright. Charlie Merritt drives slower than he usually might, but still the trees whip by. Clare can't be sure how far they've gone, which way they're going.

The wood will be wet, Clare thinks. How does one start a bonfire with wet wood?

How many drinks did she have? Jared arrived at Ray's minutes after she did, and the four of them sat at the bar, cold beer chased with warm liquor. Ray's was otherwise empty, and when Charlie reached over the bar to snag a bottle of whiskey, Donna threw a fit and kicked them out. Jared took hold of Clare as they staggered to the lot across the street, propping her up, his arm around her waist. They loaded into Charlie's truck, Sara dragging Clare up onto the flatbed though the rain had already started.

"Don't you love the wind in your hair?" Sara says.

Though her shirt is damp, Clare does not feel cold. Charlie's truck turns and slows. The clouds are backlit by the moon, the sky spinning overhead, the swirl of falling rain. Sara sits up, breathless, and makes a show of shaking out her hair. They are pulling up the Merritt driveway. Clare expects the truck to stop at the house, but instead Charlie leans out the window and calls back to them.

"Hold on!"

Both Sara and Clare look for something to grip as Charlie revs and steers the truck around the house and alongside the barn. He flicks on the high beams so the back field lights up before them. Charlie drives right for the fence posts, each still standing crookedly right where Wilfred left them. For a split second Clare meets Jared's wide eyes through the rear window.

"Slow down!" Sara yells, laughing, flat on her back.

The fence posts ping as they give way, six of them in quick succession. Clare ducks with her hands over her head, her knees raw against the bumpy flatbed of Charlie's truck, as if the posts might fly up over the cab and land on her. At the far end of the field Charlie hits the brakes so that the rear of the truck swings in a donut. Clare rolls on top of Sara. She regains her stance and looks up. They are speeding back toward the barn. Through the window Jared's voice booms at Charlie to slow down. He grabs at the wheel and pulls it to the right. They veer around the barn and stop in front of the Merritt house.

When the engine dies, Sara sits gasping, her hand over her mouth. From the cab Charlie lets out a whoop, then jumps out to open the truck bed for them, Timber appearing at his feet. Sara slaps at him, angry and then playful, and he heaves her off the truck and kisses her so deeply that Clare has to look away. A kiss like that, Clare knows all too well, can make up for whatever treason came before it.

"You're insane, Merritt." Jared extends his hand to Clare. "You okay?"

"Fine," Clare says, wobbly on her feet.

"Got rid of the fence," Charlie says, emerging from the kiss. "Let me grab some supplies. We can head down to the gorge."

"Or we could just build a fire here," Sara says.

"I'm needed down there. Be prepared, Gorman. I'm always telling you that."

Charlie disappears into the house and room by room the lights come on. Clare retreats from Jared and Sara and jogs up the hill to the trailer, prying the key from her jeans. The photographs are still strung up side by side in the kitchenette. Clare twists open the bottle of antibiotics and swallows one. In the bedroom she tears off her wet clothes and changes, Derek's bandage drooping and soaked, the wound still flaring but painless now, dulled by the drinks. She finds a warm sweater and tosses her phone on the bed. Then she bends back the wood paneling along the far wall. Her gun. Clare lifts her shirt and tucks it into her belt along the curve of her spine.

She reaches Charlie's house again just as a car turns down the Merritt driveway. Sara and Jared band together to intercept whoever has come, Timber barking wildly, tugging against his leash. The car makes a U-turn and stops pointed at them, high beams on. An SUV. Derek Meyer. He rolls down his window.

"Bad idea showing up here," Sara says to Derek, linking her arm through Jared's.

"I'm not here to see you. I came to check on her."

"Me?" Clare says.

Clare thinks of the book she found in Louise's purse, the inscription to Shayna, the profession of love. She cannot read Derek's expression.

"I wanted to see how the shoulder was doing," he says. "I need to speak with you."

"You're unreal," Jared says.

Derek ignores him, stepping out of the running car and circling to avoid Timber. "I would have called, but—"

"Where's the bouquet of flowers?" Jared asks.

"Shut up, Fowles."

The lights in the house flick off in reverse succession and Charlie appears, backpack in hand.

"Doctor!" he says. "I did not expect to see you here."

"I'm not here to see you."

"Well, good. Last thing I need is a doctor." Charlie looks around, absorbing the tension. He bends and takes hold of Timber's leash, pulling the dog to his side. "Hey," he says. "Why don't you come down with us. Big night. It's Gorman's birthday. Also, five years. We're celebrating five years."

"Of what?" Derek says.

"Five years ago Jared came back from the dead."

"Lucky us," says Derek.

In a trick of the light Jared appears to lunge

right over Sara before he lands on Derek and the two of them tumble to the ground. Sara screeches as Jared straddles Derek and punches him so that blood shoots from his nose. Derek does not fight back, only raising his arms in an effort to lessen the blows to his head. Charlie drops the bag and tugs Jared off the doctor, Timber bounding next to him, barking madly. Before he's pulled clear Jared slaps Derek across the face, a final insult, once hard on each cheek.

"I'll kill you." Derek wipes the blood from his nose on his shirtsleeve.

"Will you now? With what? Your stethoscope?"

This time it is Derek who lunges, and when they land his hands close around Jared's neck, the blood from his nose dripping into Jared's bulging eyes. Clare watches them as though they are on television, once removed, out of reach. Next to her Sara and Charlie seem frozen too, and Timber's bark has turned to a low whine. But it is the sound Jared makes, that wet gag, the muffled cough, the hiss of air escaping without a breath taken in to replace it. Clare knows that sound.

"He'll die," Clare says, elbowing Charlie. "He's going to kill him."

When Jared's arms begin to flail, Charlie winds up and boots Derek hard in the stomach. Derek doubles over, gasping.

"You're dead, Meyer." Jared massages his neck, his voice a hoarse whisper.

"Never gets old, does it?" Sara says. "You're both such pigs."

Derek paces at a distance. Then he charges at them again, his finger in Charlie's face.

"You," he says. "You're killing these people. You and that poison."

"Gear down, Doc," Charlie says, calm, Timber antsy at his feet.

"You don't think everyone knows about your little operation? You'll be taken down."

"Is that so?" Charlie takes gentle hold of Derek's hand and lowers it. "The thing is, people around here can disappear and no one much cares. You see how that works? You might want to watch yourself."

"You're a thug," Derek says.

"I might be," Charlie says. "But I like to think I'm a good friend too. And good friends don't snitch."

"I'm not afraid of you, Merritt."

Charlie laughs. "No?"

"Leave, Meyer," Sara says. "Get the hell out of here."

"You're trash," Derek says. "All of you. Junkie trash."

"You love it!" Sara yells. In the harsh light of the high beams she appears ferocious, her face twisted. She picks up a stick and moves to where Derek stands, chin up, defiant.

"I hope you all die here," Derek says.

Sara spits in his face. Derek lifts a hand across his mouth to wipe it. Then he spins and walks to the car, Sara and Jared calling to his back. As he drives past them, Jared bends to collect a rock and throws it at Derek's rear window. Though it bounces off the roof, Derek doesn't slow. His taillights fade down the driveway.

"You okay?" Sara asks Jared.

"Fine."

"You need ice?"

"No. Let's just go."

Charlie wrestles his backpack on, then grabs a box from his truck, crouching down to quiet Timber before they leave the dog and set out on foot. Clare follows the rhythms of the others, planting her feet one in front of the other across the back field, allowing Jared to guide her as they descend the steep path. Clare can't quite process what just unfolded, all of them turned against Derek with a fierceness that should scare her. Ahead Clare can see only the bob of Charlie's flashlight beam and hear peals of laughter from Sara. Though she can't see it, the sound of the creek comes to her too. Hold on, Jared is saying to her. Or maybe she imagines his voice. She can't bear to speak to him yet, she the bystander who did nothing as Derek strangled him. She had a gun. She could have intervened.

Up ahead Clare finally catches sight of a bonfire. The sleeping bag on the tree branch. When they reach the pit Clare scans the faces gathered around the fire, younger mostly. A few nod in bored acknowledgment. This is meant to be a party, people building a fire so high that it jabs at the branches, at the black sky above. But no one is talking. A girl on the far side looks like she might be fifteen, sixteen. Where is your mother? Clare would like to say to her. Charlie takes a gas can from the box and shakes some onto the flames, sending a ball of fire so high that the crowd takes a collective step back.

Jared pulls a flask from his coat and pours drops on the cut under his eye. Then he drinks, tilting whatever booze it holds straight down his throat. He offers Clare the final sip. This sort of closeness is not natural, she thinks, this pack of people shut in by these mountains. Jared takes a seat on the ground and tugs on her arm until she drops down beside him. With the heat of the embers so close, Clare can't tell if it's still raining. She thinks of Louise in her hospital bed, whether she's woken yet to find herself untied. A wave of guilt hits her. What did she do?

Once the flask has been replenished, Jared hands it to her again. The whiskey still burns long after she's swallowed it.

"What was Derek saying about your shoulder?" Jared asks.

"Nothing. I gashed it. It was getting infected."

"You went to see him?"

"He's the only doctor in town," Clare says. "I had no choice."

"I guess not," Jared says. "So why does it bug me?"

Clare keeps her eyes to the fire, offering nothing. Across the fire Charlie has taken hold of a younger man, lifting him off his feet by the scruff of his shirt. He tilts him so that the man's back grazes the flames, his boots kicking, panic on the face of the girl who stands beside them, Charlie's teeth gritted, his words an inaudible whisper. Sara yanks at Charlie's arm until he sets him down, and then Charlie just laughs, patting the man's shoulder as if he meant it as a joke. Their lap of the fire finished, Charlie and Sara take a seat next to Clare and Jared.

"So," Charlie says to Clare. "My guinea pig. I'm awaiting word on your experience."

"I lost it," Clare says. "My clothes got washed at the hospital yesterday. It was in my pocket."

"That makes me unhappy," Charlie says.

He extends a closed fist to Clare, nudging her to open her hand.

"Let's try again, shall we?"

"I don't think so."

"I do. I think so."

Clare looks to Jared. He only shrugs, but then he lets Charlie drop a baggie in his own hand.

"You're either with us or you're against us," Charlie says. "Isn't that how the saying goes?"

Sara laughs but then makes eye contact with Clare and her smile fades. A sense of helplessness washes over Clare as she lets Charlie shake a small pill into her cupped hand. Next to her, Jared downs his. They all watch her. Clare sets the pill on her tongue. If she were sober she might have the resolve, enough strength to decline it. But she was never good at swimming against the tide, at being the one to say no, especially if she was fearful of the response such a snub might incite. She scrapes her tongue with her teeth, the pill dissolved. Charlie reaches for his flask and douses the fire again, and this time the flames shoot high enough that Clare thinks the branches above might catch. They sit in silence, passing the flask until it's empty.

"Let's go for a walk," Jared says to Clare.

"It's too dark."

"I have a flashlight you lovebirds can borrow," Charlie says.

Clare blinks. She can feel it wrap her. A color comes to everything, the fire a perfect orange, tiny hues of blue shooting out of the highest flames.

"You coming?" Jared's hand is outstretched.

Clare allows him to pull her up next to him. She feels light. The plaid of Jared's shirt feels so textured, its pattern a perfect match to the angles of his body. The beam of the flashlight bounces as they walk, crisp air replacing the heat of the fire. Jared guides her to the creek. He wades through it in his boots, soaking his jeans to the knees.

"Come," he says.

"I'm not crossing that."

"You sound like her."

The bonfire is a bright ball in the distance. Clare arches to check for the steel of her gun against her back.

"Never once in my life did I see her cross the creek," Jared says. "It was a weird superstition of hers. She was afraid of the other side. My point is, she wouldn't have crossed on her own that night."

"Maybe someone carried her."

"She'd have kicked and screamed."

"Not if she was unconscious," Clare says.

Jared pivots and walks to where the gorge drops off, shining the flashlight to light a path for her to follow. Clare wades into the creek too, arms out for balance, the water numbing her feet, icy and perfect.

She should be asking questions. What did Louise say? *He's taken her. I saw him.* But Clare's wits are not about her. The disquiet has been washed away. She joins Jared at the edge of the gorge, the beam of the flashlight disappearing into the emptiness below.

"You're not scared of me anymore," Jared says.

"I'm not scared of anything right now."

Clare takes hold of two overhanging branches on either side of her and leans, tipping over the edge. She feels the skin of the gash bend open, a tickle of hot blood run down her shoulder.

"Don't do that," Jared says. "You're right on the edge."

"It would be easy, wouldn't it?"

"What?"

"To jump. To push someone."

The muddy earth gives way under Clare's sneakers. She loses her footing and dangles, the weight of her own body stretching the muscles of her arm. One leg kicks loose over the edge. Jared grabs her at the waist and swings her so that she loses her grip on the branches. Then he pins her arms to her sides, lifting her. Her back is flat against him, his face just behind hers, his breath on her neck, the flashlight on the ground beyond them. Clare kicks. Does he mean to save her? He could just let go and Clare would plunge forward and down, gone.

Clare isn't afraid. Her body is relaxed.

Jared drags her backwards and spins her. They stumble pressed together back through the creek, water kicked up so Clare inhales a mouthful that sets her to coughing. Her sweater comes loose from her waist and falls to the water, snagging and curling itself around a rock in the stream. The gun has come loose too. Clare hears the splash. By the time she regains her footing Jared has retrieved the flashlight, and they both scramble and somehow he has the gun, his hand squared on the grip. He aims the light at her face so it blinds her.

"Were you planning to shoot me?" he says.

"It's not you I'm worried about," Clare says.

With the light in her face Clare cannot detect his movement, whether the gun is lifted, pointed at her. She hears a click. Jared opens the casing and lets the bullets drop into the water.

"You always carry a gun?" he asks.

He takes a step closer, angling the flashlight up so Clare can see his face.

"It's for protection."

"From what?"

She can see it in Jared's eyes. The pieces clicking together, too obvious all along, her gun in his hand, Clare O'Dey with her questions, her pretense, coming to Blackmore with her rickety camera. They stand there at an impasse, only the sounds of the creek and the hushed chatter of those by the fire. Finally Jared takes her arm and leads her to sit on a log. He sets the gun down on the far side. Clare's eyes have adjusted. She can make out the shapes of the trees.

"You *are* a cop," Jared says.

"No."

"I never believed you just showed up here with your camera. No one did."

Clare clears her throat, her mind a muddle. "You're right," she says. "It's not that simple."

"Are you searching for Shayna?"

"I wasn't," she lies. "At first, no. Maybe I am now. Her story is . . . It's taken hold."

"You're a runaway too."

Clare doesn't answer.

"What are you running from?"

"Not what. Who."

"A him?"

Clare reaches over Jared and retrieves her gun. He makes no motion to stop her. She tucks it back into her belt.

"Of course a *him*," she says. "Don't ask me anything else."

"What's your real name?"

"Clare O'Dey."

"No it isn't. Is this man looking for you?"

"I said don't ask me anything else."

Jared sets his head in his hands and begins to laugh, quietly at first, then so deeply that his shoulders shake. He sits up again and rubs his eyes.

"You wanna know something?" he says.

Clare shrugs, the chill of her wet clothes coursing through her.

"A few weeks ago this plainclothes police officer showed up at my door to take my statement. Interviewed me in my living room. He looked bored the whole time. Irritated at having to make the drive all the way to Blackmore on a Friday. I'm wondering if he's going to arrest me, and then he says, 'Women go missing all the time.' He's sitting on my couch and he asks me if I killed my wife the same way you'd ask your neighbor for a cup of flour. He's even yawning while he takes notes. 'Did you hurt her?' he says. 'No,' I say. 'Are you glad she's gone?' he says. And you know what I said? I said, 'Yes. I'm glad she's gone.' He nods at me. Doesn't even write it down. Then he shakes my hand on his way out."

"Women do go missing all the time," Clare says.

"So they do."

"I've been thinking about what you said about Louise and Wilfred being in on it."

"I didn't mean that," Jared says. "Actually, I meant the part about Derek."

"Louise is always saying things. I think she knows where Shayna is."

"It's occurred to me to ransack their house," Jared says. "I'm pretty sure Wilfred's crazier than his wife."

The bitter taste lingers on Clare's tongue. She feels jumbled, her pulse too fast. Jared pinches a curl of her hair and pulls it straight, then releases it to bounce back into place. He raises the flashlight and touches her shoulder.

"You're bleeding a little," he says.

"It's fine. It doesn't hurt."

"One day you'll tell me?"

"Only if you stop asking."

"No one would ever think to look for you here," Jared says.

"You'd be surprised."

There is little space between them on the log.

"Do me a favor," she says, edging away from him. "Don't tell Charlie about the gun."

Clare is shivering. Jared takes her hand and guides her back to the fire. Only a few people linger around it, Sara and Charlie huddled at the far end. Jared tells her to sit and Clare obeys, and on the ground they negotiate a position where they face each other, Clare's back to the fire and Jared facing it, the yellow of it in his eyes. The quiet descends on her like a thick wool blanket, warm and calm at once. She closes her eyes. So many years since she kissed another man. Jared's breath is sweet from all the drink.

Sleep is coming. There is no fighting it. Jared stares at her, smiling, perplexed. Clare reaches for the small gash below his eye and pinches it gently closed, as her mother used to do. All healed, her mother would say. As if one touch were enough to fix anything. Her hand finds the bare skin under Jared's shirt, warm too, the beat of his heart steady and slow. Clare was never one to succumb to a first kiss. She waits for it. But when she closes her eyes, all she sees is Shayna, awake and watching them, aware. Shayna.

Sometimes, in the absolute darkness, I'm certain I can hear your voice. Calling my name. I can't be sure how long it's been. The daylight peeks through in no pattern I can discern. My head is clear, but the shadows play the strangest tricks on me.

I know his face so well, the contours of it, but there's an emptiness to him that wasn't there before. Does he even know who I am?

I understand why you've done what you've done, I tell him. I can't be sure he hears anything I say. They will come looking for me, I tell him. Please. Let me out. I tell him that you will come for me and I try to imagine it, you finally here to rescue me. But how long has it been? What if you've given up? Or worse, what if you were never searching at all?

TUESDAY

The ground cracks underfoot. The day's first light has woven through the woods, everything a dull gray. Everything out of focus.

Clare is running.

Her shoe catches on an exposed root and she falls hard against the ground. Where is the sweater she was wearing earlier? Jared had given her his coat, but now she is down to only a T-shirt. Her head throbs and the warmth of her own blood tickles her mouth. She sits up and presses her hand to her lip. The knees of her jeans are padded with mud.

Deep breaths, Clare tells herself. Deep breaths. She looks behind her, back toward the fire pit. He is not there anymore. He is not chasing her.

When Jared leaned in to kiss her, his mouth felt perfect and warm.

Run, Clare said.

Jared had pulled back and frowned at her.

Who? he said. Run? From what?

She must have been dreaming. Her eyes wouldn't open. She could see Shayna sprinting through a field flat and white with snow. Shayna locked in the cellar. Was that Shayna? When Clare woke up, Jared lay next to her, his face slack with sleep, the wood in the fire pit blackened and hissing. Next to her the creek seemed to sing, and the water curled around the rocks in a perfect pattern. Her jaw felt stiff.

Beyond the creek, just before the earth dropped off, Clare spotted movement. A figure. A man. The gold of his hair.

Where am I? Clare thought. How is it possible? Is it him?

He lunged from behind the trees.

Then, Clare was running.

Though the morning light is seeping in, she cannot see far into the trees in any direction. Clare spits blood onto the soft ground. The creek still gurgles next to her, she has traced its path, the sludge pipe beyond it slick with rain. If she stays with it she will find that upward trail, a way home, a way back to the trailer.

Behind her, the sound of someone coming. Clare fumbles for the gun still tucked into her belt. She aims it at the woods, her breath in her ears, searching.

"Charlie?" she says.

Please let it be Charlie, Clare thinks. That blond hair. Jason is not here. He can't be here.

The gun in her hand, Clare walks. Her legs nearly buckle from the effort of climbing the hill. She reaches a bend in the creek where the pipe splits into two, one branch heading down and away toward the gorge, the other up. This spot is not familiar. She must have missed the path back up to the Cunningham and Merritt properties. She must be close to the mine.

Her breath. Clare tucks herself behind a tree. Down the hill she spots another figure, another man. He is seated on a felled log, leaning against a tall stump, his shotgun gripped in both hands and rested across his lap. Wilfred Cunningham. He wears a thick coat and an army-issue blanket is draped over his legs. He seems to be asleep. Even from this distance Clare can see the wildness in him, the dirt on his face. Behind him the earth slopes downward. Only forest. No sign of anything or anyone. Only trees and rock, the creek, the sludge pipe.

Louise. Did she escape? Clare focuses, searches the woods around her for Louise. It might be that she is dulled by the remnants of the pill, that she isn't thinking straight, because Clare steps out from behind the tree and approaches Wilfred. Once closer, she can see a large flashlight at his feet.

"Wilfred?" It might only be a whisper. "Wilfred?"

He doesn't move. Clare lifts her gun and closes one eye, aiming for the center of his forehead.

"Wilfred?"

Clare thinks of Christopher, his hands up, Jason's shotgun pointed at him, Grace's voice behind her, the scene spilled out of her kitchen and into the yard. Don't shoot. Clare had only wanted the money, her share of their mother's will that he was refusing to hand over. She needed it, but not for the reason her brother thought she did. It was desperation. I am not your child, she'd yelled at Christopher. You are not my father. Seared into Clare's mind is the fear in her brother's eyes. He believed his own sister capable of pulling the trigger.

The light is upon them now. Clare steps even closer to Wilfred, lowering her gun.

"Wilfred? Are you alone?"

She cannot bring herself to raise her voice.

"Wilfred? What are you doing here?"

His hand grasps at his shotgun. The rest of his body still leans into the tree. His eyes open. Instantly Clare's senses are about her again, her mouth leathery and dry. Why did she call his name? She ducks behind a thick pine tree and holds her breath. There is no sound of him rousing. He might be fifty feet away. His eyes are open but he has not moved. He stares straight ahead, unblinking, and then his eyes close again and he tilts back into the tree.

Behind her Clare can now trace the path of the creek and the pipe clearly, back from where she came. First she walks backwards, her eyes upon Wilfred, until a screen of trees is between them, enough distance so that even with good aim, he would surely miss. Then she tucks the gun away and wills herself to go. To run.

The trailer glints silver. Inside, Clare doesn't sit on the bed, for her body aches with exhaustion, and even a small concession like sitting might lead to sleep. She does not look at the photographs that hang in the kitchen. She must clean herself up, keep moving, dance around the drop that will follow this high. In front of the mirror Clare pulls the elastic from her hair and shakes it out. A cluster of pine needles falls to the floor. She is rumpled and filthy.

Rage fills her. Clare yanks Jason's portrait from the clothespin and grips it, squeezing it at the edges, pulling it taut. Her teeth are gritted and she cannot recognize the sound that comes from her, a quiet wail. Though she tugs with all her might, the photograph will not tear. She feels as though the black and white might spill over into her hands. There is blood on her fingers. Clare crushes the photograph into a ball and throws it at the window. Then she yanks down the pictures of Malcolm, Wilfred, and Jared and does the same. Finally she collapses at the banquette and cries, the tension seeping out of her, a blast of cold sweat running up her back and along her scalp.

A shower. Clare strips off her clothes and runs outside naked. Though the air is cold, her skin cold, the water cold, Clare feels only relief as it douses her in a torrent. She dances and lathers as quickly as she can, soaping the gash, its redness already faded. Once rinsed, she darts back inside the trailer and yanks the blankets from the bed to wrap herself. Her phone, tangled as it was in the sheets, drops to the floor. She picks it up and flips it open. How alert she feels. Hungry and exhausted and too alert.

No word from Malcolm. No message. Of course not. No signal.

From her duffel bag she's able to dig out jeans and a T-shirt, a sweatshirt over it. As she wrestles with her clothes a panic sets in, a hollow pain filling her chest. She cannot keep it all straight. She keeps seeing Shayna, either dead or running, tied up. Trying to reach her. She thinks of Charlie behind the trees, it must have been Charlie. Wilfred sitting on the log with his shotgun, Derek lunging at Jared, his hands curled around his neck. Louise in her bed, the restraints undone. Clare opens the bottle of antibiotics and swallows two.

She will go to the Cunningham house. Intercept Wilfred. Louise.

Outside, there is noise. Someone is approaching. Before Clare can make it to the window, someone knocks on the trailer door.

"Clare?"

Whose voice is it? A man's.

"Clare?"

Malcolm.

Clare swings the door open and waves him in, then slams the door closed behind him. Inside the tight space of trailer Malcolm can barely stand up, and in the ensuing fumble he and Clare do this awkward dance, each trying to step around the other. By the time he sits at the banquette Clare has retreated to the bedroom door. Malcolm wears a jacket Clare has never seen before, an earthy green.

"How long have you been here?" Clare thinks of her naked dash from the shower to the trailer.

"I just arrived."

"I haven't heard from you."

"I've sent you four messages."

"I didn't get them. There's no clear signal. I told you that."

"I came here to get your things. It's time to extract you."

"Extract me? You said I had three more days."

"I've changed my mind. It's gotten risky. You look like you haven't slept."

"I keep seeing her."

"Who?"

"Shayna. I need to make sure Louise is . . ." Clare trails off.

"Did you take something? Your eyes don't look right."

"Please don't grill me."

"You have no restraint, Clare. Jesus."

"I'd love to see how you do it, Malcolm. How you show restraint."

"It's no longer safe for you," Malcolm says. "Do you understand that?"

A shrill laugh escapes Clare. "Was it ever safe?"

"I couldn't have predicted certain—"

"You did this," Clare says, her voice dropping.

"You brought me here. You knew about me, didn't you? He told you about me."

Though he evades all questions, Clare has learned one small detail about Malcolm, the way he uses simple gestures to end a conversation. He stands and fiddles with the hot plate, then sets the kettle upon it. Next to him on the counter are the balled-up photographs. Clare cannot stop fidgeting. With the tea made, Malcolm squeezes back into the banquette.

"Sit," he says.

"No."

Malcolm cups his hands around the warmth of his mug. Calm.

"How long have we known each other?" he asks.

"A week."

"Eight days. I sent you here. You're right. I did. But now you're refusing to leave."

"My head is full of things," Clare says. "I'm closing in. I wonder about Derek. Charlie too. He's trying to take hold of me. This morning I saw Wilfred Cunningham in the gorge. He was asleep against a tree with a shotgun on his lap. I really think Shayna's mother knows where she is."

"Did you spend the night at the gorge?"

"Why does that matter?"

"You're being reckless."

"I'm being thorough. And I'm not leaving yet."

"You work for *me*." There is a stark change to Malcolm's tone.

"I don't have to work for you anymore. I'll do it myself."

"It's too dangerous." Malcolm pulls his cell phone from his pocket and unlocks it. "Pack your things."

"What are you doing?"

"Checking the time."

"There's a clock on the counter."

"I can't be sure it's right," Malcolm says.

"You're threatening me. That's what you're doing. You'll call him."

"This isn't about him," Malcolm says. "We agreed on how this would go and now you're not complying. I made a mistake sending you here."

Since that snowy night when she drove away from home, Clare has taken to counting. In hours at first, and then in days. Two hundred and six days since she pulled the bedsheet off that car in the field and drove away. Two hundred and six in between. One hundred and forty motel rooms, sixty nights in her car, and six in Blackmore. Two hundred and six days worth of distance, erasable by a single phone call. Malcolm stands and puts on his coat.

"Sometimes the job doesn't get finished," he says. "I know that. I've been doing this long enough. Sometimes you find nothing. Often, you find nothing. You don't know that yet."

Clare's eyes stay on Malcolm's hand, its light grip on the phone. Then she lunges and snatches it from him.

"Jesus, Clare!" Malcolm says. "What are you doing?"

Clare shoulders the trailer door open and jumps outside. She drops Malcolm's cell phone on the rocks of the fire pit and lifts her foot to smash it.

But before she can do it Malcolm is behind her, his arms around her in a bear hug. Her feet lift off the ground. She thrashes.

"Put me down!"

"You're out of control," Malcolm says, perfectly calm, even now.

Clare throws her head so that it butts him hard in the nose. He releases her and falls backwards. The blood runs from his nose and down the sleeves of his jacket. Clare picks up the cell phone and runs to the edge of the clearing.

"Please don't," Malcolm says.

"I'll kill you before I'll let you call him!"

"You'll kill me?"

"You know nothing about me," Clare says. "You are not my savior."

There might be thirty feet between them, and the rage escapes Clare as quickly as it surged. A swell of vomit fills her mouth. She retches at the foot of the closest tree. Then she slumps to the ground and jabs at Malcolm's cell phone. His contact list is empty.

"You don't have it in here. His number's not here."

"I learned my lesson about storing names or numbers in my phone. Yours is memorized."

"You made it seem like you were going to call him."

"You aren't seeing straight," Malcolm says. "Whatever you've taken has made you paranoid."

Malcolm tilts his head back. The blood abates. It always amazes Clare how fast the human body reacts to blood loss, the clotting, the self-preservation.

She jabs at his cell phone again. The lock screen has come on. There is no photo on his wallpaper, just the swirling orange background, the factory settings. His phone the same as everything else about him, revealing nothing. Clare steadies herself and walks over to him.

"Here." She drops the phone in his lap. "I'll get you something for your nose."

In the trailer Clare gags over the sink. A cold sweat wraps her. She gargles to clear her throat, then finds a cloth and some ice from the small fridge. Outside, Malcolm sits in one of the lawn chairs. Clare hands him the cloth. He touches it to his face and winces.

"I owe you some explanation," Malcolm says. "I'll tell you. I've corresponded with him."

"Jason?"

He nods, the ice pressed to his nose.

"When?"

"He's been keeping in regular touch."

"Did you meet him in person?"

"No. I use e-mail with clients."

"What did he give you to go on?"

"Photos, mostly. Some basic history. Your features. Copies of your identification. Tendencies."

Tendencies. Clare can guess what that means.

"Did I leave an easy trail?"

"Not at all. It took me a long while to find you."

"But you did."

"I went to seventy-six motels before someone recognized your photo. Eighteen days of driving in a circle, an expanding radius from your house. Finally this motel attendant told me he'd seen you.

Maybe four months earlier, he said. Remembered your face, said you were pretty. I paid him a hundred bucks to go back through the records. Find me a name. After that, it got easier. I knew you'd gone west. You changed your last name a few times, but you never changed your first. And always the O. The O names."

The choices of O names had been plentiful. She had counted on the name Clare to be common enough to go undetected.

"You disappeared mid-December," Malcolm says.

"I went for a run. A storm was coming."

"There was no thaw until spring. They thought they'd find a body. Figured on a hit-and-run, worst case a domestic or a kidnapping. There were news stories here and there. Search parties organized by family and friends."

Clare can hope Christopher would have been the one to trudge through snow, searching for her, maybe even her father alongside, or Grace and her husband. She feels the heat of tears in her eyes.

"But they never did," Malcolm says.

"Find a body."

"No."

"And you never talked to anyone else?" Clare asks.

"You mean your family? No. He instructed me not to."

Another wave of nausea passes over Clare.

"Why did it have to be so elaborate?" Malcolm asks. "Why not just leave?"

"I don't know. I didn't think I could. I thought he'd kill me."

"Did you want them to suspect him?"

She'd imagined it more than once in the months since she left, Jason finally faced with questions he'd eluded for so long. *What did you do to your wife?* Clare angles the other lawn chair and sits facing Malcolm.

"I just wanted to escape," she says. "He needed to be fooled. Thrown off course."

"I don't think he was fooled," Malcolm says. "I think he understood very plainly what you did."

"I knew he'd come. One way or another."

"You have the instincts. They're there."

"I'm not so sure. I thought I saw him in the woods. At the gorge."

"He's thousands of miles away."

"I can't shake it. He's chasing me."

"Something bothered me," Malcolm says. "Your husband. The case. It bothered me from the start. There was something off. I thought I might find you dead. Suicide, maybe. He was clearly . . . ill-intentioned."

"So? Surely he's not the first husband who hired you to find his wife. You didn't know me."

"No, I didn't."

"So why'd you hire me instead of turning me in?"

Malcolm breaks eye contact.

"Why did you hire me?"

"It felt familiar. That same feeling you have here. You reminded me of someone."

Clare straightens up. "Who?"

"She's long gone now. It doesn't matter."

"You're not going to tell me?"

"No."

"Where'd you get that scar?" Clare asks, pointing to his arm.

Malcolm collects his ruined jacket and unravels the cloth, casting the ice into the fire pit. The lighter fluid from the other night still leans against the rocks. Malcolm lifts the can and shakes it, the contents sloshing. Still no response, always the evasion. He does not look at Clare. She will not press him.

"I need one more day," Clare says finally.

"Go inside and pack your things," he says. "I can take them with me now."

"I don't want any of my things."

"Then leave them here," Malcolm says, lifting the lighter fluid. "Burn them. You can't leave any traces."

"Okay," Clare says.

"One more day," Malcolm says. "That's it."

For the first time Malcolm appears tired, defeated, slumped back in the chair. She does not understand Malcolm Boon. The way he retains his calm no matter what, the way he shows Clare a strange loyalty because an old photograph of her struck something in him. He could have turned her in to Jason. That was his job. And instead he hired her knowing nothing of her ability to do this job, whether she could be trusted. No small thing would compel him to take such a risk on her, to keep her from Jason, even now. It must have been no small thing.

The first place Clare will go is the Cunningham house. The birch trees that split the lots look fifty years old, the bark of their trunks silvery and peeling. Clare cuts through from the Merritt driveway, carrying her backpack, only her gun, her phone, and her camera within it. Everything else she's abandoned at the trailer, the photographs burned at the center of the fire pit. Clare hovers at the tree line. Wilfred's truck is not in the drive. She must work to steady her breath before approaching the house and climbing the porch.

Cupping her hands against the door pane, Clare can see down the hall and into the kitchen, their tea mugs from how many mornings ago still on the tray on the table. She presses down on the handle. It releases but the door doesn't budge. There doesn't seem to be a deadbolt, so Clare puts her shoulder into it and the door gives readily, swinging open and banging against the foyer wall.

Trespassing is against the law, Charlie said. Wilfred could return with his gun. Clare scans the property one more time, closing her eyes to check for far-off sounds, the rumbling of an engine. Nothing. She steps inside and closes the door behind her.

"Louise?" Clare calls. She leans back against the door and listens to the silence.

She'll be waiting for me at home, Louise said.

Clare's head swirls with all the puzzle pieces collected in the days since she last stood in this front hall, Louise's cryptic pleas, Sara and Derek and Charlie. All the fingers pointed at each other. It's occurred to me to ransack their house, Jared said at the gorge.

Focus, Clare thinks. The final piece of the puzzle is here.

The floor creaks with her steps. She moves to the bottom of the stairs.

"Shayna?" she calls, slowly climbing. "Shayna?"

The second-floor layout matches that of Clare's childhood home, the standard farmhouse with small dormer bedrooms jutting off a center hall. The first room must be Wilfred and Louise's, a double wrought-iron bed unmade, clothes strewn across the floor, the vinyl blind lowered so that even in bright daylight the room is dark. An old shoe-box television sits on the dresser. When Clare breathes she feels the particles from this stale air enter her throat and lungs. She must lean against the door for a moment to stop a spin that overtakes her.

The second room is smaller, its single bed neatly made and pressed into the corner, the wooden dresser buckled with age and topped with creams and a hairbrush. The mirror on the wall is warped and gives Clare a warbled look, stretching her eyes to twice their size. Clare examines the half-full bottle of painkillers, then braces to pull the top drawer open. A check out the window. Nothing. The dresser is empty but for a few stray shirts. In the closet is a stack of boxes and a suitcase. It would have been months since Shayna left Jared and moved home, but the room has an air of transience, much as a motel room would.

Clare peers under the mattress and yanks up the corner of the rug. A cloud of dust poofs out as it drops back in place against the floorboards. If she is anything like me, Clare thinks, Shayna would keep things hidden in plain sight. Just as Clare did with the money, the fake ID, all in that tin on a shelf in the pantry. Jason made it a regular practice to go through her drawers and the boxes of mementos in her closet. He probably even tapped at the walls, looking for hidden compartments, searched her coat pockets and the mattress in the spare bedroom. But never would he have figured on the pantry, so out in the open as to be the best hiding place of all.

She squeezes the pillow and hits on something hard. Clare pulls out a large zipper bag. A mishmash of pills is divided into smaller bags within it, some pharmaceutical and others homemade looking like the one Charlie gave her. And then prescription bottles, eight of them, all empty. SHAYNA ELIZABETH FOWLES, the labels read. Methadone hydrochloride. The prescription dated a month ago. In the corner, the prescribing doctor's name: DR. D. P. MEYER. Clare opens the bottle and smells it. A drug meant to help wean the addicted. For years Grace fought for the right to prescribe it, then begged Clare to take it. Clare puts one of the prescription bottles in her pocket and tucks the bag back into the pillowcase.

At the bottom of the stairs she returns to the kitchen, its floor tracked with dry mud. By the cold room Clare kicks at a garbage bag, then pats it down and wedges her finger into the knot to loosen it. She lifts it onto one of the kitchen chairs and opens it. Clean clothing, a large bottle of water. A freezer bag with an apple and a banana, a granola bar, powdered milk. A pill bottle, unlabeled and half full, its contents mixed. Some of the pills look like vitamins, others like basic pain medication.

From this new vantage Clare can see the door to the cellar. A small padlock is hooked over the latch but not fastened. She reties the garbage bag and returns it to its place. She thinks of the cellar at her house, the captivity, the darkness that stretched from hours to days. A cellar off the kitchen, just like this one.

He can't just lock you in, Louise said.

Clare sets down her backpack and slides the padlock off the latch, setting it on the counter. Behind the door is a bare lightbulb. She tugs its chain. The stairs match those in her home, crooked and wooden, uneven in rise and tread. She yanks the door hard so it stays closed behind her, and then she descends to the dampness of the cellar.

A square window gives enough light for Clare to find the bulb at the center of the room. The ceiling is low enough that she can reach up and touch it with a bent arm. When she pulls the cord, the bulb makes a popping sound before the light flashes on. The cellar is tidy, boxes lined along one wall, a neatly sorted worktable under the window. Clare takes a flashlight from the worktable and twists it on. She grips the hammer too. On the wall is a pattern of Post-it notes, each one bearing a name.

Jared F, Andy P, Roger W, Wilfred C.

Eighteen names. The men in the mine chamber, their month-long seating arrangement re-created. The far end of the cellar is in shadow. Clare shines the flashlight into it. A black hole, a crawl space.

"Shayna," she whispers into the dead space. "Shayna?"

The space is no more than three feet high, reaching from chest height to the cellar ceiling. It stretches ten feet under what must be the cold room. The flashlight lands on something bright. Clare moves and reaches for it.

A map. Laminated. She struggles to unroll it with the flashlight tucked under her arm. She can see it's a plan of the mine. Two exits are circled madly in red, the shaft and then the egress, a tunnel aiming down the mountain so that its end point lies beyond the boundaries of the map.

Above her, the floorboards creak. Clare clicks off the flashlight and presses herself against the nearest wall. Someone is walking overhead. Clare listens, arranging the footsteps against the layout of the main floor. In the hallway. Up the stairs. Nothing. Down the stairs. Into the kitchen, right overhead. Clare tightens her hold on the hammer. She cannot confront him now, startle him. A trespasser. She clutches the map and holds her breath.

Then the footsteps are gone. Clare races to the tiny window facing the front of the house. She can make out Wilfred's form as he walks to his truck. He carries the garbage bag. She drops the flashlight and the hammer in place, then creeps up the stairs and presses the cellar door open. The light is on in the kitchen. Out the window Wilfred's truck reverses in a semicircle, then starts up the driveway. Clare fumbles with the padlock until it hooks back into place, then picks up her backpack. She darts through the dining room to the picture window. At the end of the driveway the brake lights come on. He turns left. North.

Clare pulls her phone from her backpack and types a message to Malcolm.

I know where she is.

Bursting out the door, Clare is running.

There is the crunch of wheels on gravel, a truck on the Cunningham driveway. Clare turns and sprints for the barn. The truck door slams behind her. How many times has she dreamed of him chasing her? Did Wilfred turn around? Does he see her?

"Hey!" a voice calls. "Clare! Where are you going?"

Clare stops and bends forward to catch the sob in her throat. Steve.

"What the hell are you doing?" Steve asks, approaching.

"You scared the life out of me. I thought you were Wilfred."

"You broke in?"

"No. I was . . . I came here to . . . What are you doing here?"

"Louise Cunningham went missing from the hospital last night."

Clare feels her blood funnel downward. She is certain she will faint.

"You took off her restraints, didn't you?" Steve says.

All Clare manages is a slow shake of her head.

"You've made a real mess, you know. Sara came home this morning looking like she fell down a well."

"Where's Sara now?"

"Passed out at home. With Merritt. I came up here to find Wilfred and tell him about Louise. No one at the hospital can find him."

"He was here. I think he went to the mine."

"The mine?" Steve says, puzzled.

"I think Louise might be there too." Because she's searching for Shayna, Clare thinks, though she says nothing. The weight of her words sets onto Steve's face.

"Let's go." He directs Clare to the passenger seat of his truck.

"I could go back in the house," Clare says. "Call someone."

"Who? Who will you call?"

He's right, Clare knows. There's no one to call. No one will come.

"I'll drive," he says. "We'll call if we catch a signal along the way. I've got my gun."

I have mine too, Clare thinks, feeling for its shape at the bottom of the backpack on her lap. Steve slams his truck into gear and roars down the driveway and up the road. Even through the fabric of her pack, the gun's form is easily deciphered, its chamber full should she need to use it.

There is a heaviness in the air as they approach the mine, its gate swinging open. At the bottom of the switchbacks Wilfred's truck is parked askew in relation to the buildings. Clare holds her cell phone out the open window. No signal. They pull up next to Wilfred's truck and jump out. Steve fetches his shotgun from under the backseat, then digs a flashlight from his glove compartment and tucks it into his jeans. Clare revolves in a full circle.

"I don't see him," Clare says.

Steve slams the door to his truck and walks out to the open space next to the building. "Wilfred?" he hollers, his shotgun perched on his shoulder. "Wilfred? We're here to help you!"

Aside from the caw of a crow taking flight, there is no response.

They round the corner of the building. Up close Clare can see the cinder blocks are crumbling, every window in the building broken, a double steel door at its center. She pulls on the handles. Locked.

"Give me your gun," Clare says. "Stand back."

They both take long strides away before Clare lifts the gun and aims it. When she fires, a splinter forms between the two doors. She fires again.

"You're quite the shot," Steve says.

"My father taught me."

Clare approaches and kicks the doors open. The smell strikes her first, chemicals and dust so strong she has to cough. The mess hall is dark, lockers on the walls and tables in the middle, some chairs standing, others overturned. No one is here. Steve follows, his flashlight on. To the left she can see another door, just ajar. Clare hands the shotgun back to Steve and presses the door open.

The room is set up like a makeshift laboratory, a stench of burnt rubber in the air. The light comes from the high windows facing east. Steve lifts a bag of misshapen pills off the table, an imperfect and homemade effort. Anyone can make a pill,

Grace told her once. All you need is the Internet and a chemistry set. Around the room they find more stashes, some pills crude and others pharmaceutical, and then powders divvied up into small baggies.

"This is Charlie's lab," Steve says, the rage darkening his face. "This is the crap he's giving them."

There is a desk in the corner with an old coffeemaker on top and a bar fridge next to it. On the fridge sits a large battery with power cords snaking up to the window. Clare sees a solar panel angled to catch the light. With a growl Steve swipes the contents from the table, the glass smashing so that the liquids swirl along the uneven floorboards.

"He's a dead man," Steve says.

Clare's eyes sting. Something is burning. She tugs at his sleeve. "We need to leave," she says. "We need to find Wilfred. And Louise. Now."

"I need to find Charlie," he says, gripping his gun.

"Please. I can't explain. They're in trouble."

"What?" Steve says, his eyes darting around the room. "Who?"

Clare takes Steve by the shoulders and faces him so he can't look away. "Listen to me. We *need* to find Wilfred. This is about him too. There's no time."

Steve's focus settles for a long moment on Clare. Then he nods and lifts his gun, aiming it ahead of them. Back outside they round the building to the truck. About two hundred feet away, Clare spots a faded sign pointed into the woods that marks the end of the mine clearing.

"Where does that go?" she says.

"It's the old utility road," Steve says. "Ends up down at the egress."

Louise's jumbled words come back to Clare. *Down the hill.*

Clare hoists her backpack over her shoulders and starts toward the road, Steve behind her, huffing in an effort to keep pace. The gravel road descends into the trees. To one side is a hill of rock, its angle so steep that she must scramble to climb it. At the top is a plateau, a panorama down to the mine and then out to the mountains in the other direction. When Steve reaches her, he doubles over, setting his gun on the rock, winded.

Clare forms a visor with her hand and scans below. "Where's the egress?" she says.

"Half a mile down, maybe. The lowest point of the mine."

Clare nearly loses her footing climbing back down the rise, batting away the brush that scratches her legs. They come to a sludge pipe running downhill, a foot wide and broken open, whatever bled from it dried in place.

"Look," Steve says, pointing into the trees.

Up ahead Clare sees two arms wrapped low around a tree trunk. Louise.

"How did you know?" Steve asks.

"She's looking for Shayna. I tried to listen."

Clare steps closer to the tree.

"Louise?" she says. "It's me. Clare."

When Steve circles closer, Clare lifts her finger to her mouth to quiet him. Clare takes a wide berth around until she can see the bare feet crisscrossed with bloody gashes. Louise kneels into the tree, the skin of her legs so blue that it occurs to Clare that she might be dead, frozen in this collapsed embrace.

"Louise?" There is a flutter, a small kick of the toes.

As Clare closes in Louise clenches and tightens her grip on the tree. Clare motions to Steve. Be ready. He steps closer, then positions himself like a wrestler waiting for the bell. Clare crawls until she is right next to her.

"Louise. It's okay. You're lost. We've found you. We'll bring you home."

"I'm not lost," Louise says.

Clare leans in. "This is my fault. I shouldn't have untied you. I'm so sorry."

"He shouldn't have done that either," Louise says.

"Who?"

"Wilf. We shouldn't have sent you away like that."

"Where?"

"To that place. With the white walls."

"Rehab?"

"It was the doctor's idea."

"Derek."

"He said he would take care of it. It only made it worse. Now Wilf is taking care of it. He needs my help."

Louise whimpers. Clare touches her, the cold of her skin. Louise falls away from the tree and allows Clare to catch her. She is wet, badly scratched up, her clothing torn and dirty, her lips cracked and bleeding. Clare feels a gush of shame.

"I'm so sorry," Clare says again. Louise rests against her chest like a small child. "I never should have done that."

"He told you not to worry," Louise says. "That you two would find me."

"He told who?" Clare says. "Louise. Look at me. Please focus. Where is Shayna?"

Louise searches Clare's face in bewilderment, Clare and Shayna a switch that keeps flipping in her mind.

"He told her I was lost," Louise says. "But I wasn't lost. I was upstairs in the bedroom. The window was open. I could hear them talking. I wanted to go with them."

"Where?"

"To the mine."

A barking cough overtakes Louise. Steve removes his sweater and kneels, eyes down, a reluctant witness to the scene. He hands Clare his sweater to wrap around Louise.

"Steve Gorman is here, Louise. We'll carry you back to his truck."

It will do no good with these wet clothes against Louise's skin. Clare tries to hug her again, to warm her. What could she have been thinking to undo those restraints? She figured on some sixth sense, as Derek said. *Cut her loose.* She'd needed Louise to lead her. Instead Louise wandered into the woods and nearly met her death.

"I can carry her," Steve says. "She can't be much heavier than Danny."

He hands Clare the shotgun and scoops up Louise. She tucks into the fetal position against him, her arms around Steve's neck.

"You sure made it a long way by yourself," Steve says.

"I came looking for you. You needed my help."

"Me?" Steve asks.

"You were underground for so long."

Steve looks to Clare, who mouths one word. *Wilfred*.

"It's okay," Steve says. "I'm here now. We're all safe and sound."

There might be a croak in his voice as he utters the words. The weight of Louise in his arms has no bearing on Steve's gait. I'm here now, Steve said to her. He understood right away what was needed of him, a man of few cues, able to glean so much from so little. If only his son, Michael, had had such sense that day in the mine, his father's intuition about what might come next, then he might have followed Wilfred into the chamber instead of climbing that shaft in escape.

S moke. A curl rises from a broken window. Sara's car is now parked next to Wilfred's truck. The plume of smoke is wispy, its fire soundless. High above it the sun is a blot behind the clouds.

"Jesus," Steve says, surveying the scene, Louise still in his arms. Clare opens the truck so that Steve can set Louise down in the backseat, her eyes closed, head lolling. Steve finds a bottle of water and touches it to Louise's lips. She gulps.

"She needs to go to the hospital," Clare says.

"No," Louise says without opening her eyes.

"I think she's hypothermic," Clare says.

"Sara's car is here," Steve says. "I can't leave."

Louise curls into the seat. She appears to be asleep, her breathing steady. Steve finds a blanket under the backseat and drapes it over her. He snatches the shotgun from Clare.

"She'll be fine for another minute," he says. "This needs to end."

"Charlie will kill you. Wilfred might kill you. We don't know what's happened here."

"I'll take that chance. I'm telling you. It ends."

Of course Clare knows what he means. It needs to end. The sight of his daughter-in-law staggering home this morning, stoned and caked with mud. Steve takes firing hold of the gun and rounds the corner. The version of Clare that endured her husband's wrath would surely run from this scene. That version of Clare was afraid, always afraid, accustomed to relying on her fear above all else. But now a vision of Louise staring down the cougar flashes before her. There is no point in cowering. Doing so never helped her much anyway. She checks Louise's breathing again, then closes the door to the truck and turns the corner too.

"Charlie?" Steve calls. "Sara?"

Nothing. Steve's gaze lands on something Clare cannot see. He wraps his finger around the trigger. Clare digs out her gun from her backpack and takes firing hold of it too, sidling up to Steve. Near the blown-open door of the mess hall stands Charlie, his rifle pointed back at them.

"Is Sara here?" Clare asks.

"No, no, no," Charlie says. "She's out cold. Couldn't wake her with a gong."

Finally she sees it in Charlie, the icy rage, the soul drained from his expression. Clare sidesteps away from Steve so that the three of them form a triangle.

"Should've brought my guard dog," Charlie says, deadpan.

"Can we all just put down the guns?" Clare says.

"Him first." Charlie flicks his chin at Steve.

In the sky the trail of smoke bends toward them in a breeze.

"Did you do that?" Charlie says, gesturing to the smoke. "Set my stuff on fire?"

Inside the building, the smoke has collected in a cloud that now spills out the doors. The toppled chemicals must have hit a bad wire, Clare thinks. Ignited.

"You know what they told me about Mike?" Steve says. "They told me he was obliterated down there. That was the word the guy from the head office used. Obliterated. I had to look it up in a goddamn dictionary. The ball of gas shooting up the shaft would've been so hot, the guy said, that Mikey would've turned to dust. Wouldn't have felt a thing."

"Lucky him," Charlie says.

"Your father was a stupid man," Steve says. "He owes me my son's life."

Steve wipes the sweat from his brow with his forearm, then clenches his hand to the trigger.

"Don't do it," Charlie says.

Clare points her gun at Charlie. "Don't *you* do it," she says.

But Charlie won't avert his eyes from Steve. There is a click. Nothing. Clare can't gauge where the sound comes from. Another click.

"You out of bullets?" Charlie asks, laughing.

Clare swings her gaze between the two men. Fear is etched across Steve's face. He drops his shotgun to the ground and raises his arms.

"You Gormans," Charlie says, his gun still aimed at Steve. "You never come prepared."

Clare pinches one eye closed, the soft spot on Charlie's temple centered down the line of her gun.

"Charlie?" she says. "I'm telling you. Don't do it. Put your gun down."

This time the blast is deafening, the echo darting

around them. Charlie disappears from Clare's sight line, lurching backwards. Shot.

It was not Clare who fired at Charlie. She turns. Behind Steve, Wilfred stands with his shotgun raised, the mist from the shot evaporated around him. Steve steps back until he is next to Wilfred, setting his hand gently on the barrel of Wilfred's shotgun to lower it. Clare runs to Charlie and kicks his rifle away, then drops to her knees. He is conscious, his shirt soaked through with blood.

"Old man," Charlie says, half smiling at Clare. "I think he got me right in the heart."

"Just keep talking," Clare says. "Keep breathing."

"It doesn't even hurt." Charlie's voice is a wheeze.

A sigh of hot air hits them. The flames lick out the building door. Clare sets down her backpack and tucks her own gun into it.

"We need to get him out of here!" Clare hollers.

"I say leave him," Steve says, approaching.

"If he dies, this will get a lot worse for everyone."

The pool of blood expands outward from under Charlie.

"Where's Shayna?" Clare asks. "Is she here?"

Charlie shakes his head. He tries to speak but chokes instead, his head curling up with the effort.

"Now you'll die here too," Steve says, standing over Charlie.

"Don't," Clare says to Steve. "This is bad enough already."

"You could've gone the other way, Merritt," Steve says. "Done something with yourself. Now you'll pay for it all, won't you?"

Clare lifts Charlie's shirt to examine the wound. The soft flesh just under his ribs is open like a flower and rimmed by smaller holes, blood pulsing out of it. There is a whistling to Charlie's breath now, his skin paler than his golden beard. Clare can feel his dulled eyes tracking her, but she cannot bear to make eye contact. She tucks her backpack under his head and takes off her sweatshirt to press it to his chest. Charlie barely flinches.

"We need to call someone," Clare says. "Get him and Louise to the hospital."

Both Clare and Steve look up to where Wilfred had been standing.

"Where'd he go?" Steve says.

"I think I know," Clare says. "You stay here with him. I'm going to find a cell signal."

The smoke rises in a thick column from the building. Someone will surely spot it. Help will eventually come. Before Clare turns the corner she stops and looks back at them, Steve now crouched next to Charlie, his anger replaced by a look of sad worry. The steadiness of Clare's own breathing surprises her. A sense of focus has descended, much as it did as she ran through the back field to her hidden car over six months ago. Charlie will die and Wilfred is around this corner. And Shayna? There is still a chance. Clare runs with her cell phone tight in her hand.

Wilfred is nowhere, his truck gone. In the backseat of the truck Louise is unconscious, her chest rising and falling steadily enough. Only instinct carries Clare forward now. She sprints to the far side of the clearing toward the old egress road. The mud of the road is deeply rutted now, the overgrowth bent, patterns in the tire tracks fresh. She takes out her phone. Still no signal, her earlier message still in queue. Clare types frantically anyway.

At mine. Charlie shot. Shayna here? Send help.

She accesses Malcolm's contact and presses send. If a signal picks up, then Malcolm will get her messages, and help will come.

In a stumbling jog Clare follows the tracks on the road down and around the side of the mountain. She stops at the creek as it passes under the road through a culvert. She could take a sharp turn now, follow the creek all the way to the fire pit, to town. Find help. In a dash it might take twenty minutes. She could run back to Steve's truck. Her gun is back at the building. In her backpack next to Charlie. Clare curses and wavers. There is no time. She continues downhill.

The road straightens out and comes to a fence. ABANDONED MINE: DO NOT ENTER. Its gate is unlocked. Nothing. No one. Ahead she can see a rounded hollow, like a cave entrance but with wooden doors. She approaches it. The faded sign reads, DANGER! MINE. And then, in small letters on the sign's bottom corner, BLACKMORE MINE EAST EGRESS, TUNNELS 4,5,7,9. 1979.

Clare yanks the doors but they don't budge. She presses her ear to them. There might be a voice. If she

strains she is sure she can hear it. Clare bends and
inspects the keyhole. No rust, only light scratches
to show the markings of a key trying to fit its way
in. She knocks.

"Anyone here?"

Is she imagining it? A woman's voice? Clare
holds still. Around her the woods crackle in a gust
of wind. Only then does Clare notice the signs of
life. A garbage bag tied and leaning against a tree.
Next to it, a wad of toilet paper wet and crusted
atop the pine needles. Human things, recent things.
She spins, spying among the trees for a person, a
body, some color, some movement. She follows
what's left of the road to the far side of the egress.
Wilfred's truck.

Her instinct is to run. Run! It might be that she
hears the ground crack, the sound of a stick breaking. This might be why Clare stays still instead.
Wilfred Cunningham steps out from behind his
truck, his shotgun aimed at her. Before she can
speak, before she can raise her hands, he fires. Clare
drops to her knees, crouching, the rock face behind
her exploding at the impact of the missed shot. Her
father's voice comes to her: *Never crouch. It makes a
tidy target.* Clare pushes her body hard against the
rock and clambers to standing.

"Please," Clare says, pleading to Wilfred as he
nears.

"You think you're smart?"

"No. Please."

"You're in on it all. You and Charlie."

"No!" Clare says. "No. Please. That's not it at all. I was trying to find Shayna. I'm here to find Shayna. I was hired to find her."

Wilfred lifts the gun again.

"Please don't."

Whatever daylight remains must be swallowed by the trees, because though he is closer now, twenty or maybe thirty feet away, there isn't enough light to see the look on Wilfred's face.

Then she hears it, the quiet click.

It used to be that Clare could count the beats between the blast of her gun and the instant her target would jolt at the impact. It used to feel like enough time to take a breath, to change her stance, to question whether she'd hit or missed. But when Wilfred Cunningham fires it seems to Clare that no time passes before her shoulder is pierced. She spins half a turn and tumbles onto her hands. But her arms will bear no weight, and she falls flat on her face. She can hear Wilfred's footsteps crunching toward her. She rolls onto her back and the pain that sears up from her shoulder is so sharp that she cries out. Wilfred looms above her, his gun brushing the tip of her nose.

"Louise." Clare shields her face with her good arm. "Louise."

Something might stir in Wilfred. Or it might only be that he has no rounds left, his chamber emptied in two shots. He spins the gun and holds it by the barrel before swinging the butt of it against Clare's head. The ground must be soaked with rain because Clare's back is wet beneath her,

the cold mixing with the warmth of her blood.
Wilfred swings again, and this time Clare doesn't
even feel it hit her. Just silence, the trees above her
swaying, the leaves quaking, and then everything
else is still.

Wake up. Please, wake up.
A hand on her shoulder, shaking her.

Her head. It feels like someone is stepping on her head, crushing her skull with a boot. Clare is on her back, eyes open. An earthy ceiling is in shadow above her. A woman hovers. The pain shoots down her shoulder and into her fingers, and when she goes to lift her hand, her arm flaps back to the ground. Crying. Who is crying? Clare cranes her head to the side. The woman is huddled beside her now, head between her knees. In the dim light Clare can see that the woman's face is streaked with dirt and tears. It must be her.

"Shayna?"

The woman looks up. Shayna.

"I don't know who you are," Shayna says.

Clare hears a grunt. Across from them sits Wilfred, the shotgun standing up between his bent knees. He holds a flashlight in one hand. Next to him, a propane lantern flickers.

"Wilfred?"

His jaw is slack but his eyes are lucid. The walls are dirt, held up by frames of thick timber spaced every ten feet. A tunnel wide and high enough for a vehicle. At one end Clare sees a locked and rusted grate and beyond it, through more tunnel, the wooden doors. The entrance to the mine. The egress.

In the other direction the tunnel appears to slope upward into the mountain. She can see the shadow of another grate, the space in between a holding pen. Beside Wilfred is an unmade cot, a garbage bag, a scattering of water bottles and clothing, books, something that looks like a journal.

Shayna still cries. She wears jeans and a clean blue T-shirt, her dark hair tangled. Clare tucks her right hand under her shirt and feels for the wound. The skin above her collarbone is torn open, a scream of pain. Shayna stops crying and edges over to peel back Clare's bloodied shirt. For the first time they look right at each other, Shayna's face so recognizable, softer in real life. Shayna is here. Alive.

Clare cannot feel the phone in her pocket. Did Wilfred take it? Did the messages send? What would Malcolm make of this, of Clare having found Shayna?

"She's bleeding," Shayna says. "Dad? She's bleeding badly."

"She's with Charlie," Wilfred says.

"Dad. Look at me. You need to let us out. You can't let her die here."

"She's on their side. Him and those brothers. Him and all those pills. They poisoned you. They lit the barn on fire."

"Dad, no. That was years ago. They were kids. The Merritts are dead now."

"Not Charlie," Wilfred says, his voice unsteady.

The image of Charlie on the ground hits Clare. His chest a splash of red.

"I've never seen her before," Shayna says. "I'd

know her if she was friends with Charlie. I know his people."

A surge of strength comes to Clare. She hoists herself to sitting.

"My name is Clare," she says, pausing to breathe. "I only met Charlie when I got here." She looks to Shayna. "I came to Blackmore to find you. I work for a man named Malcolm Boon. He sent me here to find you. Someone hired him. I don't know who. You've been missing for three weeks."

"Is that true?" Shayna asks.

"I swear," Clare says. "Every word."

It takes effort to speak. Clare's breaths are pinched and painful. The smell of this place. Earth, staleness, sweat, blood. Under the cot, next to Wilfred, she sees large bottles of water and a scattering of empty prescription bottles. A bucket tipped on its side. She looks to Shayna again. Though her hair is messy and her cheeks smeared with dirt, she is no longer as gaunt as in the photos. There is a brightness in her eyes. Three weeks under her father's lock and key. It makes sense.

"You were trying to help her," Clare says to Wilfred.

Wilfred says nothing. Clare looks to Shayna, who takes her cue.

"You're right," Shayna says. "That's what he was doing. Helping me."

"And you're better now, aren't you, Shayna?"

"I'm better. Much better. And Dad? You said this wasn't to punish me. That you'd let me out when I got better. When I didn't need to be here anymore."

"That's why he locked you in here," Clare says. "To give you time. He gave you time to recover."

Shayna knows what to do. Talk Wilfred down, reason with him. She looks to Clare and wipes her eyes with her bare forearm.

"He took care of me," Shayna says. "He gave me what I needed. He told me to write. It was all unclear. He kept me focused."

"You disappeared from the gorge," Clare says.

"I remember I woke up there after the party. I walked the creek to get home."

Just as Jared said you did, Clare thinks. Woke up and walked the creek home.

"You were waiting for me, Dad. On the porch. You told me Mom had disappeared and we needed to go find her. We got in the truck and then we were walking. I was begging you to take me home. I was so mad at you. You dragged me across the creek. Dragged me."

She would never have crossed it on her own, Jared said. Shayna is crying again.

"Then you brought me in here. I thought we were looking for Mom. I was so out of it. 'Why is there a cot in here?' I'm asking you. Then you locked the grates."

"He was trying to help you," Clare repeats.

"Right. Right, Dad? You were here, giving me the pills, making me drink, pouring water down my throat. And then you'd be gone. For hours." Shayna coughs and looks at Clare. "He talked to me about withdrawal. It'll take two weeks, he said. Maybe a month. Right, Dad? You dragged me outside and dumped cold water over my head. You wrapped me in blankets. I'm trying to count days. I think it's twenty days, but then I think, it can't be twenty days. I can't have been here for twenty days."

"Three weeks," Clare says. "And you're better now. It worked. Just like you promised Louise, Wilfred. That you'd take care of it."

At the sound of her mother's name, a wail escapes Shayna.

"Wasn't she looking for me?"

"Yes," Clare says. "Yes. Just not in the right places."

"No one was looking," Wilfred says. "You hear me? No one. Your mother can't keep it straight. They want us dead. We remind them."

Shayna drops her head in her hands. "Don't say that. Please."

"There's nowhere to go," Wilfred says.

"That's not true," Shayna says, the anger bubbling up. "Do you want to die here, Dad? Is that what you want? To die in the mine?"

"There's nowhere else to go."

"Stop saying that!"

Shayna picks up a clump of earth and hurls it at her father, then drops her head and wails again. Nowhere to go. What Wilfred means is that everything is lost, that there is no going back, no starting over. Clare understands. The last time Jason locked her in the cellar, Clare found a length of rope and secured it to the underside of the cellar stairs. For hours she sat and watched the noose dangle, unsure of what kept her from snaking it around her neck and kicking free the tackle box she'd placed underneath it.

Clare has known it, that deepest point of despair. Nowhere to go.

Wilfred looks up at them. "You know what I said? I said, 'If we open it, we all die.' That's what I told them."

"What?" Shayna says.

"I told them, you have to come in here *now*. There's no way out. Once we secure the hatch, it's a done deal. I told those Merritt boys, 'Don't listen to your father! You listen to me!'"

"He's talking about the mine," Clare says. "That's what you said, right, Wilfred? To the men? You were trying to save them."

Wilfred's eyes are frantic. "There was no air. Just gas. It was poison."

"You knew that," Clare says. "Jared told me the story. He said you stood your ground. That you all would've died if you'd opened the hatch."

Shayna cranes wide-eyed at the sound of her husband's name. Then she drops forward to her hands and knees and creeps across to her father. He tightens his grip on the shotgun. When Shayna touches his knee, Wilfred flinches, dropping the flashlight. The way the light from the lantern falls, Clare can see Wilfred's face but not Shayna's. He looks alert, afraid.

"Give me the gun, Dad."

"There's nowhere to go."

"I'm done with this. It's over. She's bleeding. Give me the gun."

When she reaches for it, Wilfred jolts, taking hold and firing. The blast fills the tunnel. Shayna tumbles and knocks over the lantern, snuffing it out. Only the straight, white beam of the flashlight stretches across the floor. Coughing. Shayna. The pain in Clare's shoulder stabs her as she bears weight on the arm, crawling along the dirt. She cannot see Wilfred, not even his silhouette. He makes no sound. Clare touches up against Shayna's body.

"I'm not hit," Shayna whispers. "I'm okay."

Clare finds her hand and squeezes it. From the other side of the tunnel she hears fumbling. When the flashlight reveals him, Clare lunges and takes hold of Wilfred's shirt, hugging herself against him. He must've dropped the gun because both his hands are on her, working to grab her neck, and Clare presses her weight into him, pinning him against the wall. When Shayna picks up the flashlight and shines it on them, Clare sees the shotgun dropped against the cot. She takes it by the stock and jams it into Wilfred's ribs. He buckles.

It wells up in Clare all at once. Her stance adjusted, Clare swings the shotgun like a baseball bat at Wilfred so that the stock cracks against his skull. He crumples forward onto all fours. Clare lifts the gun and swings it again, and it cracks again, and in the light of the flashlight beam Clare can see the blood in veiny trails down Wilfred's forehead.

Clare did not run, did not give up everything and run to die here in this tunnel. She will not die here.

"Don't kill him," Shayna howls. "Please stop!"

Her senses return to Clare. Wilfred Cunningham is flat on his belly, sputtering for breath. Clare feels a hand on her leg. Shayna raises the flashlight to

Clare's face, blinding her. Stop. The words come to Clare as a whisper. If this were Jason, this man bleeding at her feet, Clare would take proper hold of the shotgun and fire the last bullets into his heart.

But this is not Jason. Clare steps over Wilfred to the grate and pushes the barrel of the gun through it. Her shirt is wet with her own blood, the wound on her shoulder open. Clare sees stars. She must steady herself and take aim. Behind her Shayna's voice is a mumble, slow and deep. Clare pulls the trigger. A spray of daylight appears where the pellets pierce the wood door. She pumps and fires again, but the chamber is empty. Shayna's words run together. Clare drops the gun and tries to grasp the grate to stop herself from falling. Too late. She is on the ground. She turns her head to one side. The door is speckled with tiny dots of light, and Clare watches it as the sound fades, watches the door for some movement, something, as if someone might know to come.

You will say he is a monster for doing this to me. You'll see this place with its dank dirt walls and you'll say he had no right. He of all people.

I've thought of you every hour of every day in here. I think you'll call him a monster because he did what you couldn't do. You handed me over to strangers. You couldn't take care of me yourself. He doesn't ask me to make promises like you do. He knows it won't change anything for either of us. You never understood that part of it. Neither did my mother. She called us serious, like that's all it ever was.

He won't confine me here forever. It's hard to breathe. He did not have the right to lock me in this cage, that's what you'll say. But in the light of it, I see what he's done. He saved me. He did what no one else could do. That's what I'll tell you when he finally opens the door and lets me go.

WEDNESDAY

A hospital room. Clare wears a blue gown. There is a needle in her wrist, tubes leading to an IV. Her arm is wrapped and slung across her chest, her shoulder bandaged. Clare pats at her aching cheek. Her left eye is swollen to a squint. When she wiggles her jaw, it clicks. The door to the room is open, a chair pulled up next to her. Voices in the hallway.

"Malcolm?" Clare speaks to the empty room.

Nothing. She rests her head on the pillow. What does she remember? The egress doors being pried open. Faces over her, people and darkness, the tunnel. Someone carrying her. A stretcher. A van. Or was it an ambulance? Shayna beside her, wrapped in a blanket, shivering. A man next to Shayna. Jared. Not Jared.

Derek.

After that, nothing.

There is light out the window. It must be morning. Did Clare wake last night? Is she remembering this room in the dark? She can't be sure. Was Malcolm here? Sitting in that chair beside her bed? Watching her? That might have been a dream.

Her shoulder. The pain. Clare digs around for the bed controls and uses the button to raise herself to seated. The voices in the hallway are gone. She drinks the cup of juice from the tray overhanging her bed. It tastes sugary and cool down her throat. Her phone is on the tray too. She peels back her gown and pushes the sling aside to assess her shoulder, the black and blue of the bruising. If she runs her fingers over the bandage, she can feel the hollows where the pellets from the shotgun pierced her. She reaches over her shoulder to feel her back. No bandages. No exit wounds.

There is a quiet tap. The door opens fully. Jared stands at the threshold of her room. Clare rearranges the blanket over herself.

"Look at you," he says. "Bullet-ridden."

"Not just a gash anymore."

Jared maneuvers the door to half-closed and sits at the foot of her bed, his hand resting on her leg, the heat of it through the blanket.

"You look awfully banged up," he says. "But it could have been a lot worse."

"I don't remember much. Do you know how I got here?"

"From what I hear a crew of guys made it down to the mine. They saw the smoke all the way from town. When they got there, Steve told them where you'd gone. I guess they could hear Shayna yelling. Saw the bullet holes in the egress door. Probably took an hour to get you out."

"Is Shayna okay?"

"She is. Better than when she went in. She's got color in her cheeks, so I hear."

"Have you seen her?"

"No."

"What about Wilfred?"

"He's one floor up, under police guard. Apparently a helicopter's coming to get him. I guess they'll take him to town and book him."

"Charlie?"

Jared doesn't answer.

"He's dead, isn't he?"

"That's what I'm hearing."

Clare leans back and closes her eyes. "Poor Wilfred," she says.

"You're not the only person in town saying that. Reporters were already showing up last night. Women in pantsuits. I heard the motel's open again, flooded or not."

"And Louise?"

"She's here too." Jared shakes his head. "All I can say is I hope she doesn't understand what's happened. I hope Shayna keeps the worst of it to herself."

There are voices in the hallway again. Jared edges up the bed so that Clare must nudge over to make room for him. His fingers lace through hers, the needle from the IV shifting in her vein, tugging. Clare withdraws her hand and slips it back under the blanket.

"Will you tell me who you are now?" he asks.

"I came here to find Shayna. That's all I can say."

"I asked you that. If that's why you were here."

"You asked me if I was a cop."

"What's the difference?"

"I'm not a cop."

"If you're not a cop, why did you come?"

"I can't answer that. Honestly. I just can't." Clare repositions herself on the bed. "Your wife was missing."

"She isn't my wife. What's your excuse?"

"I don't know. I got caught up."

"Right. So you're going home then? Once they spring you from here?"

"No."

"But you're not staying here."

"No."

Clare does not look at him.

"You're a cold one, you know that? Just like Shayna. Whatever it takes to get what you need."

Jared stands. Maybe Clare deserves his vitriol, but she will not give in to it. She will not apologize or explain. All she wants is for him to leave. When he reaches the door, Clare meets his gaze. She lifts her chin in defiance or in good-bye, the only gesture she can muster.

The moment he is gone, the pain comes to her chest. Regret. When will she learn to steel herself? Even on the day she left, when she and her husband sat at the table having breakfast, she felt it, a kind of nostalgia, a pit in her stomach at leaving her home, even at leaving him. Because of course Jason knew nothing of it. It never would have crossed his mind that that morning would be the last time he'd ever see her.

The wave passes. Clare focuses on her breathing. Soon it takes effort to fend off the sleep, a familiar calm setting in. They must have given her morphine for the pain. Clare doesn't even hear Eleanor come in. She stands over the bed, tinkering with Clare's saline bag, fussing over the dressing. When she lifts away the bandage Clare can see the puncture wound clearly, a perfect cluster of dots pinched closed by flesh swollen and bruised. Her eyes meet Eleanor's but she says nothing. Clare's body feels heavy, pressing down into the bed. When Eleanor is done, she pats Clare's arm and leaves.

Clare reaches for her phone. Its screen glows blue. This is the cell phone that Malcolm gave her that morning before she left for Blackmore, the only one she's ever owned. Untraceable, he said. Encrypted. Its clock reads 11:00 a.m. At home, in the house where she grew up, the clock on the stove is probably still stuck at 11:01, as it has been for years, even though it would be early afternoon there now. Clare uses her good arm to key in her old phone number.

It rings seventeen times before she hangs up. Christopher was never one for answering machines. Next, she dials her own number. This time it rings only once before she hears the click.

"Hello?"

Clare tilts the mouthpiece away from her face so that he won't hear her breathing.

"Hello?"

Jason. The rumble of his voice, the gruffness, the hello not a question but a statement. She hangs up and holds the phone to her pounding chest. I'm not dead, she thinks. And I won't let you find me.

What feels like a blink must be a few hours of sleep, because when Clare hears the door open again, the angle of light through the window has changed. The sight of Malcolm floods her with a strange relief. He carries a plastic bag. For a brief moment he seems startled by her appearance, by what must be the bruises on her face.

"Jesus," Malcolm says. "You okay?"

"I don't know."

"Where's your gun?"

"Nice to see you too."

"We don't have a lot of time."

Clare presses her fingers into her forehead. The light seems suddenly blinding. "I think Steve has it. Steve Gorman. He must have my backpack too. But there was nothing in it. Maybe the camera but the roll was fresh. I'm not sure how the phone survived."

"I couldn't get to the trailer," Malcolm says. "Police are swarming up there."

"There's nothing there," Clare says. "Just some clothes. The darkroom kit. I burned the photographs and the fake ID."

Malcolm pulls folded papers from the breast pocket of his shirt.

"I printed this off this morning. Have a look."

Clare skims the article. "Missing Woman Found Alive in Abandoned Coal Mine." On the first page is a stock photograph of the Blackmore Mine, and then a shot of the egress, police tape zigzagged between the trees. Charlie's mugshot. Clare skims the article. Shayna Fowles, 29. Addicted. Missing for three weeks and found alive. Kidnapped by her own father, a disgraced mine foreman who fed her methadone for weeks in an attempt to detoxify her. Charlie Merritt, known drug dealer, shot dead. Townspeople shocked. Little known about second woman found wounded in the mine. Clare O'Dey.

"How did this make the news so fast?" Clare says.

"It's the Internet age. There's a picture of you."

"There can't be."

On the next page is a grainy photograph from Sara's birthday at Ray's. Clare remembers Sara taking it with her cell phone. In the picture Clare stands between Charlie and Jared at the bar. They both look straight into the lens, their eyes dewy with alcohol, but Clare's head is tucked into Jared's shoulder, so that only a profile can be discerned from under her hair.

"I turned away."

"Barely. You can clearly see half your face. It's in color online. The caption mentions you by name."

"It mentions Clare O'Dey. That's not my name."

In the picture it is Jared who catches Clare, the way she is coiled into him, his look of perfect detachment, put on as it may be. Clare is too absorbed by the photo to notice Derek Meyer come in. He stands next to Malcolm at the foot of her bed in a white coat, the look of an actual doctor, a large bouquet in his hands, his face still bruised from the fight with Jared. He sets the flowers on the table next to Clare.

"These just arrived," he says. "Someone drove them all the way up the mountain."

"Who are they from?" Clare's mouth feels dry.

"I don't know." Derek hands her the card. "I didn't read it."

Malcolm watches Clare intently. She makes a fist around the card, bending it.

"She needs a few days," Derek says to Malcolm. "To recover. They'll obviously want to question her."

"Do you two know each other?" Clare asks.

"Derek was the one who hired us," Malcolm says. "We just met in person for the first time. I've accepted payment."

Clare lies back and attempts to absorb what Malcolm has just revealed.

"So you knew all along why I was here?" Clare asks.

"No," Derek says. "I was expecting someone else. A man. An investigator. In our e-mails he said he works from the sidelines. So I didn't put it together right away."

"Not even the timing?" Clare says.

"After you left my place the other day, I went over it all. I figured it had to be you."

"But you never said anything," Clare says.

"I came to Charlie's to talk to you. But you were a little distracted."

"He was impressed by how well you fit in," Malcolm says.

"Better than I do," Derek says. "You certainly weren't acting like someone investigating."

Clare ignores this rebuke. "I found the book you gave Shayna," she says. "The Hemingway stories."

"That was a silly gift," Derek says.

"I found the letters she wrote you too. Stuffed into the book. Louise was carrying it around with her."

"It was meant to be part of her rehab. She liked to write. I'm told Wilfred gave her a journal in the mine. To calm her."

"She was married."

"Clare," Malcolm says.

"I was trying to clean her up," Derek says. "I had

her on a program. Journaling. Exercise. I was trying. Methadone. I have no idea how Wilfred got his hands on so much of the stuff."

"Why did you hire Malcolm? Why didn't you look for her yourself?"

"I had no idea where to start. This is a small town. You can't ask questions. I thought maybe an investigator could look into Jared, Charlie, follow up on things. Do what the police should have done in the first place."

"You needed to be the hero," Clare says.

"No. I needed to find her."

"She's clean now at least," Malcolm says, glaring at Clare.

"She's dehydrated, a bit undernourished, maybe. He kidnapped her, for chrissake. But she actually seems better."

"And you love her," Clare says.

"I'm not sure it matters if I do. She won't speak to me. She's asking for her mother."

"It suited you that everyone thought Jared killed her."

"Clare!" Malcolm says.

"I thought it was Jared," Derek says. "So did everyone else. Who the hell else would it be? Who would ever think her own father would lock her in a hole?"

"Listen," Malcolm says. "This could have ended really badly. Much worse than it has. By any measure this is a happy ending. Whatever comes next is up to you and Shayna. But Clare and I need to leave."

"She can't leave. She has a gunshot wound."

"We need to go," Malcolm says. "Now."

Clare motions to the IV. "What about this?"

"Do you want your face all over the news?" Malcolm says. "Do you want to talk to the police?"

"No," Clare says, tightening her grip on the card.

Malcolm comes to her side and motions to Derek to tug the needle out. Only a small bulge of blood appears. Derek jabs at the buttons on the IV machine until it powers down.

"Can you get us out?" Malcolm asks.

"I don't know," Derek says. "The two nurses are on shift change. You could probably just walk out the side door."

"Can you leave us alone?"

"She'll need pain medication. Dressings. Antibiotics."

"If you could get us some," Malcolm says. "Enough to tide her over for a few weeks. Then give us five minutes to get out."

"People will be looking for you. The police are upstairs with Wilfred. They asked me to call them when Clare woke up. What do I say?"

"You say nothing. You have no idea where we went."

Derek nods. It makes sense to Clare now why Malcolm didn't tell her who'd hired them. Clare can't be sure what she would have made of it, how it would have carried her differently. Once Derek has left the room, Malcolm dumps the contents of his bag onto the bed.

"I bought you some clothes. Not much women's wear selection at the hardware store. I did what I could."

"So you just leave? Just like that?"

"We just leave."

"You feel no obligation?"

"I met my obligations. We met them. We found her. He should be happy with the outcome."

Clare reaches for Malcolm's arm. "Did you ever call him?"

"Who?"

"Jason."

"No."

"You just dropped contact?"

"Not exactly. After I left the trailer yesterday, I sent him an e-mail saying I had no leads and would be dropping the case. I told him that you were likely dead."

Clare glances at the flowers on the side table. "Did he reply?"

"No," Malcolm says. "Why don't you open the card?"

"I don't want to."

"I don't get the impression he's particularly gullible."

"How do you make enough money to live?" Clare asks. "If Jason didn't pay you?"

"Clare. Not now. We need to go."

"I'm not allowed to ask you why you do this?"

"You don't need to know everything," Malcolm says. "It doesn't concern you."

"You know my story."

"I don't know you, Clare."

"But you knew I had a history with this stuff. That I'd been a user. Can you finally just answer me? Jason told you. You knew, didn't you?"

"He alluded to it," Malcolm says.

"Oh, come on. He *told* you. You sent me into Blackmore knowing what it might do to me. You see that, right?"

Malcolm edges to the door and looks both ways down the hall.

"We only have a few minutes."

"You see that, right?" Clare says again. "Malcolm? You put my life on the line."

"It was a better option than turning you in."

"There was the option to let me go," Clare says. "Let me keep running. But you didn't."

"I was giving you another way out."

"You said before that I remind you of someone."

"Listen. I'm leaving in two minutes with or without you."

"At the trailer. You said that."

Malcolm heaves a deep sigh, then pulls the curtain closed around the bed.

"You do," he says.

"Who?"

"It doesn't matter. She's gone."

"What do you mean by gone? Is she dead?"

"No. I don't think so. She's gone. Vanished."

"What happened? Were you married to her?"

"Yes," Malcolm says.

There is a sour taste in Clare's mouth. Malcolm Boon, married. A wife disappeared. Gone. A story he refuses to tell.

"Do you know who sent the flowers?" Clare asks.

"Read the card," Malcolm says, losing patience.

"I don't want to read it. I'm not reading it. Was it him?"

"Listen," Malcolm says. "I'm going to find Derek and get your supplies. Can you get dressed on your own?"

"I think so. Malcolm?"

"Clare. We have to go."

"Where? Where will we go?"

"I haven't figured that out yet."

They watch each other in silence, Clare exhausted and parched and propped up in this bed, Malcolm at the foot of it, ever composed. Clare thinks of Jared's estimation of her, a cold one, how it fits Malcolm too, the sparseness of him, how he does not temper his words to account for her injured state. In all his coolness Malcolm is the only person with any sense of Clare's true history, the only one to have glimpsed the indignity of her life before this one. Still, Clare cannot decode him, what his ulterior motives might be, whether he means to protect or discard her. But he is right. She cannot stay here, and Malcolm Boon is her only way out.

"Okay," Clare says finally. "Let's go."

When he leaves the room Clare presses herself up, then swings her legs over the edge of the bed and stands. She will have to change quickly, ignore the shudders of pain that come with even small movements, whatever drugs she'd been given wearing off. It takes two tugs for the string of her hospital gown to come loose. Before she can grab hold of it, the gown drops to the floor. Clare wears only underwear, the chill setting upon her instantly. She fumbles with the clothes on the bed, sitting to pull on the pants, tucking her head into the shirt. Malcolm even brought her a pair of shoes, a sort of tennis slipper one size too big.

The nausea from the pain passes. Clare feels steadier. She stuffs the unopened card into her back pocket. Then she throws the flowers in the garbage. If they are lucky, Derek will run interference for them at the nurses' station. They will make it out of here undetected, out to Malcolm's car and back down the road, away from Blackmore. No one will see them going, everything Clare had left behind in the trailer anyway, even the name O'Dey to be cast off. All these people left behind to sort out the aftermath, puzzled by Clare's disappearance, left to question whether she existed at all. If they are lucky, it will be like they were never here, the short life of Clare O'Dey abandoned in the egress of an old mine.

The stucco on the motel room ceiling is peeled in places. Clare lies on her back, the bandages on her shoulder tinged with blood. According to the glow of the alarm clock, it is nine. Despite the bedside lamp this motel room is dim, the bathroom in shadow at one end, another double bed empty beside her, the heavy curtains pulled shut. How many hours have passed since she and Malcolm drove away from Blackmore? Clare can barely envision the exodus, the flight of hospital stairs to the car, then the click-clack of the windshield wipers, how Malcolm sped around the turns though the road was slick with rain. There was the cold of the mountains out the window, their snow-dusted tops peering in and out of the clouds.

The day now reveals itself to Clare in hazy scenes. She cannot pinpoint exactly when the mountains gave way to rolling hills and bright sun, to earth brown and scorched, and then to a lush and flat green that must have signaled the nearing of the ocean. She has no memory of securing a room or navigating from Malcolm's car to this bed. There is the vague image of Malcolm standing over her with a glass of water and a pill, setting some food on the bedside table, then sitting in the chair, watching the muted TV while she swayed in and out of sleep. Now Clare can see that the food is still untouched in its takeout container, that she did not imagine him setting it there, this her only sure clue it wasn't all a dream.

From the next room comes the clang of old plumbing. Maybe Malcolm is there, taking a shower, washing his face, brushing his teeth. Clare tries to listen for more noises, but her head hurts. The corner of her forehead where the butt of Wilfred's gun landed is sore even to the lightest touch. When her eyes close she sees the barrel of Wilfred's shotgun, that perfect circle of black, the halo of trees above it.

Salty tears burn down the swollen skin of her cheek. There was no lucidity as she lay on the wet ground under Wilfred, his gun aimed down at her, no awe or incredulity that death might be what came next. The only death Clare ever witnessed firsthand was her mother's, a peaceful enough departure, a tube in her arm to feed her a drug that might have spared her any sense of what was unfolding. It must have been like sleep, thoughts weaving in and out like dreams, so that her mother might have figured her own death to be imaginary. Clare remembers marveling at death then, how it might take its time, plucking life away over weeks or years, a slow decay, or how it might choose instead to barge in, a truck on the highway or a blast at a mine, a cooked needle in the wrong vein, a shotgun aimed just so.

A bottle of the small pills is on the bedside table next to the food and a glass of water. Clare's legs and toes feel numb. Whatever momentum has driven her these last months seems to have left her. All she wants is to stay in this bed under the yellow light of this lamp. The taste of it is in her again. She will have to work hard to ration the pills, to keep herself to a regimen, to avoid that slip back to a place where this dullness is the welcomed norm.

"Malcolm?"

Clare sits up.

"Malcolm?"

It takes some maneuvering to get out from under the blankets and fend off the dizzy spell that follows. Clare stands and flicks the switch next to the door, washing the room in a harsh light. The light fixture hums, its bowl speckled with the black dots of dead insects. Clare can't be sure what she is looking for until she sees it, the card that came with the flowers on the dresser next to the television, a yellow envelope and the cell phone Malcolm gave her on top of it. Clare limps over and opens the yellow envelope. Inside is a wad of fifty-dollar bills held together by an elastic. The Post-it note tucked in with the bills offers only two words. *Your share.*

Your share. The wonder of it, Clare thinks, this life as a paying job.

Next, Clare picks up the card. She knows. She knew the moment she saw the bouquet in the hospital. Some instinct must have been honed these past months, because a pulsing pressure fills the space between her ears. She nudges the card open. A folded paper falls to the carpet. Clare struggles to pick it up. She unfolds it. The greeting is set apart from the rest of the text so that it catches the eye at first glance. Typed.

My Clare.

Clare must sit back on the edge of the bed to stop herself from vomiting. She turns the paper over in her hands. It is blank but for the printed words. *My Clare.* In the early days of their courtship she'd taken this call as a gesture of dreamy intimacy, but in time she grew to hate it. I do not belong to you.

Clare crumples the paper in her fist, then stands and goes to the window, yanking the curtains fully open. The sight of Malcolm's parked car fills Clare with resolve. The motel sign is lit. SEASIDE INN AND LIGHTHOUSE. On the far side of the parking lot is a drop-off beyond which Clare assumes is the ocean. A wash of pink sky. She can taste the salt in the air. On the desk next to the phone Clare finds a pack of matches embossed with the motel name. She slides the chain lock and steps outside into the dusky light.

It is the noise of the ocean that surprises Clare the most. The roaring hum of it. The light in the room next to hers is on. Malcolm. Malcolm is here. Clare walks across the parking lot to the guardrail. Below, the water froths up, then curls back over itself, a steep drop down to a rocky shore. The sun has just dipped behind the horizon. Clare holds her sore arm to her chest and climbs over the guardrail, balancing with her legs pressed back against it. There is the sensation that the wind is rocking her. She pinches the card between her teeth while she works to strike a match. The corner of the paper lights up and the heat curls up the page. Clare watches it, working to steady her breaths, about to toss it, unread, into the sea.

No.

Just as the flame is about to take hold, Clare

blows and pats at the paper until it's extinguished. She sits on the guardrail and runs her finger along the charred edge of the page.

Two hundred and seven days. That was her reprieve. Clare thinks of Jason plucking at the keyboard of their old computer, searching for a florist, e-mailing this note to be tucked into the card. The gravel in his voice, how he might have uttered the text aloud as he typed, never one to give her the last word.

My Clare.

So many things can change in a day. That e-mail telling me he couldn't find you. That you're probably dead. The world works in such strange ways. Timing, you know?

I sent him to find you. I've been awaiting his word.

I've been looking for signs. Every day I search online for news. So many missing women. And then there you were! You're turned away but I'd know your face anywhere. That smile of yours always broke my heart.

I took the picture to your brother. She's not dead. See? Like I told you? That's what I said to him. She's in the mountains and she's in trouble. Again with the drugs. I don't know what I expected him to do. He just stared at the picture and handed it back to me. And Grace. Poor Grace has been the worst. Telling the cops to come after me and question me. Calling the precinct. Telling them I'm a violent criminal. I found Grace in her backyard this morning. She was pushing her little guy on a baby swing. She said the picture might not be you. Then she got a sad look on her face. Some people give up more easily than others.

I told them everything, Clare. About the pills and all the drinks you had that night. How hard you fell off the wagon. About the baby. How you wouldn't let me drive you to the hospital. About the night you disappeared. It made me cry to finally tell it.

It was hard to see Grace's little boy, to think of our son, how he'd probably be sitting up by now too.

You know I was never good at letters. Or flowers. My Clare. You aren't dead. I knew it.

I don't know why everyone here is so willing to forget about you. It's like that's what you wanted. To be forgotten. Like you knew no one would come after you, like you knew they'd be glad to see you go. But not me. I can't forget you, my Clare. You're still mine.

I hope he gives you this, that he doesn't want to keep you for himself. I hope he believes me. Because I need you to know how hard I've been searching. I need you to know that I will come find you. I will. I'm right behind you. I promise.

J

ACKNOWLEDGMENTS

I HAVE BEEN humbled by the support and generosity shown by so many over the time it took me to write this novel. Above all, I owe a lifetime of gratitude to my parents, Dick and Marilyn Flynn, for their love and encouragement, for their sacrifice and hard work, and for the help and logistical backup they've offered in so many forms over the years. Also to my sisters, Katie Flynn and Bridget Flynn, and my sister-in-law, Beth Boyden, for their cheerleading from start to finish, and to my in-laws Mark McQuillan, Chris Van Dyke, Jamie Boyden, Tim Stuart, and Anne Wright, as well as my nieces and nephews and my extended family, with much love and thanks.

To the talented team at Simon & Schuster Canada for all they've done to put this book into readers' hands. A big, huge thank-you to Nita Pronovost, my skillful and tireless editor, for her warmth and her willingness to toil with me page by page, as well as to Kevin Hanson, Sarah St. Pierre, Brendan May,

Amy Prentice, and the amazing editorial, sales, and publicity teams.

To my wonderful agent Chris Bucci, for reading several drafts and for championing this book to so many, and for his patience and good humor in the face of my writerly angst. Thank you also to Martha Webb, Anne McDermid, and Monica Pacheco for their support.

My profound gratitude to Martha Sharpe, for her advocacy and her friendship, for recognizing something worthy in this book and for pushing me so hard to make it better.

To my UBC Creative Writing instructors and fellow students for the community they provide, to Andrew Gray for leading the pack, and most especially to Lisa Moore, my kind and diligent thesis advisor. To the Toronto Arts Council and the Ontario Arts Council for providing financial assistance and for their ongoing work in promoting and supporting artists in our city and province. To the editors at *FreeFall* magazine, for publishing my short story "Damn Animals," which inspired an early chapter in this novel. To those who indulged my constant search for quiet by providing me with space to write, including Mitch Kowalski and Yvonne Lai at the Toronto Writers' Centre, the staff at Artscape Gibraltar Point, the Gladstone and Robarts libraries, the McQuillan family at Rowntree Beach, and my parents for converting their bunkie in Dwight, Ontario, into an ad hoc writer's studio.

To my students and colleagues at the TDSB, especially at Contact and Beverley schools, for always being so supportive of writing as another love and pursuit. A special thank-you to Jeffrey Caton, Anna Gemmiti, Grant Fawthrop, Mike Gurgol, Vivian Meyer, Michelle Balcers, Dexter Abrams, and Tina Kotsilis for upholding my efforts to strike the balance between two careers.

To my fellow writers at the Muskoka Novel Marathon, where early first chapters of this novel were written in one harried weekend, for the amazing work they do and their continued interest in this book. To my band of scribes for their companionship and commiseration, especially Jonathan Mendelsohn, Mary Kim, Monica Lin Morishita, Paulette Bourgeois, Stefan Riches, Yakos Spiliotopoulos, Marilyn Boyden, the Salonistas, and my birthday twin Claire Tacon.

A shout from the rooftops to my friend Kendall Anderson, who for many years has offered helpful advice on the writing life, and on life in general, who planted the original seed for this novel, and who has read more of my writing than anyone else. To Elisa Schwarz for her unflagging belief in me and for a lifetime of friendship, and to Sarah Faber for understanding the trials of writing and for supporting me from the very beginning.

To my dear friend and favorite retreat and treat partner Mariska Gatha, who engaged in endless hours of plot/life discussion with me, who debated smiles and slight nods and shrugs, and who swiftly answered my panicked mid-draft text messages, and to Jeff Beer for graciously letting me take up so much of Mariska's time. To the women in my book club for over ten years of food and drink and for keeping my nose in books no matter what. To my friends and family who read drafts along the way, sometimes twice, and provided invaluable feedback and airspace for my rambling ideas: Paige Lindsay, Allyson Payne, Deanna Wong, Kirsten White, Meagan Cleary, Erin Cunningham, Sarah Martyn, as well as the aforementioned Katie, Bridget, Marilyn, Mariska, Claire, and Kendall, this novel has been much improved because of your insights.

To Ian, with all my heart, for pretty much everything all the time, for his love and conviction, for his steadfast good nature, for his heroic efforts in carving out space and time for me to write. Much love to our boys, Flynn, Joey, and Leo, for offering in their joyful wildness a strong antidote to the solitude of writing, for their hilarious questions and their vivid stories, and for keeping me in line with their great enthusiasm for the little things in life.

To Susan Stuart, the reader I always kept in mind as I wrote. I am forever grateful to her, and for her.

ABOUT THE AUTHOR

Amy Stuart's debut novel, *Still Mine*, was an instant national bestseller, and was nominated for the Arthur Ellis Best Crime First Novel Award. In 2011, Amy won the Writers' Union of Canada Short Prose Competition. Amy's writing has previously appeared in newspapers and magazines across Canada. She lives in Toronto with her husband and three sons. Visit her at **AmyStuart.ca** and follow her on Twitter **@AmyfStuart**.

Turn the page for a sneak peek at
Amy Stuart's next novel

STILL WATER

Now available from Gallery Books!

Sunday

Clare jolts upright, her hand at her mouth to stifle a scream. This room is blue with moonlight. Clare is on a single bed, its rusted joints creaking beneath her as she adjusts to sitting. She blinks. Bare walls, high ceiling, cobwebs wound tight in the corners. There is an open window, a hot wind lifting the corner of her bedsheet. The door is closed. Another single bed is pressed to the far wall, a woman lying facedown, asleep, as still as a corpse.

A voice in Clare's head. *Do you know about this place?*

The woman in the bed lets out a long whine. Clare studies her in the low light. She looks to be in her mid-thirties, her face gently lined but tense even in sleep. She rolls onto her back, one arm flapped over the side of the bed. There is a zigzag of scars on her forearm and palm. Defensive scars, Clare knows. The kind that come from fending someone off. They spoke only briefly after Clare arrived last night, shook hands, maneuvered around each other in the small space. Raylene, she'd said. Her name is Raylene.

The painted hardwood is warm under Clare's feet.

She stands and tiptoes to the window. This room is on the second story, a porch roof extending below her. Two hundred feet ahead, a river churns. A willow tree is perched so close to the water that its thick roots curl over the edge of the bank. A wooden cross has been nailed askew to its trunk. Clare twists her hair into a bun, then crouches to catch the breeze on her neck.

Do you know about this place?

Yes, Clare thinks, eyes on the wooden cross. I know about this place.

This morning, there was the ocean. Two days ago, Malcolm Boon in the doorway of Clare's room, a folder in hand.

I have a new case, he said. A woman and her child have disappeared.

How many days since she and Malcolm absconded from the hospital in Blackmore before the police could question them? How many days and nights did Clare spend in that motel room, drifting in and out of fitful sleep as she healed from the gunshot wound? She can muster only flashes. Bandages peeled back, the angry pink of her shoulder. A meal eaten on an unmade bed. A dusty glass of water Malcolm gave her to wash down the pills. The tide in and out on a beach. Malcolm there, Malcolm gone. And then, Malcolm arriving with the folder, offering her a new assignment.

I think you'd be good for this case, he'd said. It's a place called High River. A place for women like you.

Something had roused Clare then. Her second case. A chance to right the wrongs of her first effort, to prove she might actually be good at this work. For twenty-four hours she'd pored over the folder: Sally Proulx and her two-year-old son, William, swept away days ago by the same river Clare watches out this window now. She'd papered the wall of her motel room with the timeline and backstory, photos and police reports. Photos of Sally in her previous life, before she and William arrived in High River. As Clare worked, a strange energy bolted through her. She couldn't sleep. She wouldn't talk to Malcolm. She cut back the pills, holding her breath against the waves of pain and nausea. This time, she would be prepared. She would invent a version of herself that fit in at High River. Go undercover. Learn from her mistakes. It only occurs to her now that Malcolm probably chose this case because he knew it would hit too close to home for Clare to refuse it.

With a gasp, Raylene sits up in bed, eyes wide. "No!" she says. "No."

Her eyes search the room until she spots Clare crouched at the open window.

"It's okay," Clare says.

Raylene's eyes are unfocused, afraid.

"You were dreaming," Clare whispers. "Go back to sleep."

As if never awake, Raylene slides down the bed until her head lands softly on her pillow.

Rain. Clare extends her hand through the open window to catch the first drops on her palm. She can never remember her own dreams. It used to suit Clare to forget, to abandon the details of her life before this one, those many months on the run before she met Malcolm Boon. Before Malcolm hired her to this strange work of searching for lost or missing women, before her first case in Blackmore. Before the bullet wound and the blur of days spent recovering at that seaside motel. As they drove to High River yesterday, southward to this thick heat, Malcolm kept such quiet that when he spoke his voice startled Clare.

Remember, he said. We got lucky on the Blackmore case.

We got lucky, Clare repeated, hand resting on the shotgun wound just inches from her heart. *Lucky*.

What I mean, Malcolm said, is that missing women don't always turn up alive.

Forget luck, Clare wanted to say. Instead she looked out her window in silence, any change in the landscape masked by the gas stations and fast food joints on repeat at every interchange. Mile after mile she mulled the details of the High River case. The little boy and his mother. Fixating on the details of the case distracted Clare from the pain in her shoulder, the panic, the need for one more pill to take the edge off. She committed everything in that file to memory, every detail of Sally Proulx's story absorbed, Clare an actor learning her part. This time, she will play Sally's friend, a more direct route into the story than she took last time. But now that she's here in High River, Clare feels uncertain she's made the right choice in agreeing to take this case on. She stares at the white cross, at the swaying tentacles of the willow tree. Her chest hurts. Her shoulder hurts. It feels hard to breathe in this heat. She thinks of the letter from her husband that she carries in her bag.

I can't forget you, my Clare. You're still mine.

Eighteen, Clare thinks. Eighteen days since she left Blackmore with Malcolm, driving west to the ocean and that motel, the letter from Jason in her back pocket. Two hundred and twenty-five days since she left Jason, sprinting through the snowy backfields to the car she'd hidden under a sheet. A long-planned escape from a vicious husband. A life left behind months ago. But no matter how much time passes, she can't seem to stop counting the days.

Do you know about this place?

It was Raylene who'd asked her this question as they lay in the dark last night, hours after Clare first arrived. Clare had feigned sleep instead of answering. Yesterday she'd felt certain she was equipped for this. She'd felt certain she'd learned all she could about High River, that this time her ruse would be rock solid. Clare looks over her shoulder to Raylene, curled into a fetal position, a pained look on her face as she sleeps. Clare looks back at the river, then presses the window all the way closed, her hands shaking with pain or withdrawal or panic, she can never tell which anymore.

It doesn't matter if I'm ready, Clare thinks. I'm here.

BOOK CLUB FAVORITES

READER'S GUIDE

STILL MINE

AMY STUART

1. Before sending Clare into Blackmore, Malcolm Boon hastily decides that her alias will be O'Dey, meaning "servant" or "maid." Discuss the significance of this name. What do you think Malcolm meant by it? And was he right in this choice? Why or why not?

2. As she immerses herself in the little mining town, Clare is forced to think back on past "versions" of herself. There is nineteen-year-old Clare, happy and on the cusp of adulthood with her best friend, Grace. There is the married Clare, close to broken at the bottom of her cellar steps. What version of Clare do we see at the beginning of the book? At the end? How are they different?

3. Blackmore is both strange and utterly familiar to Clare. She empathizes with the cold nature of the tight-knit community toward strangers, even as they ruthlessly keep her at bay. Do you think that empathy is ever returned? When, and why?

4. Shayna writes that her mother, Louise, believes that tragedy can alter a constitution. But Shayna

thinks otherwise. She posits that there is a core in each of us that can never be changed; it separates the good from the bad. Whose side do you think Clare would take? Why?

5. Clare momentarily envies Louise's dementia as Shayna's case brings on a wave of overlapping memories in Clare, even causing her to relapse. But what is the cost of oblivion or sedation as a coping mechanism? Who do you think suffers more: the confused Louise or the very lucid Wilfred?

6. Clare revises history to imagine a world in which she had stayed in art school, or had forced Jason to hold their dead baby in his hand. Discuss the role of regret in the novel. How much do you think one decision can alter a life?

7. Framed pictures and photography figure heavily into Clare's quest. At one point, she studies a picture of Shayna with Jared, Sara, and Charlie, and wonders whether they are less "friends" and more "characters in her story." What does she mean by this? Do you think she feels this way about her best friend, Grace, or her brother, Christopher?

8. If, as Clare surmises, Shayna left a "hole" or a "vacancy" in the town of Blackmore, she is not the only one to do so. What other holes did you see widening? And how did these characters go about filling them?

9. Before she succumbs to cancer, Clare's mother tells her that no matter what, she needs to keep moving forward. In Blackmore, Clare feels lost in "the empty distance between nowhere and here" (p. 207). Does that change? If so, at which point does that forward motion begin?

10. When Jared finally tells Clare what happened in the mine, Clare says that it's "hard to blame the dead for anything" (p. 227). Discuss the scene Jared describes, and the interplay of grief and blame. Are they necessarily inseparable in this case? Why or why not?

11. Derek has very personal feelings about addiction. He watched his mother die of alcoholism and believes that her death resulted from a lack of will. Wilfred, of course, believed he could force his own will on his struggling daughter. Where does Clare, now (relatively) clean, come down on recovery? Do you agree with her?

12. Malcolm Boon drives Clare crazy. She feels that he is the only person in the world who really knows her, even as she fails again and again to decode him. Discuss their relationship. Is Malcolm manipulative? Or protective? Is this a mutually beneficial partnership? Why or why not?

13. Based on her writings, what perspective did Shayna gain from her time in the mine? How do you think this will affect her future, now that she has survived traumas similar to those of Clare's?

14. Jason, an omnipresent threat throughout the novel, becomes all too real when he sends Clare flowers. In that final note, he emphasizes that her loved ones are more than willing to let her be forgotten, even as he promises never to forget. Unpack this threat, so carefully threaded between loving words. Can Clare ever truly escape him? How?